WHAT DIVIDES US

THE KILTEEGAN BRIDGE STORY - BOOK 2

JEAN GRAINGER

GOLD HARP MEDIA

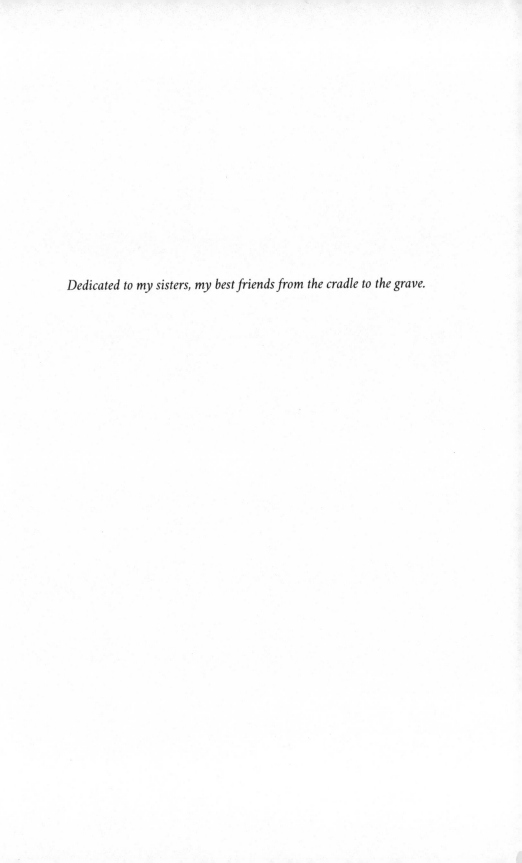

Dedicated to my sisters, my best friends from the cradle to the grave.

FOREWORD

The story so far...

In *The Trouble With Secrets*, beautiful Lena O'Sullivan, who lives on a small farm near Kilteegan Bridge in the west of Ireland, is only seventeen when she falls in love with green-eyed Malachy, whose father August Berger owns the magnificent local estate, Kilteegan House.

After a promise of marriage, Lena becomes pregnant but Malachy abandons her. Heart-broken, she confides in her godfather "Doc", the local doctor who has been there for her ever since her father Paudie died, leaving Lena and her sister Emily and brother Jack to manage the farm while caring for their unstable mother, Maria, and Maria's newborn twins, Molly and May.

Doc arranges for Lena to go to friends of his in Wales, where she will put her baby up for adoption. There she meets Eli Kogan, once a Jewish war refugee and now a newly-qualified doctor. They marry and return to Ireland, where Eli takes over Doc's practice in Kilteegan Bridge, and raises Lena's baby, Emmet, as his own. But then Malachy returns from America to see his dying father, and dreadful secrets are revealed. August Berger was no "hero of the French resistance" but a committed Nazi. Lena's father didn't die in a shooting accident but was murdered by Berger's devoted servant Phillippe Decker, because Berger was convinced his wife Hannah was in love with Paudie. The reason Malachy abandoned Lena was because Berger falsely claimed she was sleeping with other men.

Malachy, realising Emmet is his own son and still in love with Lena, begs her to leave her husband and come back with him to America. But as much as Lena has dreamed of this moment in the past, now that it has come she realises she loves her husband Eli with all her heart.

Now read on....

CHAPTER 1

'ammy, I need another slice of bread and jam. Mammy? *Mammy!*'

Lena blinked and raised her head from the solicitor's letter. Around her, the kitchen of Kilteegan House swam into focus, bright with vases of bluebells from the garden. Five-year-old Sarah was sitting at the long pine table, happily licking rich butter off her own slice of bread, while two-year-old Pádraig lolled in his high chair, chewing on a crust.

'Mammy!' Emmet, her seven-year-old son, frowned at her from the far end of the table. 'I said I want more bread and jam!'

'Oh, sorry, my love. I was miles away.' Her brain still in a fog of panic, she set aside the stiff ivory linen sheet of headed notepaper and, with shaking hands, spread butter from her brother Jack's farm on a warm slice of soda bread and handed it to her oldest son.

'I said *jam*, Mammy!'

The door opened, and the local girl they employed as a part-time nanny appeared, smiling broadly. 'Is that Prince Emmet's voice I hear, demanding jam?'

'Katie! Katie!' Sarah jumped down and rushed to hug the red-

1

haired teenager, Pádraig clapped and squealed with delight, and Emmet's frown became a gap-toothed grin. Katie was a huge favourite with the children; she was always up for wild games and teddy bear picnics on the extensive grounds on the days she took care of them.

Lena stood up shakily. 'Katie, can you take over the children from here? I need to attend to something.'

'Of course, Mrs Kogan, no problem at all.' The girl expertly wiped Sarah's face clean of butter, then unstrapped Pádraig and lifted him out onto her hip. With her free hand, she pushed the pot of blackcurrant jam towards Emmet and handed him the jam spoon. 'Now, Your Majesty…'

Lena crossed the wide sunny entrance hall into the library, where the heavy dark drapes and large mahogany furniture from August Berger's time had been replaced over the last few years with pastels and pretty florals. She stood by the fireplace, rereading the letter again from the beginning, trying her best to take in the words.

It was from Hayes, Kilgallen and Moran, Solicitors at Law, with an address on Merrion Square in Dublin, and it was addressed solely to her, without a mention of either Eli or Emmet.

Dear Mrs Lena Kogan,

We are writing to advise you regarding your current occupation of the property known as Kilteegan House. The legal owner as per the last will and testament of Mr August Berger, drawn up and placed in trust with us, wishes to assert his right to use or dispose of this property as he sees fit. Further to this wish, he desires you to vacate the property with immediate effect. Refusal on your part to comply will lead to legal action.

Yours faithfully,

Ignatius Hayes,

Bachelor-at-Law

Lena felt her pulse beating in her temples. *Calm,* she urged herself, but she was anything but calm. How could Malachy Berger do this to her? How could he do this to Emmet? *There must be some mistake.* Malachy had left the house in trust to Emmet, with Lena and Eli administering that trust until the boy turned eighteen. Was it even legal for him to change his mind after signing the contract?

She needed to ask Kieran Devlin. He was the town solicitor, late fifties, good at his job and someone who told the truth with no frills. Or perhaps she would go to the hardware store to show the letter to her sister Emily, who knew the truth about Emmet's parentage and was always the voice of reason.

No, stop. It would be better if she talked to Eli first. Her husband had gone to Cork, where there was a meeting at the South Infirmary of all rural doctors about TB vaccination services – the disease was still a problem in rural Ireland, even in 1966 – but she'd wait and talk to him about it tonight. He would know what to do, and he would keep her calm. Eli had a way of soothing people, helping them through the hardest times in their lives. She would need every ounce of his skill now.

Mrs Shanahan, their housekeeper, would be in in a while. She'd be grumbling about the school holidays because the children 'would be constantly under her feet', even though Lena knew the old woman loved all the Kogans, especially chubby little Pádraig.

She looked quickly around the room, then folded the letter, replaced it in its thick luxurious envelope and stuck it out of sight behind the big wooden clock on the mantelpiece. It could stay put until Eli got home. The awful poisonous thing. She imagined it pulsating there in the dark, its hateful contents dragging up memories so painful that she'd suppressed them for years now. How August Berger had lied to Malachy, telling him that Lena was a girl of loose morals who'd offered herself to all the local men. And how Malachy had foolishly believed his father and abandoned her. He never even had a conversation with her to end their relationship. So it was a terrified, lonely, lost Lena who took a boat to Wales to have her baby away from prying eyes. She was forced by an intolerant society to give Emmet up for adoption, until Eli Kogan saved her by marrying her and adopting Emmet, treating the little boy as his own.

Before turning away from the mantelpiece, Lena caught a glimpse of her face in the large gilt-framed oval mirror that hung over the fireplace and paused to gaze at it. She wondered if she looked so much different to the starry-eyed girl of seventeen who came to this house, thrilled to have caught the admiring eye of the local gentry. Malachy Berger had asked her to dance at the Lilac Ballroom in Enniskean, and she had felt like all her birthdays had come together. If only that wide-eyed girl had known then what lay in store.

Running around after three little ones had kept her trim, and her brown eyes remained unchanged. Her hair was still dark, but she wore it back in a sedate bun most days now, having decided that her signature Audrey Hepburn high ponytail was too young and flighty for a respectable doctor's wife and mother of three. Was there a silver thread to be seen? She turned her head slightly. Eli had claimed she was imagining things when she asked him that question as she'd brushed her hair before bed a few nights ago, but she still wasn't sure. That was the trouble with being so dark-haired – the greys were more obvious. She remembered her daddy having grey temples in his thirties, so it ran in the family.

Paudie O'Sullivan. She felt that old familiar pang of longing. He wouldn't even be old now if he'd lived, still a middle-aged man, fit and strong, caring for his family, playing with his grandchildren. But he wasn't here and never would be again, more work of that murderer Phillippe Decker and his employer, August Berger.

Like a tongue pushing a sore tooth, she felt the wave of grief. Her father was gone for so long now, but some days it felt like yesterday. Her eyes dropped once more to where the letter was tucked out of sight behind the clock. Malachy giving Emmet this house had enabled her some peace. It would never make up for her father's murder, but it was kind of a symbol of moving on.

On the front lawn outside the long windows of the library, Katie and the children were playing with a ball, and their laughter filled the air. This magnificent manor was Emmet's birthright. He and his sister and brother saw it as their home, and they loved it.

Was their peaceful, happy life about to implode?

No. There was no way on God's green earth she would have this place taken from them. She would write to Malachy in America and beg him not to change his mind about the house. Or maybe it would be better if she called him. But she dreaded the thought of hearing his voice. She was glad that in the last few years, she had become able to gaze into Emmet's green eyes and stroke his dark-red hair without once thinking of the man who had fathered him. She never wanted to go back to a time when Malachy Berger's voice and face were constantly in her head, dominating her every waking thought.

CHAPTER 2

*L*ater that evening, Lena tried not to get frustrated with her husband.

Eli was rolling around on the floor of the library with the three children, who were cackling like witches as they climbed all over and tickled him; he whooped in mock horror. They had already been bathed and were in bed when he came home, but they'd instantly piled down the stairs in their pyjamas. Now it would take ages to settle them again, because they would be high as kites after all this horseplay.

Normally Lena wouldn't have minded at all. She appreciated how her husband never used a long day at work to duck the hard task of being a father. He was a very modern man in that regard. Other women, including her mother and sister, were astounded to hear how he changed nappies as well as bathed and dressed and read to the children. So much so that his example had led some other men in the village to push their babies in the pram down the main street of Kilteegan Bridge, a sight previously unseen. The whispering went on for weeks.

Still, tonight she needed Eli to be a husband, not a father. She needed to talk to him alone and in peace. 'Eli, please...'

'I'm not Eli, I'm a lion!' His normally neat sandy hair was standing on end, and he had all three children on his back as he pretended to rampage through the Serengeti. Although he was so slim and tall, she thought he looked more like a giraffe than a lion. He had never put on an ounce of weight in all the years Lena had known him. He loved ice cream and cake and Irish butter and cream, and while she and her sister bemoaned regularly how they only needed to look at a cake to feel the pinch in their skirts, Eli could somehow eat whatever he liked.

'Daddy, don't eat us!'

'I'm not going to eat you. I'm a friendly lion!' He let out an incredibly realistic roar, to their hysterical screams of laughter.

Lena rolled her eyes. He was impossible to stay cross at.

'Right, you intrepid explorers.' He reared up gently, each child sliding to the carpet. 'Time for bed. Mammy is giving me the evil eye.' With yelps of protest, they rushed to climb up on him again, but he rolled away and stood up. 'No, that's enough fun for one evening. Mr Lion has got to go and munch on a few gazelles now, so off with you. Go and explore your bedrooms.'

'But, Daddy, we had shepherd's pie for dinner.' Sarah giggled. 'I think that's all there is.'

'You're wrong. Mick Cronin had a special offer on minced gazelle this week, so that's what was in the pie.'

'Urgh, no…' The little girl turned pale and looked like she might be sick.

'I'm only joking, pet,' said Eli hastily, kneeling down again with his arms out. 'Come here to Daddy for a hug.'

She ran to him. 'Are you sure you were joking?'

'Of course he was joking,' said Emmet, so sharply that Lena rather suspected he'd believed it for a moment himself. 'You only get gazelles in Africa and India, which you would know if you ever learnt to read instead of just playing with your silly dolls.'

'I can't help it I can't read…' Now Sarah did start crying. 'And I love my dolls.'

Eli frowned over Sarah's shoulder at the boy. 'Don't be mean to your little sister, Emmet. Tell her you're sorry.'

'I'm not being mean. I just said she should learn to read.'

'And I just said, "Tell her you're sorry," so do it.'

'But –'

'Emmet, say it now or you won't get a bedtime story from me – only Sarah and Pádraig will have one.'

'Fine, I'll read my own story. Because I *can*.' And the red-headed boy stormed out of the room and up the stairs.

Eli breathed heavily for a moment, then looked at Lena with a forced smile. Lena didn't smile at him in return.

He turned back to Sarah. 'Right then, my clever little daughter, since we are nowhere near either Africa or India, I think we can safely say we don't eat gazelles. Now, up the stairs, you two, and no more shenanigans.' He stood and swept Pádraig up in his arms, the toddler throwing his fat little arms around his daddy's neck, and took Sarah by the hand. 'Sarah, will I tell you a story about your dolls?'

'And do the voices?' Her tears had already dried as she trotted out of the room beside him.

'Of course I'll do the voices,' Eli answered in a falsetto warble, which made Sarah giggle again.

Slowly taking the letter from behind the mantelpiece clock, Lena moved through an internal door into the small sitting room. The days were warming up, being April, but the evenings were still chilly, so she lit the fire that Mr Shanahan, the housekeeper's husband who looked after the grounds, had set in the grate.

When August Berger lived here, there had been a pair of large heavy leather chairs either side of the hearth, but Lena had given them away and bought a lovely blue and pink chintz-covered sofa with some cream embroidered scatter cushions. The floorboards had been stripped back to the bare wood, and there was a ten-foot-square Persian silk rug on the floor, a wedding gift from Eli's parents.

She sat waiting on the sofa, the letter in her hands, her thoughts with Emmet in the bedroom above. She hoped her husband would relent and let him come into the younger children's room to listen to the story. Eli teased her sometimes that she let the older boy get away with too much, and Emmet did love to lord things over his younger siblings as if he were their superior. She didn't think she let him get away with bad behaviour, and she would have said something to him tonight about the Sarah incident if Eli hadn't done it first.

Twenty minutes later, Eli joined her. 'Emmet apologised to Sarah for being mean, though I think he regretted it when he found out the story was about her dolls,' he said with a grin as he plumped down on the sofa and put his arm around her. 'You look lovely.' He nuzzled her neck.

She pulled away from him slightly. 'I really don't think Emmet meant to be mean. He thought he was just telling the truth.'

Eli shook his head. 'There are ways and means of telling the truth nicely, Lena, and he should have stopped when she cried. Sometimes Emmet acts like he's better and cleverer than other people. Maybe he doesn't mean it to come out that way, but it does, and it's going to make life hard for him if he continues. So we need to stop it, for his own sake as much as for the other two.' His voice had deep, strong, lilting tones. He was German by birth, but he and his mother and uncle had arrived in Cardiff as Jewish refugees during the war. He had developed a Welsh accent and never lost it.

'Emmet *is* very clever, but he doesn't think he's better than other people.'

'He does, and it's not just me that's noticed. I mean, only the other day, Emily was saying...' He stopped, pressing his lips together.

Lena looked at him sharply. 'Saying what?'

He shook his head. 'Nothing, it doesn't matter. Anyway, what did you want to talk to me about?'

'No, Eli, that's not fair. If this is about Emmet, then you have to tell me. I'm his mother, and if Emily had anything to say about him, she should have said it to me, not to you.'

Eli's hurt was clear as his brown eyes met hers full on. 'Why shouldn't Emily speak about Emmet to me, Lena? I am his father.'

She swallowed, flustered. This was all Malachy's fault for upsetting her and getting into her head with this crazy letter. She touched her husband's arm pleadingly. 'I know, of course you are, and I didn't mean Emily shouldn't talk to you about your son. But please tell me what it was about. I'm worried now. Did he do something wrong?'

Eli sighed and relented. 'OK. She said he was very haughty with Nellie and talked to her like she was beneath him, even though they're cousins and the same age.'

'I'm sure he didn't mean –'

'Lena.' He took her hand, laid it on his knee and patted it gently. 'Lena, listen. I know you love Emmet with all your heart, and so do I. You don't like to listen to anything being said against him, but he told his cousin she was only a shopkeeper's daughter while he lived in Kilteegan House, the most important house in the town.'

'Oh…' She dropped her eyes, embarrassed, then raised them again hopefully. 'Did Emily hear him say it? And why didn't she tell me if she did?'

'Honestly, Lena? Because she thought you wouldn't believe her. You see, you're right, she didn't overhear it herself. It was Nellie who told her.'

Lena felt a sense of relief. 'I thought so.'

'No, Lena, you know Nellie wouldn't make up anything like that – she's an honest little girl. And when I spoke to Emmet about it, he didn't deny it, just asked me not to tell you. So now I've broken my promise to Emmet, and I'd like you not to mention it to him because he needs to trust me. Anyway, it's fine now, it's dealt with. I took away his books and had him out weeding the garden with Mr Shanahan. I told Mr Shanahan that Emmet was under orders to do exactly as he was instructed, that he wasn't to let Emmet boss him around and that he was to tell him off if he was rude. And you'll be pleased to hear Emmet behaved perfectly. Mr Shanahan said he was a great help and very polite.'

Lena sighed. She knew she should be angry with Emmet for upsetting Nellie, if it was true, and she knew Eli as his father had a right to tell Emmet off. And nobody could say a few hours helping in the garden was a harsh punishment. But she still hated the idea of Eli talking about her son like that to Mr Shanahan. The social workers had stolen Emmet from her before and she'd had to fight to get him back, so she hated the idea of anyone having authority over her son apart from herself. Of course, Eli had fought for Emmet's return as well. If it wasn't for him convincing her it would be possible to get him back from the adoption services, her precious boy would be with another family now, strangers. She knew how unusual and lucky she was, and she was so grateful that Eli was Emmet's father in every way that mattered, but still...

Sometimes she worried that Eli, and her sister Emily for that matter, were too much on the watch for Emmet showing traits of his real grandfather – the haughty, supercilious August Berger, who had certainly thought himself better than anyone else.

Eli broke the silence. 'Ah, he's a good boy at heart, and he's exceptionally clever, just a little too autocratic. It's a good thing he doesn't know this house will belong to him one day. I hope he'll be mature enough at eighteen not to let it go to his head. I sometimes wish we could leave it until he's twenty-one.'

She suddenly remembered the letter she was holding, which had got momentarily pushed from her mind. 'I got this in the post today, Eli. I've been waiting all day to show you and see what you think.'

She handed him the letter. He looked perplexed at the fancy envelope addressed to her, then pulled out and unfolded the single stiff sheet and began to read.

As he scanned the words, Lena waited for the same indignation, the same fury she felt at Malachy's betrayal to be mirrored in Eli's handsome boyish features, but instead her husband's face remained calm and unlined.

'Well,' he said eventually, folding the letter and replacing it in the envelope, 'if Malachy Berger has changed his mind, so be it. I can't say I like the idea of him moving back to Kilteegan Bridge, but hopefully he's just in financial difficulty and wants to sell.'

Lena couldn't believe her ears. She leapt up from the sofa and turned to face him, standing square in the middle of the beautiful silk rug. 'If Malachy Berger has changed his mind, "so be it"? We just pack our bags and leave our home, after all the time and effort I've spent on it?' She could hear her voice rising on every word.

'Do you seriously want to fight him in court?' Eli asked quietly, gazing at her from the elegant sofa. 'With everything that would have to come out about who Emmet's father is? Everyone in the town thinks we bought this house from Malachy, and they think Emmet is my biological son. Only you and I and Emily and Jack know the truth.'

Something dawned on Lena, something she'd been ignoring since the day she'd persuaded her husband to move from their cramped accommodation above the surgery in the town to Kilteegan House. She fixed her dark-brown eyes on his accusingly. 'You don't want to live in this house, do you? You resent it.'

'Ah, Lena, don't be silly, that's not it –'

'I'm not being *silly*, as you put it. But I *am* furious. And now I realise this is exactly what you want. You never wanted us to live here – you hate it, in fact – and this is the perfect solution for you.'

He gazed at her in bewilderment. 'Lena, what on earth are you going on about? I do like this house. Who wouldn't? It's beautiful. But I just think that if Berger has decided, for whatever reason, that he wants it back, then why not move? It's not worth the hassle. It's not like we're penniless these days. We can buy a nice house – not as big as this one of course, but big enough to be happy in – and save ourselves all the trauma of a court case. We could just walk away –'

'And as an added bonus to your fragile male ego, we won't have to live in the house of a man who slept with your wife?' she finished for him, frustration, hurt and disappointment fighting for supremacy in her tone.

Eli paused and gathered his thoughts. He was maddening to argue with in that regard. He wasn't as fiery and passionate as she was, and it always meant he sounded more reasonable and rational, even if he wasn't. 'Lena, this has nothing to do with what you call my "fragile male ego". But since you mention it, yes, I'd be happy to leave here. And I know you've done an amazing job with the place – it looks beautiful – but would a home entirely of our own, with no past, not be a nice thing to consider? And don't you think it might be good for Emmet too?'

'Good for *Emmet*?' Lena couldn't believe her ears.

'Lena, listen…' Eli continued to sound calm and rational. 'It's just a thought, and I know you might think it's a selfish one, but if we don't have to explain to Emmet about the house, then we won't have to tell him about Malachy being his biological father if we decide not to.'

'Not tell him?' She was astonished; she'd had no idea this thought was in Eli's head. 'You've never suggested that before. I thought you agreed it was the right thing to do when he was eighteen. No more secrets, remember?'

'I agreed we should tell him because he would have to know why he inherited the house. But the truth is…' He sat forwards on the sofa, his elbows on his knees. 'The truth is that every day I dread that moment in the future when we have to tell Emmet he is not my biological son. That day, when you gave him up, I *saw* the pain there, Lena. My heart broke for you. But I felt love for that little baby boy as well, because he was yours and part of you, and I swore then that if I could convince you to marry me, we would get him back, and we could raise him as our son. Emmet feels like he's mine, he thinks I'm his father, and honestly, it hasn't been hard. I worried when you were pregnant with Sarah that I might feel different, having a biological child, but it changed nothing. I love Emmet and Sarah and now Pádraig all the same – I make no distinction.'

'I know, Eli.' Although sometimes, like tonight, she wondered.

'And I don't think you should make a distinction either.'

'What do you mean?' She was astonished. 'They're all my children, and I love them all equally!'

He shrugged. 'Maybe so, but I worry the fact that Emmet will inherit this house alone will come between him and his siblings. It singles him out, Lena, makes him different. I wonder sometimes if he senses that, or if unconsciously you treat him differently because of it.'

'How dare you! I don't treat him differently!'

'Lena, I'm not criticising you.' He reached for her, trying to grasp her fingers, to pull her back to the sofa, but she stepped away, thrusting her hands behind her back. 'I'm just saying, maybe it's better if he doesn't inherit.'

'No! This is Emmet's house, and I'm not giving it away on his behalf. I *want* it for him. It's to make up for everything Malachy never did for him.' Her blood was pulsing in her ears, her cheeks were burning, and hot tears were forming and threatening to fall.

Eli's face went dead. 'You want to keep it for him because it's his "real" family's home.'

The words cut through Lena like a knife, yet as painful as it was, Eli was right. He might be raising Emmet, and doing a wonderful job, but this house belonged to Emmet because it had belonged to Malachy, and Malachy's father, and Malachy's mother's family before that. And now Lena wanted to keep it for her son. 'We're his family, but this house is his birthright, don't you see that? It has to be Emmet's.'

Eli stared at her for a long time. The flames danced in the grate, but she shivered, like the room around her was growing cold.

Finally he said, 'Like I told you, I don't discriminate between our children. But you do. I see it now. You always have done.'

Her heart twisted. 'Don't be ridiculous, Eli. I just meant –'

'Except I'm not being ridiculous, am I? Lena, it's written all over your face.'

'That's not what I'm saying at all. You're not listening.'

'Oh, I'm listening. You want to keep this mausoleum to the past because you think it's our son's birthright, that he should have something from his *real* father, and not any inferior house that I can buy him. I very foolishly thought I was Emmet's father and we were his family. I thought that we were enough, that *I* was enough. Clearly not. The child I decided to raise as my own son –'

'And I'm grateful to you, of course I am, but –'

Eli bolted to his feet, towering over her, his normally kind brown eyes glittering now in hurt and rage. 'Grateful to me? That's what you feel? The foundation of our marriage is gratitude? Then you do what you must to keep your favourite child's birthright, Lena. I know better than to stand in your way. You think you know better than anyone, and we wonder where Emmet gets it? You know my feelings. If you choose to go against them, I can't stop you, but I won't have anything to do with it.'

Without saying another word, he stormed out of the room, slamming the door as he left. A moment later, the front door also slammed, and she heard the car start. It was something he did on the rare occasion that he lost his temper with her; he would go for a long drive while he calmed down and then come back and apologise for his behaviour and they would kiss and make up.

This time he would surely do the same, and then they would talk and he would forgive her and understand.

CHAPTER 3

*P*hillippe Decker bought his bread at a different *boulangerie* each day. There were several dozen in the city of Strasbourg, and if he wasn't a regular at any of them, he felt he was less likely to be noticed or recognised. Besides, the price of bread often varied a few centimes and he liked to hunt down the cheapest bargains.

He had returned to his old village of Eguisheim after leaving Ireland as it seemed to be the only thing to do, but he knew the moment he set foot in it that it was a mistake.

In other parts of France, the war dead were honoured as *enfants de France*, those who died for their country. In Alsace, where the Germans conscripted the male population, there were two different ways that soldiers were remembered. Those who were forced to join up were considered exonerated. They had no choice. They might have died in a German uniform, but they were Frenchmen in their hearts and souls and could be recalled with love, just as if they'd died under the *tricolore*, the emblem of the fifth French republic.

The other way was for people like him, those men who'd volunteered for whatever reason before being conscripted, and they were seen as traitors, worse even than the Germans, because they'd turned on their own without reason.

In Eguisheim, his parents' *patisserie* was closed and the Loebs' house over the road was shuttered. War did nobody any good on either side; everyone suffered. Why couldn't everyone just forgive and forget? He wasn't August Berger; he didn't hold a grudge.

Peering into the unwashed windows of his parents' glorious bakery made him feel hungry, and he went into the nearest café to buy a meal. To his disgust, the woman there did her best to give him the tiniest ladleful of soup and then served it with yesterday's bread. No butter, no offer of coffee, only a generous dollop of spite and venom. He wondered how she knew about him...but then everyone knew everything about everyone in that village.

The next day, he decamped to Strasbourg and rented the best room he could find with the bulging satchel of money August had sent him away with.

Today the sun was shining, and a group of tourists were admiring Strasbourg's own Cathedral de Notre-Dame. It was a feat of engineering and architecture that would be incredible to achieve now, let alone in the 1400s when it was built. His mother and father used to take him and his sisters there to Mass whenever they visited the city, and it was always a treat. The huge clock in the right-hand chancel of the vast cathedral, where the little mechanical man came out and rang the bell, delighted him as a child.

He wished he could be a child again, before the war. He and his sisters grew up over their parents' *patisserie*. The smell of sugar and butter, the tinkle of the shop bell, the sound of his parents greeting customers who dropped in for something sweet for after their dinner. A *tarte aux pommes*, perhaps, or a *pain au chocolat* for breakfast, and occasionally a more elaborate cake for a birthday or Easter or Christmas. He recalled making the Easter lamb cakes, the *lammele*, in a mould with his mother and dusting them in sugar powder and tying a red bow around their necks; they'd be devoured by families on Easter Sunday.

He'd learnt to bake when he was only seven or eight, and he made a *lammele* especially every year for the little girl across the road, Rebecca Loeb. She'd loved them, licking her fingers clean of the icing sugar once she'd finished. He'd loved Rebecca as much as she'd loved his cakes, ever since she stood up to Jean Yves Kuger when they were nine years old. Jean broke the strap on Phillippe's school satchel, swinging it around his head while his henchmen laughed. She'd kicked Kuger hard on the shin and took the satchel from him, returning it to Phillippe. Sometimes he thought that had been the happiest moment of his life.

He liked to remember how things were before the war; these were the only comforting thoughts he had. The idyllic past, before everything changed. Yet there were days he found it hard to visualise himself that young. He felt so old. He'd seen and done so much, most of it pointless, ineffectual, much of it bad, he supposed, although none of that was his fault. He'd done what he must to survive.

There had been a time, when he'd realised he was never going to see Rebecca again, that he had considered suicide. Sometimes even now he thought about it. He was so lonely. And if he killed himself, not one person would even mourn his loss. If he hung himself in his room, his landlady would notice the stench after a while, but other than that, nobody would care. He didn't much care himself either. Yet something stopped him.

All that talk of heaven and hell he was subjected to as a child was somehow embedded in his memory, even if he'd seen too much to truly believe in God. If there was paradise or eternal damnation, he knew unequivocally where he was going if he committed suicide. To take your own precious life was a mortal sin, with no chance of repentance. He wouldn't even get a Catholic burial. That was probably what stopped him putting his old Luger in his mouth – sheer cowardice.

He had always been weak. Not in body – he was strong and sturdy, or had been when well fed – but in his mind. He'd always needed someone to follow, someone to tell him what to do. As a bullied child, it was Rebecca Loeb, that slender, wonderful, energetic girl who had saved him.

Where was she now? He knew she hadn't died. August Berger had got her transferred from Auschwitz back to Alsace, where she was cared for and fed in Natzweiler-Struthof camp. He knew this because August had brought him a photograph taken of her just before the end of the war; she'd been smiling at the camera and not at all thin or ill. It would have been so difficult for August to do something like that, but he did; he was a good friend.

If she'd come home, he would have sought her out and proposed, but August told him she had gone with her parents to America. The Loebs were like all the rest of the Jews who survived the carnage of the war, abandoning Europe like it was a sinking ship and leaving no forwarding address.

He crossed the square. The cafés were just setting out their tables and chairs for the morning trade. People liked to have their morning coffee in the square, or perhaps a beer in the sun, with the cathedral providing a sense that all was well with the world. It wasn't just the locals; the many employees of the Council of Europe also milled around the city. It gave the place an added layer of anonymity that suited him. Still, he kept his eyes front and slightly down, a two-decade habit now, avoiding eye contact just in case.

He wondered how it would feel to be like other men. To sit and meet a friend or a lover for a coffee, to chat about weather, the harvest, the wine, whatever came up. Sometimes he was tempted to sit, order a drink, take his hat off and feel the sun on his face, but however tempting the idea, he always immediately dismissed it. That was a luxury for others – loyal Frenchmen, foreigners, diplomats and their staff – not for the likes of him.

He darted down the Rue des Juifs, as he did most days. It was stupid, he knew, but something, a final ember of hope, refused to go out in his heart. Might she come here to revisit an old haunt?

The Street of the Jews. It was so narrow that when he looked up, he could see only a strip of blue sky. The architecture all had a uniformity to it in Strasbourg that lent the entire city a sense of beautiful cohesion, but these houses were not just architecturally pleasing to the eye. These buildings were once home to people who everyone was saying had been killed by people like him. Yet he'd never done any such thing, nor seen it happen. And nor had August, even though he'd been in Auschwitz for a while.

Phillippe hadn't been in the labour camps himself; he was a mere soldier in the army. He had only joined the Waffen-SS at August's suggestion. August Berger had it on good authority that Hitler was planning to conscript all the men in Alsace, and August had been advised by his SS friends that anyone who volunteered ahead of time could avoid being sent to the Russian front. The Bergers knew people, they mixed in high social circles, so Phillippe knew it was prudent to believe it. It was a cowardly thing to do maybe, but August said it was the best way to survive, which was all that mattered. Besides, Rebecca's family had left by that stage, so she would never know…

Anyway, it turned out to be a good thing, because if they hadn't joined the Waffen-SS, August wouldn't have been sent to the Auschwitz labour camp, and then he wouldn't have been able to help Rebecca and arrange for her to join a convoy of other Jews who were sent back to the well-run camp in Alsace, where they lived out the rest of the war in comfort.

He knew he could never voice his opinion out loud, people were so sensitive these days, but honestly, he thought, everyone went on like the Nazis had deliberately tried to kill the Jews, but Rebecca's photo was proof that wasn't true. Some did die, like lots of people died in the war – he wasn't saying they didn't – but this idea that it was the mission of people like him to get rid of them was just propaganda. History was written by the victors – wasn't that what they said?

He paused for a second outside 335. This is where he'd come with her, in 1935, to her cousin Herschel's bar mitzvah party. Her uncle and aunt, Monsieur and Madame Loeb, were remarkably alike, he recalled. Both tiny, wiry people, he with dark hair and a beard, she fairer, but looking like brother and sister.

Rebecca had asked permission to bring her Gentile boyfriend to the event, and her parents had agreed. They knew he and Rebecca were sweethearts, and while he was sure they would have preferred a nice Jewish boy for their daughter, they respected her choice. She was an only child, and they were old when she was born. He used to tease her that she had them wrapped around her little finger, unlike his own father and mother, who were tough, hard-working Alsatians who took no nonsense from their children.

Rebecca's parents, Josef and Ruth Loeb, were wine merchants in the little village of Eguisheim, where they all lived, just like August's parents – if not quite as wealthy. Everyone there was involved with wine in some way; it was as if Pinot Gris ran through their veins, not blood. That was the happiest time of Phillippe's life.

He sighed. These reminiscences were the only indulgence he allowed himself, thinking about the past, when everyone was happy, he and Rebecca were in love, and he was friends with August, who was popular, clever and rich. The past, before everything changed.

A million regrets buzzed briefly around his brain – if only things had worked out differently – but he mentally dismissed them; no good came of that.

He hurried on past the Hotel de Ville and arrived to the Place Broglie. He entered the *boulangerie* there.

The young man behind the counter looked up, bored. *'Bonjour, monsieur, je peux vous aider?'* Though he said the words, helping Phillippe with anything looked like the furthest thing from his mind.

'Une baguette, s'il vous plaît.' His own voice sounded strange to him. Many days this was the only thing he said. He lived on bread, some jam or cheese and coffee. Very occasionally he treated himself to a sliver of meat, but only once a week or so. His budget didn't allow for anything else these days. His money was running low, and he'd have to pay up for that supercilious solicitor in Dublin. When August sent him away from Ireland, Phillippe was sure the satchel of cash would tide him over until he established himself again, but that had never happened. People didn't want to offer him work, or friendship, or any kind of welcome. In hindsight he should have left, tried his luck in America or Australia, somewhere the perception of his past wasn't a barrier to getting on. But that was just another regret to add to the rest.

He had taken to doing some gardening for an elderly widow, out near the Jardin d'Orangeries, in return for a few francs. She never spoke to him after that first day when he called in response to an advertisement on the post office noticeboard looking for a gardener, and he never spoke to her. He knew, of course, who she was. And he suspected that she knew if not *who* he was, then *what* he was. Neither acknowledged their shared past. It was better that way.

He resisted the urge to nibble the bread on the way back to his room. That was all right for children but not adults. But his stomach grumbled.

He wondered if he would always be hungry and lonely from now on, or if things would change. The greedy solicitor in Dublin must have sent the letter by now.

CHAPTER 4

*L*ena woke, feeling cold. The sun was just up, and a few birds were chirping sleepily outside her window, limbering up for the dawn chorus. Shivering, she rolled over on the feather mattress, looking to warm herself against her husband's lanky body, but his side of the big double bed was cold and empty. The horrible row they'd had last night came flooding back to her. After storming out of the sitting room, Eli had slammed out of the house and gone for a drive, presumably to cool down. She had waited and waited for him to come back before crying herself to sleep.

Now it was dawn – the hands on her bedside alarm clock pointed to five thirty – and he still wasn't here. Her eyes filled with tears. He must have slept on the sofa bed in his dressing room, something he only did when he got called out to a patient in the middle of the night and didn't want to wake her when he returned.

She slipped out of bed and felt for her sheepskin slippers, then took her dressing gown from the hook on the back of the door. She would go there, crawl into the bed beside him, kiss him and make up with him. She'd tell him how much she loved him, and he would forgive her, as he always did.

She crept along the landing, avoiding the squeaky floorboard for fear of waking the children. The door opened with a creak, but to her dismay, the sofa hadn't been pulled down into a bed; no one had slept there. Outside the window, where Eli's car should be parked, the gravel was bare.

She felt sick, like there was ice sloshing in her stomach. She was convinced he'd had a fatal accident, crashed the car and bled to death in a ditch in the dark. And it was all her fault for behaving so badly.

What should she do? Her instinct was to race down the driveway, but of course that would be foolish. She would get dressed, try to think clearly. As she went out to the hallway, something caught her eye.

He must have known exactly what she would do, because there was a note pinned to the inside of the front door, written on the back of a sheet pulled from his yellow prescription pad.

Lena, I'm fine, don't worry. Stay calm, and I'll be back this evening. E x

Her worry was replaced by a wave of frustration. What was he doing? Her life was imploding, and he was chasing around the countryside and staying out all night. And now she was awake, and cold. She stomped into the kitchen and threw open the door of the range, the fire she had damped down last night bursting into life. She threw in a few pieces of turf from the wicker basket near the door, then got down some white flour, currants and baking soda from the high cupboard. She fetched a jug of Jack's buttermilk from the pantry and set about making soda bread, taking out her furious feelings on the dough as she thumped and twisted it on the floured board.

Don't worry? Stay calm? Did Eli expect her just to hang around all day doing nothing, with this threat of eviction over her head? Surely he could see this wasn't just about Emmet; it was about all of them. Sarah and Pádraig would be broken-hearted to leave this house. It was the perfect place to grow up, with room for their ponies and trees to climb in the orchard and spring lambs bouncing in the fields. That was another thing Eli hadn't considered. If they let Malachy take this place from them, what would happen to those fields? At the moment, Lena's brother, Jack, and his American friend, Skipper, used them to graze lambs and cattle, cut silage, grow grain, all rent-free. The fields of Kilteegan House had more than doubled the size of the O'Sullivan family farm, and this made it possible for Jack to turn a sizeable profit and then reinvest that money to improve the farm. Losing it all would be devastating.

And Jack deserved that land, because August Berger had Jack's father murdered. The fields were recompense to Jack, as the house was recompense to her and her family. Emily also benefitted; she and Blackie used the dry, secure outhouses for storage, which freed up the whole of their shop for selling goods and meant they could bulk buy in a way they hadn't been able to before. Because of that, they were in the middle of buying another premises in Bandon and even talking about expanding into Cork eventually.

No, Malachy couldn't do this to her family. It was wrong and cruel. She flung two loaves into the range and slammed the oven door.

In bad temper she ran upstairs, got dressed and went back down to the kitchen. She figured she might as well get on with the day at this stage. Perhaps a cup of tea and a slice of the bread from the oven would improve her mood. She stood, mug in her hand, a million miles away, trying to imagine how this whole mess would be unravelled. She jumped at the sound of a voice and whipped around.

'Are you all right, Lena? You look a bit...I don't know, upset?' Jack was lounging in the kitchen doorway, holding the earthenware jug of fresh milk he delivered to her house every day. At twenty-one, he still looked like their mother. He'd always had Maria's light hair and eyes, but now he was broad and tall like their father as well. He'd also got less nervous as he got older, and now he exuded that same quiet confidence Paudie O'Sullivan had possessed in spades.

'I'm fine, Jack, I'm not upset.' And it was sort of true, because just his gentle presence made her feel calmer. For a split second she thought about confiding in him, but she didn't want to worry him over losing the land if it turned out not to be the case. So instead she said, 'How is Mam? Is she feeling steady? Not too...happy?'

All these euphemisms. A bit low, not great, needing a rest. Steady, normal, on an even keel. Happy, a bit too happy, definitely too happy. Maria O'Sullivan had suffered from manic depression all of her life, and despite several courses of treatment, even electric shock therapy, nothing had really worked. Her family had come to accept that there were times in the year when she was fine, able to care for her youngest daughters, Molly and May, cook for them and Jack and Skipper, run the house, even sew Irish dancing dresses for Emily to sell in the shop. And then there were times when she wasn't able for anything.

Like the last three months, for instance. Maria had spent them in St Catherine's, the psychiatric hospital in Cork run by the nuns that she'd been going to for as long as Lena could remember. She'd only come home last week. Lena had called to the farmhouse on Maria's first day home, and while Maria wasn't manic or anything, she had looked tired and deflated. Her poor mother was tormented by her own mind. Lena loved her, but she could never wholly trust her.

'Mam is feeling much better, very steady, so she said to tell you she'd give the kids their tea, and I can drop them back in time for bed.'

'That's wonderful. Do you think she could take them any earlier? I have a few things to do, and Katie is at her cousin's wedding today.'

'She'd love it, I'm sure. The days are long for her. I just have to check on the lambs, then I'll go back home and send Skipper down for them with the trap.' Though Jack had a car and a tractor, which Skipper used as well, he still preferred a horse and cart, poor old Ned the donkey had been retired and died a few years ago happily in the field after a long life, but Susie the mare had taken over and the children loved travelling in it.

'Are Molly and May around to help Mam?' Her ten-year-old twin sisters were wild about Pádraig and loved dressing Sarah up, although they were a little more distant with Emmet for some reason.

'The twins have gone over to play with Lucy – they've spent nearly the whole Easter holidays there. Deirdre and Bill don't mind, and the girls are so mad about farming and animals and everything about the land, but they'll come running home when they find out your gang are visiting. And Klaus is coming down from Cork too, so don't worry – there'll be plenty of hands on deck.'

'Oh, that's good news about Klaus. He's a lovely man, and he always cheers Mam up. I know we only put them in touch about her trying to find her brother, but it's nice they've become friends. He's a dote but seems a bit lonely, I always think.'

'He's been great to her all right, and she seems, I don't know, kind of calm around him. He's a restful type of person.'

'Well, Emmet will be delighted too. He loves history, and Klaus always makes time for him, takes his questions seriously.'

Klaus Rizzenburg was a historian from Cork University who Lena met on the ferry to Cardiff several years ago. He'd been in the Wehrmacht in France and was so ashamed of his role that he'd devoted his life since the war to finding out what happened to their Jewish victims, whether they had died in the camps or miraculously survived. He'd even offered to help find Maria's beloved brother, Ted, who was living in Leipzig when the war broke out. Nothing had come of that so far, but in the process, Klaus had ended up a good friend of the family and was wonderful about visiting Maria, whether she was in the psychiatric hospital in Cork or home at the farm. He was an unusual man in so many ways, and the years he spent in a Russian gulag after the war had not embittered him but had made him incredibly resilient and self-contained. He was able to manage Maria's illness in a way that others couldn't; he had patience and didn't expect too much. And when she lashed out, he didn't take it personally but accepted it was part of her condition and was willing to wait gently till the storm passed.

Jack set the jug of milk on the table. 'Now how about some fresh soda bread? There's a fine smell and I'm starving.'

'Sit down. I'll make you a cup of tea.' She busied around setting the kitchen table, fetching homemade jam and butter from the pantry and throwing on a pan of rashers, which had been smoked by Jack's good friend Skipper.

Before long, the smell of frying bacon brought the children downstairs, and Jack took Pádraig on his knee, feeding him off his own plate, while Sarah and Emmet tackled the fresh-baked soda bread on the table, with Emmet helping his sister by buttering her slice. Lena was pleased to see her daughter and oldest son getting on so well together and even better pleased when Emmet showed Sarah the word 'butter' on the butter dish and Sarah spelled out the letters. 'B-U-T-T- E-R.'

'Now see how clever you are,' said Emmet. His little sister beamed, delighted with his praise, and Lena felt her heart grow warm.

* * *

TWO HOURS AFTER BREAKFAST, Susie clopped up the drive with Skipper sitting up behind her in the trap holding the reins; he was dressed as usual in a plaid shirt and canvas trousers held up by a belt with a huge buckle, his outfit topped off by the leather Stetson that he always wore; apparently he'd won it in a game of poker from 'a guy in Salt Lake City, Utah', and it made him look like a cowboy from a Western.

The American ranch hand was practically a part of the O'Sullivan family now. Seven years ago, he had come back with Jack from the States, where they'd met when Jack was in Montana researching natural pesticides and herbal veterinary medicines. At first Lena thought the flamboyant cowboy had just come for a holiday, but he'd stayed on until she stopped wondering when he was going home. He seemed to love farming as much as her brother did, and their milk, butter, meat and vegetables were in great demand. The two boys used the alternative natural farming methods Jack had learnt from the Travellers and then at the Montana ranch, and as a result, all their produce was wonderfully tasty.

Squealing with delight, the children chased down the front steps and rushed to pet the old horse. Paudie's old Border Collie, Thirteen, who had a lot of arthritis in her joints now, was happy to curl up beside Skipper's feet. She was as old as the hills, but much loved.

'Wait, wait, your coats!' Lena went running out after them with their coats in her arms. Emmet had already climbed up beside Skipper, and Skipper handed him the reins. While Lena passed up a dark-blue woollen coat to her son, Skipper jumped down to help Sarah and Pádraig on with their little red duffel jackets and then lifted them into the back of the trap, where he covered their knees with a rug.

'Skipper, I can spell "butter"!' Sarah shouted happily. 'B-U-T-T-E-R!'

'Well, isn't that just swell.' Skipper grinned, tipping his hat to Lena as he climbed back into the front beside Emmet. 'Looks like your little gal is following in her brother's footsteps, Lena. Two smarty-pants in one family! Now, kids, wave goodbye to your lovely mama and off we go.'

'Thanks, Skipper, you're a great help.' Lena turned to the children. 'You three be good now,' she said, standing out of the way as Skipper turned the cart to face the gates. 'Do what Skipper and Jack tell you, and don't run your granny ragged. Skipper, tell Klaus I said hello, and tell Mam I'll pick them up after dinner.' She gave Thirteen a rub on the head, and the old dog licked her hand.

'I'll bring them back down to you. It ain't no trouble.' He grinned again.

'Are you sure? You're such a help. Bye, Emmet! Bye, Sarah, and take care of Pádraig, make sure he doesn't fall in the nettles again…'

'Bye, Mam, bye, Mam, bye Mam!' they called as faithful Susie plodded off down the driveway and the irrepressible Skipper flourished his hat in the air by way of farewell.

CHAPTER 5

*B*ack in the house, all was quiet. Mr and Mrs Shanahan were at the same wedding as Katie; it was a grandson of theirs who was marrying Katie's cousin in the local church. Out of loyalty to the Shanahans, and to save the family some money, Lena had offered to host the reception at Kilteegan House, with a marquee in the garden and food from Jack's farm. But the bride had set her heart on the posh new hotel in Bandon, where everyone seemed to be having their weddings these days. Mrs Shanahan had mentioned once or twice that the young lady in question had lots of ideas above her station and the wedding was costing a fortune, but Lena didn't comment. It was all right for Mrs Shanahan to criticise her own, but woe betide anyone else who dared. Now Lena thanked her lucky stars Katie's extended family hadn't taken her up on her generous offer; she didn't know how she would have coped today if she'd had to organise a tea for two people, let alone a reception for maybe seventy.

After clearing away the breakfast things and the children's toys, she went into the small sitting room and sat down to read the letter again.

It still made no sense.

Dear Mrs Lena Kogan...

Why was it only addressed to her? Did Malachy Berger want to punish her personally?

We are writing to advise you regarding your current occupation of the property known as Kilteegan House. The legal owner as per the last will and testament of Mr August Berger, drawn up and placed in trust with us, wishes to assert his right to use or dispose of this property as he sees fit...

Perhaps Malachy was in financial trouble and had been advised by his accountant to do this. Yet he was a wealthy man. She remembered him telling her, 'My father's told me I'm going to be rich when he dies. Apparently his parents were wealthy and their money came to him and will then come to me, so I'll have plenty enough for both of us.'

Further to this wish, he desires you to vacate the property with immediate effect. Refusal on your part to comply will lead to legal action...

On that dreadful night of his father's death, Malachy had told her he still loved her, so how could he act so brutally towards her now?

Yours faithfully,
Ignatius Hayes,
Bachelor-at-Law

That was another thing she didn't understand. Malachy's solicitor was Kieran Devlin, the town solicitor for Kilteegan Bridge. So who was this Ignatius Hayes of Merrion Square? Absolutely nothing about this made sense.

She sat, frowning at the letter, twisting her wedding ring around her finger. Eli's note had told her to wait, that he would be back that evening and she wasn't to worry. But the idea of spending a whole day just waiting...

With an impatient snort, she jumped up from the couch and went to her writing desk, a lovely little rosewood antique she'd picked up for half nothing at a house clearance sale in Cork. She opened the top without needing to unlock it. Although there was a keyhole, the key had been lost before she bought it; she'd never had another made because they didn't keep secrets in their family. The untruths August Berger told had nearly destroyed them all, so complete transparency in everything was their motto.

Although that wasn't strictly true, was it? A pang of guilt washed over her. Eli would never go snooping; he trusted her.

When Kieran Devlin had called them to his office to tell Lena and Eli that Emmet was now the legal owner of Kilteegan House and that she and Eli were to hold it in trust for him until he was eighteen, Kieran had told them that Mr Berger wished no further contact on that or any subject. However, in a private moment with Lena alone, he had slid a business card across his desk, a fancy one with gold embossed writing.

Malachy Berger, BEng
Director
MBE Construction
226–229 Pike Street
San Francisco
Telephone: San Francisco 4-35456

'Mr Berger asked me to give this to you, Mrs Kogan, and only to you, in case you should ever need it.'

And she had taken the card and put it in her purse, fully intending to show it to Eli at the right moment. Except the right moment never seemed to come, and the further it got from when she was given the card, the more difficult it became to tell her husband about it. She had kept it in her purse for two years, and then she had bought the rosewood writing desk and discovered it had a secret drawer, and for the past three years, that is where the card had stayed.

ELI HAD HAD a telephone installed in the house, in the library, in case of emergency calls. Lena now picked up the heavy Bakelite receiver, then set it down without dialling. Then lifted it and set it down again. This was impossible. She wished she didn't feel so furtive. She wasn't doing anything wrong, of course she wasn't, but it felt like she was.

Anyway, if she dialled America from their house, she wouldn't be able to hide the fact even if she wanted to, because it would show up on the next bill. And that was fine, because she wasn't planning to lie to Eli, was she?

Although if she'd had the car, she might have driven as far as Cork to make this call. The General Post Office in Cork had several telephone booths outside, most of which smelled of something unsavoury – she dreaded to think what – but at least she wouldn't risk being overheard by the local postmistress. But Eli had taken the car, so she would just have to trust Geraldine Cronin, who as well as being the postmistress was also the telephone exchange operator for Kilteegan Bridge. Geraldine was a discreet woman, to be fair to her, and she loved Lena because she was Doc's goddaughter. Doc had loved Lena, and Geraldine had loved... Well, it was pretty obvious she would have said yes to Lena's godfather if he'd ever asked.

Sometimes Lena wondered why Doc had never asked, though she suspected it might have something to do with Anthea O'Halloran, the woman friend he went to see in Dublin a few times a year, and who he'd asked Lena to write to when he was dying. Anthea had written a pleasant letter back, asking Lena to give Doc her love, and then another letter after he died, sharing a few memories of the loveable country doctor, his pithy sayings and warm-hearted common sense.

Lena picked up the receiver for the third time, dialled zero and asked Geraldine to book a trunk call to the number in San Francisco. There were two numbers on the card, one said Office, so she assumed the other was his home number. The postmistress managed not to betray the remotest hint of surprise, and she rang back half an hour later to tell Lena the call would start in four minutes. 'Hang up, Lena, and when the telephone rings, you will be connected.'

It felt like hours as she waited for the ring, and when it came, it sounded so loud, her heart leapt in her chest. She grabbed for the heavy receiver, but then raised it slowly while a crackling voice on the far end of the line repeated, 'Hello? Hello?' He sounded sleepy.

She put the receiver to her ear. 'Hello? Hello?' She wished her voice didn't sound so hesitant, so nervous.

'Hello? Is that Mrs Kogan? I was told this was a call from a Mrs Kogan of Kilteegan Bridge.'

'Yes, it is. Is that you, Malachy?' She had no need to ask; she knew it was him. Malachy had never had a West Cork accent, the years of posh boarding schools had seen to that, although now there was a slight American intonation to his voice.

'Oh...' His voice softened and deepened with pleasure. 'Lena?'

'Yes, it's me...' She stopped. It was strange. She'd expected him to sound embarrassed or defensive, but he actually seemed happy to hear from her. 'Malachy I'm sorry, I've woken you...' Her voice trailed off again.

'That doesn't matter. Lena? What's happened? Is Emmet all right?'

The concern in his voice surprised her. It was as if the father in him needed to be sure Emmet was safe, even though he had only met the boy once, seven years ago. 'Yes, he's fine, we're all fine.'

'Oh, thank God. So how have you been, Lena? It's so good to hear your voice. I'm so happy you called. How are you? Are you well?'

'I'm fine,' she repeated. She knew she sounded like a simpleton, but she was getting more and more confused. She'd been planning to berate him or plead with him about the house, but now she wasn't sure what to say.

'You don't sound fine to me, Lena.' The concern crept back into his voice. 'Do you need my help? Has something happened to upset you? Has Eli... Is everything all right at home?'

Malachy using her husband's name jolted her. It was like two parts of her life suddenly touched and sparked off each other. 'Eli is fine. We're very happy.' Whatever might be going on between her and Eli, she would not betray him to Malachy or give Malachy any reason to suspect a crack in their relationship.

'Then what is it?'

Come on, Lena, she berated herself, *stop acting dumb and say what you have to say.* Maybe Malachy was playing games with her. He'd betrayed her before, thanks to his lying father, so why wouldn't he do it again? 'Listen, I've had a letter from your solicitor that says you want us to leave this house...'

'Hello, Lena?'

The line was awful, crackling and buzzing. Perhaps she should have written instead – this was too hard. 'Malachy? Are you there?'

'Yes, I'm here.' His voice came over stronger and clearer. 'You got a letter? What letter?'

'A solicitor's letter.'

'From Devlin?'

'No. From a firm of solicitors in Dublin. And it says you want us to leave Kilteegan House because you want to sell it or live here or something – it wasn't clear.'

'The letter asked you to leave Kilteegan House?' All trace of the enthusiastic, friendly tone had vanished from his voice.

'Yes. Because you want it back.'

He said flatly, 'I don't understand.'

'Neither do I, Malachy.' It was beyond frustrating. 'It says here in black and white that you want us to leave the house right away or you'll set the law on us.'

'Read it to me, Lena.'

She blinked. 'I'm sorry?'

'Please read me the letter. Slowly.'

'But you must know what it says –'

'Read it.'

It was disconcerting; she could hear in his imperious tone an echo of her own son's voice when he wanted something.

'Fine then, wait a second.' She pulled the letter from the pocket of her skirt and spread it on the telephone table. 'It begins, "Dear Mrs Lena Kogan".'

She read it aloud until the end, having to stop and repeat words to him several times when the line crackled too much. When she'd finished, there was a pause that went on for so long, she wondered if she'd been cut off.

'Malachy? Are you still there?'

'You rang me because you think that letter came from me?'

She experienced a surge of irritation. 'Well, what am I supposed to think, Malachy? It does say "the legal owner as per the last will and testament of Mr August Berger". Are you trying to say that's not you?'

'You really think I would ask you to leave Kilteegan House?'

'The letter says –'

'How could you think I'd do that to you? Lena, for God's sake, how could you be so foolish as to think –'

Lena was fed up with men telling her she was being silly, or over-reacting. The whole lot of them could go boil their heads as far as she was concerned. How dare he? 'You're seriously asking me how I think you could do that to me?' she snapped. 'After the time you abandoned me without a word?'

'Lena, you know what happened. My father lied to me –'

'You didn't have to believe him!'

'If you'd only told me you were carrying my child –'

'Eli's child.'

His voice sharpened. 'Come on, Lena. You know I know the truth. Why else would I leave Kilteegan House to Emmet and allow you to live there?'

Allow them indeed. Lena felt her blood boil. *The audacity of this man.*

'I don't know, Malachy. As compensation for your father ordering Phillippe Decker to murder *my* father?'

There was a long, long silence, and again she thought she'd been cut off. But he came back.

'Lena, let's not do this. My father was a sick, evil, lying old man. We don't even know if he was telling the truth about your father's death. Doc Dolan even thought it was an accident, the shotgun backfiring.'

'Stop trying to change history, Malachy. Doc had his suspicions all along, and well you know it. He never voiced them because he couldn't prove them and he didn't want to upset my mother.'

'And how will dredging all of this up now help anyone?'

This time, Lena said nothing, because in a way, Malachy was correct. Long ago, Emily had persuaded Lena that it would be better if their mother continued to believe Paudie had died in an accident. Lena had wanted to go straight to the guards, tell them it was murder, but her older sister was more practical and said there was no point in distressing Maria when there was no way to bring their father back or Phillippe Decker to justice even if they could find him. Doc had put 'accident' as the cause of death, and the only evidence against Decker had died with August Berger.

'Lena, are you there?'

She sighed. 'Yes. Malachy, if this letter is nothing to do with you, then who sent it?'

'I swear, I don't know. Maybe my father playing tricks on us from beyond the grave? I wouldn't put it past him.'

'Then what is the trick? It's scary, Malachy. I don't understand what's happening.' She hoped she didn't sound stupid, but it was the truth.

'It's a stupid mistake. Ignore it.'

'I can't ignore it.' How typical of Malachy, always running away, never wanting to confront a painful situation. 'I have to do something. I was thinking of going to Kieran Devlin, but maybe I should just call this Ignatius Hayes direct and try and find out from him who's behind this.'

'No.' He became decisive. 'Hayes will only hide behind client confidentiality. Take it to Devlin and ask him to ring Hayes himself. He'll stand a better chance of getting an answer from a professional man.'

Again she detected that imperious tone. Why would a grandiose lawyer talk to a mere woman? When Malachy was giving orders, he sounded a bit like his own father. She wondered if he'd got more like August as he got older, the way sons often became more like their fathers whether they liked them or not.

Still, he was right; it was the obvious course of action.

'All right, I'll do that this afternoon. Will I get Kieran to ring you?'

'Yes, and if it's something more than a mistake, I'll get involved. Nobody is cheating my son out of his birthright.'

Lena froze, the receiver clutched in her hand. She knew Eli would hate to hear Malachy saying those words. She should end this call. 'He's not your son, Malachy, I told you.'

'Just tell me what he's like, Lena?' The voice at the far end of the line, from way across the Atlantic, was wheedling. 'I'm not trying to take him off you – I just care about him because he's yours. Is he a clever boy?'

She hesitated. She shouldn't do this. But it was nice to talk to someone who wanted to hear only good things about Emmet, who wouldn't go on about him being too proud or haughty, or not being kind enough to other people. 'Yes, he is clever. He's the most intelligent child in his class. He's really well read, he loves the library here, and he knows all sorts of stuff that even I don't know.'

'That's wonderful. I loved books at his age. Is he good?'

'He is, he's lovely, very sensitive and affectionate, always giving me hugs. And he adores living in Kilteegan House. He's got a little pony of his own called Ollie, and he can jump him over a log already.'

'Make sure he doesn't fall off.'

'He won't. He's got an amazing sense of balance – Mr Shanahan says he's a natural.'

'Books and horses, I like that.' Malachy's voice swelled with pride. 'I had ponies and horses until my mother died, and I could jump a five-barred gate. And do you remember, my mother loved to ride that stallion of hers, even when he went wild in the spring with the fresh grass.'

'I do remember. My father used to soothe him for her.'

'Yes…' He fell silent.

Lena guessed, like her, he was remembering that night when August Berger told them how Malachy's mother, Hannah, had committed suicide and blamed it on Lena's father. Apparently Hannah had some kind of a passion for Paudie, and when she discovered that Maria was pregnant with the twins, she felt rejected or something. The whole thing was mind-boggling. Then he told them how he'd ordered Phillippe Decker to kill Paudie and then tricked Malachy into abandoning Lena. The sins of the father and mother visited upon daughter and son.

Malachy said softly, 'I hate that my mother killed herself, Lena. But love…well, unrequited love is very hard to live with.'

She needed to end this call. 'I have to go, Malachy. I'll talk to

Kieran Devlin, and I'll make sure he lets you know what's going on. Hopefully, like you say, it's just some stupid mistake.'

'Wait, don't go…'

'I'm sorry, Malachy, but I have to.'

She knew what he was trying to do; he wanted to draw her into talking about love, implying there could still be feelings between them. There weren't. Love was simple. She loved her husband and didn't love Malachy. She didn't hate him any more, if she ever had, but she didn't love him.

'Lena…'

'Goodbye, Malachy.'

CHAPTER 6

*L*ena sat waiting in Kieran Devlin's outer office while he made the phone call to Ignatius Hayes from his inner sanctum. She hoped he would be able to deal with the Dublin solicitor; Hayes's firm was based in prestigious Merrion Square, and he was probably a slippery cosmopolitan type.

Land grants and probate, will-making and farm disputes were Kieran's area mostly, with an odd criminal case now and again if a local person got on the wrong side of the law. Still, she trusted him. He was a monosyllabic man in company – she had the misfortune to get stuck beside him on a train once, and getting small talk from him was like getting blood from a turnip – but that was exactly the trait required for a legal man in rural Ireland.

After a while, the murmur on the far side of the heavy door ceased, and she heard a chair being scraped back. Kieran opened the door and beckoned her in. He showed her to a leather chair in front of his desk, while he returned to his seat behind it. On the desktop was the letter from Hayes, Kilgallen and Moran, Solicitors at Law. Kieran placed his fingertips upon it, hooded eyes half-closed as if gathering his thoughts.

The silence hung in the room that smelled of old paper and dust.

Motes danced on the shaft of sunlight coming through the tall Georgian sash windows. The shelves that lined two walls held binders, each marked with a letter and number code so there was no way of knowing what each one was about. On the bookcase was a picture of Kieran's wife, Monica, who was at least a foot taller than him and who sang enthusiastically in the church choir, off-key.

Lena's eyes wandered back to the letter, where Kieran's fingers still rested, stubby and hairy. As a child, she had always marvelled at his hairy hands, and how the dark curls seemed to peep out over his shirt collar, while his hair was quite thin on top. Under his suit she imagined him quite monkey-like. She prompted him. 'So did you manage to talk to Mr Hayes?'

Kieran sighed and tapped on the letter slowly. 'I'm afraid I did, Lena.'

'Afraid...?'

When it came to his work, Kieran was more verbose, thankfully. 'He's a right clown, speaks like he's got a boiled egg in his mouth. He reminded me we were in the same year at university – I thought I knew the name. I had the misfortune to hear him in court a few times. He could drone on for Ireland, and he loves to win a case even if it means getting a right nasty piece of work off scot-free and trampling some poor woman into the ground.'

Lena stared at the county solicitor in astonishment. It was quite a speech for a man who never passed comment on anyone, and for the first time, she realised Kieran was angry. Really, really angry. A shiver ran up her spine. 'Kieran, what did Hayes tell you? Isn't this all a terrible mistake?'

'He told me...' He stopped, inhaled deeply through his nose and carried on. 'He told me that August Berger had made a second will, after he made the will I hold in this office. In the second will, held by Hayes, Kilgallen and Moran, the house in Kilteegan Bridge is left to...' – he ran his hand over his sparse hair – 'Phillippe Decker.'

The solicitor's office faded to a whirl of grey, like a reflection in dirty water going down a plughole. She was in a bad dream; any minute now she would wake up and it would be a normal spring day in Kilteegan Bridge and…

'Lena?' The solicitor's voice came from far away. 'Lena, are you feeling faint? Will I ask Monica to make you a cup of tea, maybe throw a dash of whiskey in it?'

The room steadied and came back into focus. It wasn't a dream. 'Kilteegan House…' Her throat was so dry, her voice came out in a squeak. 'But surely that can't be right. It's our home, Kieran.'

'I'm so, so sorry, Lena, and I wish that was true, but it isn't,' Kieran said bluntly. 'The second will was made after the one August made with me, so that's the one that takes precedent. The house belongs to Phillippe Decker.'

She wanted so much to blurt, 'Decker murdered my father,' but after all this time, it would sound mad, desperate, like grasping at straws. She missed the next thing Kieran said, and tuning back in, heard him say,

'…was probably in the Waffen-SS, like his employer.'

Lena stared at the solicitor, amazed. Up to this moment, she'd believed no one living but her, Malachy, Eli and Emily knew August Berger had been a committed Nazi. It was another one of those terrible secrets that wove themselves around Kilteegan House.

'Malachy told me, Lena,' explained the solicitor simply. 'He needed me to know why he wanted nothing to do with anything his father left to him.'

'And did you tell that to Ignatius Hayes?'

'Believe me, I made sure Hayes knew who he was dealing with. But it made no difference. Like I said, Iggy Hayes doesn't care about morals as long as he's winning.'

She pressed her hands to her temples. How *dare* Decker do this to her! The barefaced audacity, the arrogance. Could he not stay in whatever rathole he'd found for himself? Leave her alone? But no, like a poisonous snake he was back, looking to wreak even more havoc and misery. Well, over her dead body would that awful man ever come within a hundred miles of her or her family.

'Can't we just write to Decker and threaten him we'll tell everyone in Kilteegan Bridge what we know about him if he doesn't go away?'

'Under client confidentiality, he won't give me contact details. We can write to Hayes and he can pass it on if you want to, but...' His tone of voice told her he didn't think that would do any good.

Lena grasped at another hope. 'But the house was a Fitzgerald house, not Berger. August only married in. It belonged to Malachy's mother until she died, and her parents before that. Surely Malachy must have been entitled to inherit his mother's family home?'

'Hannah died without a will, so it became her husband's property. And Malachy wasn't left with nothing. There was the huge legacy from the Berger line – there was a chateau in Alsace, and they were big wine dealers so their cellar was worth millions of francs.'

'Millions? For a few bottles of wine?'

Kieran smiled slightly. 'We don't really get what all the fuss is about wine, sure we don't? I wouldn't thank you for it – give me a nice creamy pint any day – but apparently owning a really good bottle of wine is like owning an old master. Berger told me a good bottle can go for thousands of pounds, and apparently there were a lot of bottles.'

He's right, thought Lena in astonishment, *the Irish really don't understand about wine.*

'Anyway,' continued the solicitor, 'the point is that people can do as they please with their fortunes once their nearest are catered for adequately, so I doubt any court would see this as a miscarriage of justice. Hayes said Decker was bequeathed the property in return for services rendered to Mr Berger during the course of his life and, in particular, in his later years when he was dependent on the other man for his care. I'm afraid the court would see it as a faithful servant being paid for his work.'

'Even if we tell them he was a Nazi?'

'There's no direct proof of that. Only Malachy's word, and he stands to gain. Besides, Decker's not been prosecuted for any war crime, so in the eyes of the Irish courts, he's an innocent man entitled to live his life.'

Once more, she bit back the urge to blurt out the details of Paudie O'Sullivan's murder. She pushed away the image of her father lying in a pool of blood in a field. 'There must be something we can do…'

'I'm going to write to Hayes and request that he hold off proceedings for a month. Iggy Hayes won't mind, because the longer this takes, the more Decker will have to pay him in legal fees. Then I'm going to contact Malachy to explain what's happened and see if he wants to mount a legal challenge on behalf of Emmet, and if he does, I'll give him what support I can.'

Though he'd never said it, Lena knew intuitively that Malachy had told Kieran Devlin the reason he gave them Kilteegan House. If anyone else knew the truth of her son's parentage, she would have been worried, but Devlin was like the tomb. Eli joked that he'd barely tell you the time if you asked him, he was that closed.

She felt a flicker of hope. 'And you'll advise him to contest the will?' Although the thought of Malachy Berger acting as Emmet's champion made her feel nervous, and she doubted if Eli would approve.

'Frankly? No, because that would be unprofessional of me. The challenge will probably fail and cost him a great deal of money.' Kieran was nothing if not honest.

'But if he doesn't challenge it…'

'Then I'd expect Decker to sell the house through Hayes without ever surfacing in Kilteegan Bridge. I'm sorry, Lena. I'm so sorry about all this.'

'It's not your fault, Kieran.' The faintness was coming back; she had to get out into the open air. She stood and picked up her handbag off the desk.

He stood too and walked her to the door. 'I'll stay in touch. And you know where I am.'

CHAPTER 7

*L*ena walked where she always did when she needed to think:
through the village of Kilteegan Bridge that had barely
changed since she was a child, up the hill on the far side of
the village, to the graveyard looking all the way to the sea.

Here in a remote corner lay her father and godfather, lifelong
friends, side by side under the spreading chestnut tree, an idyllically
peaceful spot with a wide view of the distant bay.

Her father's stone read:

Paudie O'Sullivan

1914–1955

Beloved husband and father

Ar dheis Dé go raibh a h-anam dílis

His soul is at God's right hand.

Doc's headstone was a simple limestone.

Emmet 'Doc' Dolan

1913–1960

Beloved doctor, godfather, friend

Ar dheis Dé go raibh a h-anam.

May he rest in peace.

Usually, if the day was dry, Lena would sit on the grass between their graves and announce herself with wry humour by saying, 'Hi, Doc. Hi, Dad. I'm up to you with my problems again. You'd be forgiven for thinking that dying should relieve you both of that responsibility, but alas, no...'

Although when she was pouring out her troubles, it was Doc she addressed the most. She loved both her father and godfather, but she was only fifteen when Paudie O'Sullivan died and Doc had known her as an adult. He knew the whole story of Malachy and Emmet and Eli and had never let her down.

Today, as she approached their corner of the graveyard where the chestnut was slowly unfurling its spring-green leaves, she saw she was not the only visitor. A woman, dressed elegantly in a camel coat and a cream hat, was placing a pot containing a purple and white orchid on Doc's grave. Lena thought this must be the owner of the beautiful maroon Ford she had noticed parked outside the gates.

And maybe it was the same person who had left an orchid on Doc's grave three times before. His former patients often left flowers, so Lena hadn't thought too much of it, even though the orchids had struck her as very exotic.

The woman glanced up as she approached. She was probably in her fifties, Lena thought, tall and very slim, with large hazel eyes. Her coiffed dark-auburn hair had a few silver streaks, but it suited her.

'Hello?' Lena smiled, her natural West Cork friendliness and inquisitiveness coming to the fore despite her inner turmoil. 'Are you a friend of Doc's?'

'Ah...yes, I...' The woman seemed tense. Her accent was cultured, English almost, or at least very posh Dublin. Not Cork anyway. 'I was a...friend of Emmet's. Yes.'

'Nice to meet you. I'm Lena, his goddaughter.' She extended her hand, and at that, the woman relaxed and smiled. She was wearing dark-red lipstick, and her mouth was a beautiful shape.

'The famous Lena. It's nice to finally put a face to the name. Emmet talked about you all the time, and all your family. It feels like I know you already. Oh, I'm sorry, I suppose you're wondering who I am?'

Lena did have an inkling, but she waited politely to be told.

'I'm Doctor Anthea O'Halloran.'

So Lena had guessed right. This was the woman her godfather had visited in Dublin several times a year yet never brought home or even talked about except briefly when he was dying. 'Then you're very welcome to Kilteegan Bridge, Dr O'Halloran.'

'Thank you, Lena, and please, Anthea.' The woman still had hold of Lena's hand. 'Emmet told me all about you. He loved you so much.'

Though she knew it to be true, Lena felt a warm glow at hearing it from someone else. 'I loved him too. My father died when I was young, and Doc stepped into his shoes.'

'Yes, he told me.' Anthea glanced at the simple headstone and then back to Lena. 'I was so sorry to miss his funeral, but I often drop by if I have a medical conference in Cork.'

As much as Lena wanted to be alone, it felt wrong not to offer a proper Cork welcome to a friend and colleague of her godfather's. 'Can I buy you a cup of tea in the village? I was going to go and say hello to my dad over there and I'll leave you with Doc, but maybe afterwards?'

The woman smiled. 'I can't, I'm afraid. I've had my chat with Emmet, and now I have to hurry back to my patients in Dublin. But here.' She dug in her handbag and produced a card. 'This is where I live. It's an odd address because it's a sort of rest home for the disabled and terminally ill, but I have a house on the premises, so you'll find me. If you're ever in Dublin, please do visit me and stay the night, or as long as you like as I've plenty of room, and we'll have a lovely time talking about your godfather. He was a great friend of my husband's as well. We all trained as doctors together, but now Michael has gone...' She stopped and sighed. 'Well, I have no one who talks about Emmet any more, so it would be lovely to spend some time with you, remembering him.'

Lena took the card. 'I'd love that.'

* * *

AFTER ANTHEA LEFT, Lena sat down between the graves as she always did. Yet somehow it didn't feel right today; the orchid distracted her. Was there some big secret in Doc's life he had hidden from her? Something felt strange about Anthea. Not *wrong* – she seemed like a lovely person – but...mysterious.

'Doc?' But it felt like he wasn't talking to her.

'Dad?' Another silence.

Sighing, she got back to her feet. 'OK, you two, keep your secrets, and I'll go and talk to...' She had been going to say 'Eli' but then remembered their terrible argument and realised that, far from wanting to go home and share her troubles with her husband and best friend, she was dreading having to face him. She'd have to tell him about Malachy, and Devlin, and Decker, and it was all too horrible and hard.

But she had to talk to someone.

It crossed her mind to confide in Klaus, who Jack had told her was up at the farm today. The historian was a lovely, helpful man, and he might even be able to use his contacts to get some information on Decker. Maybe he could find out the man's address, so Lena could... Well, she wasn't sure what she could do, maybe set Nazi hunters on him. But Klaus was with Maria, and she and Emily had agreed that Maria was to be kept in the dark when it came to Phillippe Decker.

Emily. She would talk to Emily.

She would have thought of her sister before if she wasn't so annoyed about Emily complaining to Eli about Emmet. But she and Emily were very close and always forgave each other everything, and besides, how could she not tell her sister that their father's murderer was alive and might turn up in Kilteegan Bridge? Devlin suspected the Waffen-SS man only wanted to sell the house, but if he had the nerve to do that, then who knew what he might do next.

* * *

THESE DAYS CREAN'S HARDWARE, on Kilteegan's main street, was more like one of those fancy places up in Cork or Dublin. Emily had turned the whole thing around, transforming a dark, dingy place selling buckets and yard brushes and treatments for roundworm into a bright, sunny place with lovely tea sets, cheerful oilcloth you could buy by the yard to brighten up the kitchen table and nice pots and ornaments for the garden.

All the boring, necessary stuff that farmers and builders needed over and over again, sacks of cattle and sheep feed, tractor parts, lengths of timber, things like that, were stored in the extensive outhouses of Kilteegan House, saving Emily and Blackie Crean a fortune between not having to rent storage space and being able to free up the whole shop to look inviting and attractive.

There was even a large section devoted to their mother's sewing: elaborate dresses for Irish dancing, women's dresses, christening gowns. They sold lengths of material and patterns too, along with wool, needles and crochet equipment. When Maria was feeling well, she often helped out in the shop and gave advice and assistance to women who wanted to make their own dresses.

When Lena entered the shop to the ring of the bell, Emily looked up from behind the counter with a smile that turned into an expression of guilt. She straightened up, touching her long fair hair that, like Lena's, was twisted into a bun. She, like Jack, looked so much like Maria these days, her eyelashes and eyebrows so light they were almost invisible, her body long and graceful. 'Hi, Lena.'

Although she'd come here to warn her sister about Decker, Lena felt annoyance surface in her chest again; she couldn't get past Emily talking to Eli behind her back. 'Hi.'

A silence hung between them.

'Look, I don't want to get into a fight, but Eli said you were talking to him the other day about Emmet?' Lena let the words hang, waiting to see what her sister would say in return.

Emily winced. 'Lena, I'm sorry. Eli probably told you what I said to him about Emmet. I don't think he was being bad, just a bit silly, but

Nellie did get upset, so I was upset, and Eli was just there right in front of me because he had come round to see to Blackie's mam's bunions. Otherwise I would have said it to you directly, although I know you're protective of Emmet, which I understand, I really do. I would be too if… Well, anyway, I'm really sorry.'

Lena's heart melted. Emily was such a sweet, gentle woman. She knew all about Emmet's start in life but had never murmured a word about it. As far as Emily was concerned, Eli was Emmet's father and the less said about anything else, the better.

Lena realised she had bigger problems and decided to forget it. 'It's fine, Em. His father set him weeding with Mr Shanahan to teach him a lesson about hard work, and I'll talk to him myself about it if you like.'

'Ah sure, an afternoon weeding is grand, poor lad, and Nellie forgot about it straight away. Herself and Emmet are thick as thieves anyway, and sure they're bound to have the odd squabble.'

The air thoroughly cleared, Emily called out the back to her husband. 'Blackie, I'm just having a cuppa with Lena upstairs, so keep an eye on the counter, will you?'

Blackie emerged, his dun-coloured shop coat over his clothes. Emily said she was tired of trying to get all kinds of stains out of his shirts.

'Howra, Lena?'

'Grand, Blackie, and yourself?'

'Sure she has me worked to the bone, but apart from that, I'm fine.' He chuckled.

'Go way outta that, you chancer. Who got up this morning to get our daughter's breakfast and check all the deliveries?' Emily raised an eyebrow.

'Ah, fair enough, I suppose. Go away and have yer natter. I'll be advising on all the latest fashions.' He laughed good-naturedly and returned to whatever it was he was doing.

'Come on. Mrs Crean dropped over some porter cake yesterday. Save me from myself by eating a bit of it.'

They climbed the stairs to the family home over the shop, and Lena took a seat at her sister's table in the long kitchen that ran the full length of the building overlooking the main street. They chatted about the weather and Emmet and Nellie's new teacher as Emily spooned leaves and poured hot water from the kettle simmering on the range into a Royal Doulton teapot.

'What a beautiful teapot,' Lena said admiringly.

Emily blushed. 'Oh, I wouldn't usually bother with such fancy ware, but there was a small chip on the handle when it arrived...see?' She pointed to a near-invisible blemish. 'So I wrote and complained to the supplier, and they sent a replacement and I get to keep the old one. It isn't saleable, but it's still nice, isn't it?'

'It really is.' Emily and Blackie worked so hard and were saving all their money to help them expand into Bandon and, later, Cork, so it was nice to see her sister enjoying something elegant of her own, even if it was only a second from the shop.

'So what's up?' asked Emily.

Lena winced. 'I'm here with some very bad news about the "big house" as it happens.'

'What is it?' Emily pulled up her chair and poured out two cups of tea. 'Don't tell me you've a hole in the roof or something. That will cost you a fortune with the size of the place. But don't worry, Blackie will get you all the materials you need. We know how much we owe you for letting us use the outhouses for storage.'

Lena added milk to her tea. 'You don't owe us or anybody anything, Emily. You deserve to benefit from Kilteegan House as much as I do. August Berger had our father murdered, and giving the house to Emmet was the least Malachy could do by way of making amends. And so does Jack.'

Emily shot a startled glance towards the open door, her finger to her mouth. 'Shh! You haven't told Jack, have you?'

Long ago, the two sisters had agreed not to tell their brother about the murder, at least for a while. Jack still shared a house with their mother, and Maria had an uncanny ability to ferret out a secret. She always seemed to know when someone wasn't telling her something and would get upset if they continued to hold back. And Jack was no good with lies – he was as honest as the day was long – so it wouldn't be fair on him to make him carry such a heavy secret.

'No, I haven't. But, Emily, it might come to that yet. Phillippe Decker might be coming back to Kilteegan House.' And as Emily listened in open-mouthed horror, the whole story came tumbling out.

By the time Lena finished, Emily was seething with fury. 'Are you saying he could come back here to stay? No, I couldn't bear it. We just can't have him back in our lives, wandering around here, rubbing our noses in what he did to us.'

'I know.' She felt Emily's outrage. 'I could just about live with the idea that Daddy was gone if it had been an accident. I'd put it to the back of my mind, get on with my life. But this is my town – not just the house, that too – but Kilteegan Bridge. I couldn't bear knowing that the man who killed our father could be in the post office or buying meat in the butcher's. Knowing I could run into him any time… We can't let Phillippe Decker destroy us all over again.'

'Maybe that…that…awful man…will just sell it and not come back. Which would be terrible for you and Eli, of course. I'm so sorry, Lena.'

'Not just for us, I'm afraid. Eli and I can buy another house, not as grand but a nice home to raise our children in. But it also means you losing the storage sheds and Jack losing half his farm when he's done so much work on the land.'

'Oh, you're right.' Emily went white, the enormity of the problem now dawning on her. 'How am I going to tell Blackie? We'll never afford the premises in Bandon now, and poor Jack, and poor Skipper as well.'

'I know, and it can't be allowed to happen. Kieran Devlin has told this man Hayes we need a month to sort things out, and maybe Malachy will contest the will, which might draw everything out for years.'

'But you said Kieran thinks Malachy would lose?'

'Yes, and to be honest, Em, I don't think Eli would even want

Malachy to get involved. He's going to be upset enough as it is when I tell him I called Malachy in California.'

'Mm. Yes.' Emily was too kind to offer an opinion, but she clearly knew what Lena meant and she was likely to be on Eli's side.

Lena rushed to reassure her, feeling bad for worrying her about something that might never happen. 'We won't let him do this to us, Emily, I promise. We'll find a way to stop him.'

'But how?'

'I don't know, but we'll find a way. And when we do, we're going to make sure that man will rue the day he ever got involved with the O'Sullivans of Kilteegan Bridge.'

* * *

WHEN SHE GOT HOME AROUND six, Eli's car was outside the front door. She stepped softly into the hall, listening. No sound of children's voices, so Skipper must not have brought them home yet. No sign of Eli either. He was in the library probably, reading the newspaper over a tumbler of whiskey. They kept a decanter on the dresser, and while he wasn't a heavy drinker, Eli did enjoy a glass after work while he was catching up on the news and doing the crossword.

Lena tiptoed across the hall and up the carpeted stairs. After her long day, she felt grubby in mind and body, and she wanted to get clean and changed before she tried to explain things to her husband. In her dressing room, she stripped off her dusty clothes, washed herself at the sink and brushed her dark silky hair until it gleamed. She buttoned on a black blouse and then a fine-knit green sweater and a black skirt, shorter than a lot of women wore around here but that was all the rage in Cork and Dublin. She didn't bother with stockings. She had skin that took the sun easily, like her father – even on her legs it wasn't that milk-bottle white most Irish people were – and once the spring sunshine warmed up, her light natural tan would get darker. She tied up her hair in a ponytail, knowing Eli loved it like that, and she wore a little dusting of makeup.

Then she descended the stairs, her stomach in knots of anxiety, and entered the library.

Sure enough, Eli was there, sitting by the fire, reading his paper and sipping whiskey from a crystal tumbler. He looked up with a start when he saw her. 'I didn't hear you come in. I thought you were out with the children. Where are the little monkeys? Normally by now they'd be climbing all over me.'

'Skipper took them up to the farm for the day. Mam is giving them their tea.'

He nodded, setting down the newspaper and feeling in his jacket pocket. 'Good, because I wanted to talk to you in peace, without interruptions.' He held out a cream envelope.

'What is it?' She eyed him warily. No kiss, no smile. So things were still strained between them.

'Take it, Lena. It's something I thought might help. But before you open it, remember I'm just giving this as an option. It's not what I'm saying you have to do – I just thought it might solve the problem.'

Stepping forwards, she took the envelope. Inside was a cheque for the sum of 4,000 pounds, made out to cash. She stared at it stupidly.

'I just thought, if we paid Malachy Berger off...' Eli's voice was hopeful. 'That's what I was doing all day. I got the house valued and raised that much between money my Uncle Saul put in a fund for me, money he managed to get after the war from my family's estate, funds from Charlie's bank and then our own savings. We can't raise a mortgage on this property since technically Emmet owns it, but Charlie was able to pull a few strings and assured the board of his bank that I was a safe bet to lend money to. We had about 1,200 in our own savings, Saul's fund was worth around 1,500, so I borrowed the rest. And so I thought maybe if it was just about the money, Berger could take that and use it for whatever he wanted, far away from us, and that would be an end to it.'

Lena raised her eyes to him but she was still speechless, and her lack of response seemed to make him nervous.

'I know the way I reacted last night was wrong,' he said anxiously. 'I was jealous and... Look, I'm so sorry. And if you think this is a mad idea, or you think I'm trying to tell you what to do again, we can forget it obviously. But I just thought maybe as an option...'

'This is so kind of you.' Her voice was choked.

His boyish face brightened. 'Lena, darling, I'm not being kind. I'm standing by my wife and trying to help her get what she wants. It will clean us out for a while, but so would buying a different house, and you don't want a different house. So this way we can draw it all up legally and everything, so we own the house properly and can never lose it again. He takes the money instead of the house, and that's the end of it all. And we go on to live happily ever after, never having to hear the name Malachy Berger again for the rest of our lives.'

Lena put the cheque back in the envelope. 'But I'm afraid it doesn't solve the problem, Eli. I rang Malachy in California, and he knew nothing about any solicitor's letter. He said it didn't come from him at all, so I went to Kieran Devlin and...'

'You rang Malachy?' Eli was staring at her grimly. 'You had his number?'

She felt like stamping with annoyance. 'Yes, Eli, Kieran Devlin gave me his card a long time ago. And I'm sorry I never told you I had it, but it never seemed like the right time.'

'I can't believe this.'

'If you could hear yourself carrying on, you would believe it. How am I supposed to tell you things when you don't trust me?'

'You never told me you had his card. You've been in contact with him.'

'Just the once, Eli, and that was today, because I *had* to do it, not because I *wanted* to. God's sake, he lives in America, California –'

'And now he wants to come back to Kilteegan Bridge? To be near you?'

'Stop this nonsense and listen to me!'

He started to say something else but then caught himself and just looked at her.

She sighed. 'Malachy said he knew nothing about the letter. He told me to speak to Kieran Devlin. So I spoke to Kieran, and he rang the Dublin solicitor. And it turns out August Berger made a second will that takes precedence over the first, and the new will left the house to...' As Eli stared at her, finally listening properly, she forced herself to say that hated name once more, the one she'd uttered more times today than she'd spoken it in the last five years. 'Phillippe Decker. For services rendered.'

Silence. The Nazi's name hung in the air. The clock on the mantelpiece ticked, and a family of rooks that nested in the old sycamore tree outside cawed loudly. Eli rose from the sofa and came to put his arms around her. He kissed her forehead and stroked her hair.

'Oh, Lena. I'm sorry. I'm so sorry.'

And that was when she finally broke down in tears. The phone call with Malachy, Devlin's discovery of who actually owned Kilteegan House, even the mysterious meeting in the graveyard that had only added to the stress of the day, it all came crashing through her brave façade, and she sobbed against Eli's shoulder, gasping out deep howls that seemed to come from her very bones. Her husband guided her to the sofa and gave her his linen handkerchief, and she leaned against him as he patted and stroked her, whispering affectionate words, trying his best to calm her.

'It's OK, my love,' he kept murmuring. 'We'll get through this. We'll find a way.'

'But how?' she sobbed. 'If he moves back here, how can I stand it? Or Emily? And even if he just sells the place...'

'If he sells it from under us, we'll buy another house. I even know which one. The Munnelly place out towards Skibbereen is coming up for sale – they're moving back to Roscommon to be near her parents – and it's got a little lake and lots of gardens for the kids. The house isn't as big or as grand as this one, but it's bright and sunny and it's got five bedrooms. And if that devil does move back to Kilteegan Bridge, we'd be far enough away not to run into him. This house is nearer to Castletownorben than Kilteegan Bridge, so the children could go to school there, we'd shop there and live there, but you'd still be close enough to your family to drive over whenever you wanted. We'll get a second car...'

She pulled away from him, angrily scrubbing her face with the handkerchief, ruining her makeup. 'So we run away from him? He just decides he wants to come back here and live happily ever after despite what he did, and we just scurry off like mice?'

He sighed, hurt. 'I'm just trying to think of what's best to do in bad circumstances.'

'It's not just about us, Eli. It's more than half of Jack's farm, and it's all of Blackie and Emily's storage. It will crush everyone's plans. And maybe you and me could run away and buy a nice house, but we can't afford to buy Emily new sheds or Jack a new farm around Kilteegan Bridge, even if they could be got – which they can't. And Emily can't move away from here, and do you think she wants to run into Decker every day if he comes back? It would break her heart.'

Eli let her hand go and turned to face the flickering fire, his forearms resting on his thighs, dark shadows chasing across his face. Finally he said, 'Then let's give Decker the 4,000 pounds.'

She glared at him in astonishment, unable to believe her ears. 'Eli, no. It's kind of you, but we can't live with the knowledge that he ended his days in luxury from the proceeds of his crime! Because you can bet the biggest "service" Phillippe Decker rendered to August Berger was the murder of my father.'

'I know, Lena. But you say you don't want him here, and I agree with you, but short of tracking him down and shooting him or something, what else can we do? If we pay him off, then Emily and Blackie and Jack get to keep everything they have, and you can too.'

For a moment, she could see the sense of his argument 'Yes, but –'

'We can't control what other people do, Lena. We can only control how we react to it. So if that means this man Decker has a legal right and we have to legally go along with this, all I'm saying is, there's a way to salvage the situation.'

She knew there was a kernel of truth in her husband's words. They could indeed decide to accept this awful new reality and work with it to get the best solution possible. Eli was good like that; he could see how to walk around a barrier instead of trying to climb over it. But the thought of paying off her father's killer... 'I don't know, Eli.'

He reached over and took her hand again, smiling his boyish smile.

'Just think about it for a few days, Lena. We can get through this, and we can move forwards, with hope.'

Before she could answer, there was a rush of feet and the door flew open, and the children piled into the room shouting, 'Daddy! Mammy!' The two youngest threw themselves furiously on Eli, and Emmet climbed sleepily onto her lap and wound his loving arms around her neck.

CHAPTER 8

STRASBOURG

*P*hillippe Decker struggled up and down the lawn, shoving along the ancient contraption that passed for a mower. After a while, he stopped to wipe the sweat from his neck with the handkerchief from his pocket, and when he looked up, he saw Madame Faber watching him from behind the curtain in the window above.

He nodded to her, raised his hand in a slight wave, and she turned away hastily. The wealthy widow had barely spoken to him since the day she had taken him on as a part-time gardener. She acted like there was this great gulf between them, but he didn't care; he knew they were cut from the same cloth and knew she knew it too.

On his first day, she had brought him into the hall of her house, and while she was giving him his instructions, his eyes had drifted to a small framed photograph on the wall of a fat fisherman holding up a large pike. With a start, he'd recognised that man, despite the hat nearly covering his face. It was Ernst Faber, or Standartenführer

Faber, as Phillippe Decker had known him back then. A jovial colonel, florid-featured and full of fun, who looked like he wouldn't hurt a fly. Unless that fly was Jewish, and then, well, then he was capable of untold cruelty.

Normally Decker's path would not have crossed with someone like Colonel Faber, who was so far above him in rank, but August, by virtue of his higher breeding, had dragged Decker with him out of the anonymous world of the NCOs into the ranks of the Untersturm-führers. The Berger name meant something in Alsace; they were cele-brated wine merchants. Plus August was always happy to smooth the way for the two of them with bottles of vintage Crémant or Pinot Gris. Not that the bottles contained what they said they did. August's parents were a cunning old pair, and they had taken the precaution of relabelling all of the best vintages as cheap ones and vice versa, as well as building a secret vault in their huge cellar near Colmar to hide the most expensive stock, which was worth many thousands of francs a bottle. Luckily the Boche would drink any cheap old stuff, and if the label said Grand Cru, they were happy.

To be admitted to the Untersturmführers, August and Phillippe had to be physically, politically and socially screened to ensure they were of clean Aryan blood and had no connection to the Jews. Decker was questioned closely about the Loebs, but he explained they'd been people he barely spoke to, 'just neighbours', nothing more.

It reminded him of the story in the New Testament where the Roman soldiers ask Peter if he knows Jesus and Peter says three times that he does not. Peter acted like a coward, but later he repented and all was forgiven. And if Phillippe had seen Rebecca Loeb again, he would have told her he was sorry too. And she would have forgiven him, like Jesus forgave Peter, because what would have been the point in sacrificing himself for nothing? Standing up to be counted, admit-ting he loved a Jewess, would have meant one thing only: a bullet against a wall at dawn.

So instead he had denied her, and he and August were both shipped off to SS-Junkerschule Bad Tölz in Bavaria to train for their commissions.

He would never forget the ceremony where they, along with their graduating class, were incorporated into the SS officer corps and presented with their insignia and SS sword. Nobody did pageantry like the Nazis; they could give the Catholic Church a run for their money when it came to pomp and ceremony.

He remembered seeing pictures of the rallies at Nuremberg when he was a lad, when he'd been concerned only with impressing Rebecca and dreaming up ways for them both to escape the oppressive social constraints of Eguisheim. People were sniggering at the Germans then, goose-stepping and all marching like little tin soldiers, paying homage to that stupid little Austrian. Not one of them knew the fate that lay in store, not just for Germany but for almost the entire world, the havoc, misery, pain and death to come. Hitler might have been little, and he was Austrian, but he wasn't stupid. Mad definitely, but stupid, never. He knew just the buttons to press, just the things to say to stoke the fires of German national pride so decimated by Versailles. He needed someone to blame for the loss of the Great War, the destruction of German industry, the annihilation of their armed forces, the savage reparations that were keeping the proud nation on its knees economically as well as culturally, and the Jews were as good a target as any.

Decker gave up on the mower and sat on the stone surround of the fountain to eat his lunch of greasy cheese, tomato and half a baguette grudgingly given by the sour-looking housekeeper. He then spent the rest of the afternoon trying to cut through a clematis that had wound itself around some old trellis that was disintegrating. As the sun set, his hands scratched to pieces because blackberry bushes and dog roses were also in the tangle of vegetation, he went as usual to the front door to receive his pay. He thought it odd that she insisted on paying him herself rather than letting the old bat in the kitchen do it.

Madame Faber always paid him at the door, without inviting him in. She was stingy in her recompense, but he always took whatever she offered and promised he would come back the following week. This time, however, she beckoned him inside, something she hadn't done since the day he'd started. Though once he was in the house, she didn't seem to know what to do with him. For what felt like an interminable time, she fidgeted around the hall while he stood patiently waiting. An Egyptian vase, three feet tall, rested on a polished table at the foot of the stairs, and the smell was of lavender wax polish and something else, a kind of musty, mothball smell, maybe from the Turkish rug beneath his feet.

He wondered how old the woman was. As she fussed around him, he thought she smelled like the house, of camphor and dust. She was thin and tall, her skin was so dry it looked almost papery, her grey hair was drawn back in a bun over her skull, and age spots dotted her pale complexion. Yet she could have been any age. The war did that. It did it to everyone, in equal measure. He'd noticed it as he and August had made their way across France to get to Ireland at the end. French, English, Americans, Canadians – it didn't matter; the war aged everyone far beyond their years.

Eventually the old woman stopped dithering and took down the photograph of the fisherman from the wall, her bony ringed fingers clasping it tightly, and held it out to him. 'Do you know him?' she asked. Her voice was tremulous and high-pitched, the voice of someone who never went outside and barely ever spoke. 'I saw you looking at him once, on your first day here.'

Phillippe met her eyes and inclined his head.

She held the photo against her almost flat chest. 'I never learnt what happened to him. I would like to know where he died. Do you have that information?'

Clearly she'd been mulling this over since that very first day. She was his kindred spirit, used to being very cagey about who she was, what her past connections were. This was dangerous for her; she must have been desperate. He wondered why she cared. What was the difference? She knew her husband was dead, clearly, and he was, so why was finding out how it happened worth exposing herself like this? Was she harbouring a secret hope he was still alive?

Phillippe knew exactly where Ernst Faber died and how he died as well. The story of Faber was almost legendary, and there was a certain schadenfreude to the retelling. Faber was not well liked. Phillippe had heard the story from August, who'd heard a bunch of Waffen-SS officers laughing about it one night after too much wine.

A group of maquisards had detonated a bomb under a railway carriage, destroying vital supplies to Northern France in 1940. Faber had, along with the Gestapo, investigated the attack, and once they found the culprits, or who they imagined were the culprits, they shot them in the town square. A man came forwards to bargain for the life of his twelve-year-old son, who had already been beaten badly by Faber. 'Shoot me instead,' he'd begged.

Faber had complied.

The son survived, but he grew to follow in his father's footsteps and tracked Faber down in a brothel in Paris in 1944. The young man, now sixteen, along with some compatriots, tortured Faber with the full compliance of the girl he was paying and left him to slowly bleed to death, naked and alone in a tart's bedroom.

The story had spread like wildfire through the Waffen-SS ranks, eliciting indignation on the face of it but a certain degree of satisfaction in private. Faber didn't care to get his own hands dirty but did enjoy dreaming up elaborate and brutal methods of torture for his victims that he would then instruct his subordinates to carry out. He seemed to derive some dark pleasure from watching. His death was fitting.

'The last time I saw him was in Baden-Baden, at a conference. That was in late '42, early '43 maybe. I never saw him again after that.'

Phillippe was telling the truth. He was never again in his life going to lie. He'd made himself that promise once he left Ireland. He'd keep silent, never volunteer information unless asked a specific question, but not lie. Why should he? He had done what he could to survive. He had nothing to be ashamed of; everyone had done what they needed to survive. Like Peter in the Bible, who had been forgiven by Jesus.

'So you don't know where he died?' Her blue gimlet eyes in her old careworn face were like chips of ice.

'I heard something about Paris.'

'In action?'

'I think he was.' Again, not a lie; he was on top of a prostitute.

'So he died with glory then, with honour.' It was a statement, not a question, so Phillippe remained silent. What good would speaking up do for her or for him? None. Plus it would probably lose him the only job he was likely to get.

Without another word she hung the photo back on the wall, fussed around at the sideboard, then passed him a small brown envelope. It felt a little heavier than usual, not much, but perhaps she'd thrown in a few extra centimes for the information. Then as he turned to leave, she tapped him on the shoulder and handed him a dusty bottle. A bottle of eau de vie, a strong spirit made from the remains of the crushed grapes.

'Thank you,' she said.

'*Merci, madame.*' He took the bottle and left.

He waited till he turned the corner to open the envelope, and yes, to his relief there were two francs extra. A baguette was thirty-five centimes, so it meant he could afford some meat for his dinner as well. He stopped at the *boucherie* and asked for a *saucisson*; the hard salted sausage was strong-flavoured enough that a little went a long way. He'd fry a few slices with onions, and the fat in the sausage would render down and flavour the onion beautifully. He would have that with the last of the brie he'd bought yesterday when the *fromagerie* at the corner of his street was selling it cheap. It was overripe, so he'd only paid a few centimes for it, but it was still delicious.

He was salivating as he walked. He dropped in at the small post office to see if there were any letters for him. He never gave anyone his real address; he only ever used this place. Sure enough, there was a letter for him. It was slightly wrinkled and damp; either it had been delivered in the rain or the postmistress, intrigued by the Irish stamp, had steamed it open. She was a nosy woman, but it didn't matter if she'd tried to read it – she wouldn't have been able. The address was written in perfect French, but he knew the contents would be in English. He decided not to read it himself until he got home, just savour its possibilities, so he stuck it in the pocket of his threadbare coat.

Half an hour later, he entered the dark hallway of the house where he had a single room on the top floor. The familiar odour of *choucroute garnie*, the local dish of cabbage and pungent garlic sausage, assailed his nostrils. Madame Muller prepared the exact same meal every single night for her and her husband, and the aroma often made his stomach grumble.

Soon, if the letter said what he thought it would, he would be able to afford such luxuries.

With it nearly burning a hole in his pocket now, he quickly climbed the three flights of rickety stairs, passing the floor where a woman he suspected was a prostitute lived with three children, one an infant. There had been no sign of a husband as far as he was aware, and they only ever nodded to each other if they met on the stairs.

She wasn't bad-looking, considering, and she wouldn't charge much, based on where she was living. Maybe once he got hold of his money…

He let himself into the only room on the top floor. It was spartan in its décor, even by army standards. A single bed with one set of sheets, a woollen ex-army-issue blanket and a pillow that even when folded over raised his head a bare two inches from the thin mattress. There was a scarred table and an old chair liberated from a bistro, he imagined, that served as a desk, dining table and food preparation area. He'd invested in a Primus stove, again ex-army issue, in a second-hand shop in Ribeauvillé one day, so he could heat soup or make coffee in his one pot. It was necessary in the winter when the room, without a fireplace or any kind of heating, was bitterly cold.

He sat on the bed and took out his letter, all thoughts of his dinner forgotten. He kicked off his boots, leaned back on the iron bedstead and savoured the moment. August Berger had left him Kilteegan House in his will, and he'd promised that Malachy would organise the sale after his death and send the money to Phillippe's bank account. Yet over the years, as the money August sent him away with dwindled, the bank account remained empty.

He had no address for Malachy to ask what the hell was going on, and he was reluctant to go back to Ireland to track him down. Who knew what a dying man might have blurted out on his deathbed?

Then, a few years ago, he had picked up a copy of the *West Cork Chronicle*, which an Irish tourist had left on his seat in a café, and to his absolute fury, there was the christening photograph, posed on the steps of Kilteegan House, and a headline screaming that the local doctor and father of three had recently been appointed the Chief Medical Officer for the Munster region. There was the girl, Lena O'Sullivan, and all her inferior family: the mad mother, the pervert brother, the shopkeeper couple. And of course, her Jewish husband, Eli Kogan, whose family must have cut and run from Germany before the war, as all Jews did if they could, saving their own skins like anyone else with an ounce of sense. Did anyone blame the Jews for what they had to do? Of course not. All the blame was reserved for the Germans.

He thought again what a pity it was that Rebecca's parents had been so foolish, ignoring his advice. The Germans would have allowed them to leave, but instead they had come back to Alsace, clinging to their belongings. Which was why it had been down to him in the end – well, August – to rescue their daughter, Rebecca, from Auschwitz.

After seeing the newspaper article, he had written to the Dublin solicitor, and the last of his savings had gone to paying that oily Ignatius Hayes, who had promised to sort everything out, to contact Malachy if he could find him and also write to Lena O'Sullivan, ordering her and her family to leave the premises. Perhaps this letter was to tell him the house had been sold already. Perhaps it contained a cheque for thousands of pounds.

Licking his lips in anticipation – first stop, the prostitute on the second floor – he gazed at the envelope for the longest time, then slit it open.

Dear Mr Decker,

I am writing to advise you that Malachy Berger, the only son of August Berger, is refusing to recognise the last will and testament of August Berger.

While we do not expect him to mount a serious legal challenge, his opposition will lead to some delay and unfortunately will incur further legal fees. Please deposit in our account...'

He gazed at the letter for the longest time, until eventually the words swam before his eyes.

CHAPTER 9

*L*ena drove Jack's Morris Minor towards the University of Cork through twisting, narrow streets crammed with student accommodation, buzzing cafés, bookstores and second-hand clothes shops. As she passed the glass windows of Jackie Lennox's, the famous fish-and-chip shop, in her mind she heard the voice of a teenage boy, coming back to her from across the years.

'There's a gorgeous chipper up behind the college, Jackie Lennox's. Or maybe you'd prefer a restaurant? Sorry, Lena, I wasn't thinking...' Malachy had been humbler then, with less of his father's autocratic tone.

'I love chips, and I can't think of anything I'd rather do than eat chips in a car with you,' she had assured him. She wouldn't have minded what they did or ate that day; she was so happy just being with him.

How things had changed.

Now, with the gates of the university looming ahead of her, she parked the car on the cobbled street and wondered how she was going to find Klaus Rizzenburg in this huge ancient building.

She had never visited Klaus at the university before; they'd always met in a restaurant or else at Kilteegan House or her mother's farm. The history professor had been a country boy in Germany before the war, and he loved an excuse to get out into the country-side. And besides, he had developed a particular fondness for Jack's potatoes, boiled until they were fluffy and then dolloped with rich farm butter by Maria. Maria had told her with a giggle how Klaus loved all food, though he was rake thin, and he never left even a crumb on his plate.

Today was exactly two weeks since she and Eli had talked about paying Phillippe Decker the four thousand pounds. She had called Klaus the day after their discussion.

She hadn't told the professor why she wanted to know what she did, because everyone except Emily and Jack and Kieran Devlin thought she and Eli had bought Kilteegan House. All she said was that she wanted to know about the two people who had lived in the house before her, that they were from Alsace but she'd heard a rumour they'd been in the Waffen-SS and she couldn't get it out of her head, that it was haunting her and she needed to know one way or the other.

Klaus had been sympathetic and said he knew an amateur histo-rian in Alsace who might be able to help. 'He's on a committee that is part of the International Refugee Council. Of course with every year that passes, the chances of reuniting people become more and more remote, but he won't give up. They still have had breakthroughs, and they are tenacious. But lately he's been working with the Nazi hunters as well, tracking war criminals. Who knows, he might have what you need on file already.'

She wasn't sure what she would do even if she found out more about Decker, but at least having Klaus contact his historian friend made her feel like she was doing something. Maybe a miracle would happen and they would find Decker had been accused of war crimes or something. Then they could rip up the cheque for 4,000 pounds that still sat tucked out of sight behind the clock.

Five days later, Klaus rang her back. 'Both Phillippe Decker and August Berger are listed in Pierre Laroche's records. He's posted me a copy of their files. It's all too long and complicated to explain on the phone, but I can drive down to you with them as soon as they get here.'

'No, don't do that. Call me when they arrive, and I'll come to you.' She didn't want anyone else to know what she was up to, not even Eli. 'I've promised Mam to buy her some dressmaking stuff. There's a big wedding coming up in July and she's been asked to make the brides-maid's dresses for Professor Lamkin's oldest daughter, so I need to go into Cork sometime this week anyway.'

Klaus called back two days later to say he had received the files, not long after Eli had left for work. Lena waited until Katie arrived. She left Pádraig with her and asked her to pick up Sarah and Emmet from school, then walked up to the farm through the hawthorn-filled country lanes.

It was Wednesday, washing day, and Maria was washing sheets in the new twin tub with spinner that had made washing day a much less laborious affair. Skipper was helping hang them on a line strung across the yard.

'Skipper, can I have a loan of the Morris Minor today? I've to go to Cork, and I'm going to get some shopping for Mam.' Eli had taken their car because he had a lot of home visits that day, and the Bandon-Cork railway line had closed three years ago, to everyone's anger.

As she'd known he would, Skipper tossed her the keys with a grin and a tip of his hat, while Maria wiped her hands on her apron and went into the kitchen to write out her shopping list. 'Four lengths of lace and white satin, twenty yards of pink shot silk. Mrs Lamkin wanted satin, but that's a very unforgiving fabric. I can ruche the silk better to fit. Thanks, Lena.' Maria handed her some money. 'That should be enough, but if not just let me know what I owe you. And drive safely, won't you?'

'I will, Mam, don't worry.' Lena kissed her mother's cheek and called her goodbyes to Skipper as she started up the Morris.

People like Katie's cousin and Adele Lamkin were spending huge amounts of money on weddings these days, which Lena thought was daft, though she knew it was good for Emily's business and Maria loved the work – it kept her 'steady' for long periods of time.

Once in Cork, Lena went to the sewing shop first, where she found everything Maria needed. She even had the woman throw in some ribbons and sequins for the Irish dancing costumes, because apparently you could never have too many ribbons and sequins on a dancing dress these days. Then she drove to the university, with the goods parcelled up in brown paper on the back seat.

She got out of the Morris Minor and locked it, then turned to face the college gates. She was holding two fresh buttered scones wrapped in a white cloth, which her mother had insisted on giving her 'in case you get hungry on the road'. She knew Klaus would be delighted to help her out eating them; he loved all her mother's cooking.

He'd explained that she should enter through the elaborate black wrought-iron gates and walk up the willow-lined avenue, keeping the river to her right. The hill was not steep, and Lena marvelled at the beautiful university grounds. Old cut-limestone buildings were dotted here and there, the Department of Humanities, the Department of Engineering, and she daydreamed what it would have been like to come here to study. It wasn't a place really for people like them – it was expensive and elitist – but there was no doubting it was gorgeous.

As she came to the top of the hill, she saw the president's residence, a Victorian two-storey with the most exquisite rose garden outside it, and in front of that, a large verdant lawn where students sat in groups, some reading and studying, others chatting animatedly. Was she ever that young and carefree, she wondered?

The large library was to her left, and then she entered the quad where Klaus had his rooms on the second floor. The grassy quadrangle was manicured to perfection, topiary hedging in each quarter, and all around it was a gravel path where a weed didn't dare raise its head. Gothic wooden doors with black cast-iron decorations at intervals in the limestone walls were surrounding the lawn. She entered and found herself in a corridor lined with ogham stones. She remembered the teacher in school explaining to them about the stones that the university had acquired, marked with the ancient Celtic form of writing and telling their own stories. There was a time she would have stopped, tried to decipher what the stones said, but not today.

The steps up to Klaus's rooms were worn in the middle from years and years of feet, and the walls were adorned with huge oil paintings. In the corners stood suits of armour or marble statues, and the whole place was so impressive, it almost took her breath away.

Eventually she found his room, a tidy space lined floor to ceiling with books behind an ornate brass grille and with two comfortable chairs either side of the fireplace. The leaded diamond windows didn't leave as much light as a normal window might, but the effect was like something from a storybook.

The kindly professor beamed when he saw her. 'Lena! *Willkommen*! Welcome!' He still had a very strong German accent despite having lived in Ireland for years.

'How is your dear mother, Lena? Keeping well, I hope. Sit down, sit down. Can I make you tea?' He had a little area in the corner with a kettle and some cups.

'Lovely.' She smiled and gave him a hug. 'I have two of my mother's scones if you would like one.'

'Splendid! *Wunderbar*!' With twinkle-eyed delight he placed a pretty patterned side plate and two bone-china cups and saucers on the table between the chairs, on the corner of which was a pile of papers he'd been marking when she arrived. He then made the tea and brought the pot, a jug of milk and some sugar in a brass bowl to the table. 'I'm afraid it is not as good as your brother's milk – I suspect the college waters it down – but if you can bear to lower your standards...'

'I'm sure it's perfect.' In her tea the milk did taste thin, but she drank it. She was glad of the scone, and Klaus was clearly glad of his, devouring it as if it were the first thing he'd eaten that day. Between mouthfuls, he asked questions about all Lena's family, and she told him about Emmet's project on the Industrial Revolution and the changes to technology as a result. He was so young to be interested in such things, but he loved finding out how things worked.

'Remarkable boy. Perhaps one day he will come here and study with me.' Then he checked his watch. 'I have a lecture to deliver in less than an hour, so perhaps we had better get to your questions, Lena.'

He rose and went to the large roll-top desk in the corner of the room and extracted a manila envelope addressed to him. Lena watched as he moved. He was stealthy; his height of over six feet didn't make him awkward, and he reminded her of a tall lion.

'Now, my friend Pierre is a very organised man, so all his files are in alphabetical order, and by a miracle, the men you are talking of were clearly unashamed of using their own names in Ireland.' He looked at her enquiringly.

'I suppose they felt so out of the way,' she said, 'living in a remote village in a neutral country. It wasn't that people accepted them – it was just that nobody knew. My godfather had worked as a doctor in Liverpool during the war. He was called to treat Berger for shock one day, and he thought he recognised the signs left by removing a tattoo of the Waffen-SS, but he couldn't be sure.'

Klaus nodded. 'Your godfather was right. Both the previous occupants of your house were members of Hitler's elite, although neither was ever charged with any war crimes, so that might be some consolation to you.'

It wasn't – it was horribly disappointing – but the history professor wasn't to know that. 'Surely every member of the Waffen-SS is a criminal?'

Klaus nodded. 'That's true in a way. The Waffen-SS at the Nuremberg trials were found to be responsible for countless atrocities. They were considered a criminal organisation because of their racial policies and the close links they had to the Nazi party, and a Waffen-SS veteran is denied any rights afforded to other former soldiers.'

'Then why wouldn't Decker and Berger be charged as war criminals?'

'Because there were so many of them, Lena, I am sad to say. There are people who track down the top Nazis, the ones who oversaw the mass murder of the Jews, but someone like Phillippe Decker would be of little interest to them because he was only ever a soldier. The other man, August Berger, is a different matter. Berger was promoted after reporting a conversation in a café between two saboteurs speaking in Alsaciene, who assumed that Berger, in German uniform, wouldn't have an idea what they were saying. The saboteurs were arrested and shot, which meant Berger had averted the death of some very senior German officers and the destruction of a critical bridge over the Rhine. After that he was transferred to the SS-Totenkopfverbände, known as the Death's Head Units, who were responsible for the management of the concentration camps. He seems to have passed through Auschwitz at some stage, and may have been briefly involved in a project in which selected prisoners were well fed and medically looked after for months, then gassed and plaster casts taken of their bodies, the idea being to create a museum displaying the inferior physiognomy of the Jewish race.'

Lena felt sick. She had heard stories about the death camps, though Eli never talked about them. She'd once seen a short film in the cinema of emaciated people being released from Auschwitz. But what Klaus was saying made it much more real. People actually did that to fellow human beings, gassed them in cold blood. And August Berger had been one of those murderers.

Klaus watched her sympathetically. 'Is that enough or do you want to know more?'

'I never wanted to know any of this… But yes, I do want to know. Go on.' These men had murdered her father. One of them was Emmet's grandfather. It felt necessary to understand them.

Klaus shuffled some papers and cleared his throat. 'It looks as if August Berger and Phillippe Decker grew up in the same village, not far from where my friend lives in Alsace, a little place called Eguisheim. Berger's family were wealthy. He was an only child. His parents were Germans who settled in Alsace after the Great War.'

He looked up at Lena over his reading glasses. 'Alsace is a small place with a long and complicated history, sometimes French, other times German. The Bergers were always able to transcend that, though. They were wine dealers and mixed with the aristocracy, both in France and Germany. Everyone wants good wine, and they were the people to know if you wanted to get it. The Bergers were cunning. There is a saying I heard in Ireland that sums them up – they ran with the hares and hunted with the hounds.'

He allowed himself a small smile at having mastered the colloquialism, then continued. 'Decker, on the other hand, was the son of a baker, six children in the family. It's not clear how he became friendly with August Berger, who was far above him in social class, but it's possible they went to the same school. Berger left the country for a while to study art in Dublin, leaving Decker to help out on his family's estate. Then in September 1939, Germany rolled into Poland and Berger returned to Alsace. By the following May, France had fallen, but the Alsace-Lorraine region wasn't invaded and subjugated as the rest of the country was. They were annexed, treated as German citizens who were welcomed into the warm bosom of the fatherland once more. The Germans thought the people of Alsace would be happy to see them and join the army, and there were indeed a small number of volunteers. Including Berger and Decker.'

Lena burst out, 'Why would they volunteer if they didn't have to?'

'Probably not for ideological reasons,' said Klaus, glancing from one file to the other, turning pages with both hands. 'More likely to escape being sent to the eastern front. Have you heard of the Malgré-nous?'

'Never. Who were they?' It was strange how little she knew about the war. It had taken place while she was alive, and it wasn't like she was an old woman. Ireland was one of the few places in the world not directly involved in the Second World War, though many Irishmen and women joined the Allies. She knew Switzerland had been neutral too, but geographically it had no choice but be in the middle of it. Portugal and Spain refused to take a side either, but again, people escaped through those countries so they weren't ever truly neutral. But Ireland wasn't in any sense a theatre of war. Of course her country had helped the Allies, rescuing downed airmen and things like that, but her little green island off the coast of that troubled, scarred and battered continent had managed to maintain a verdant lush-green peace.

'Malgré-nous means "against our will", and it was what they called the men of Alsace who didn't volunteer but were conscripted into the German forces, over 130,000 of them.'

'And they went on to fight for the Germans?' Lena was transfixed.

'They did. Most of them ended up on the eastern front.'

'So they were traitors to their country?'

Klaus smiled wryly. 'Well, when it comes to the Malgré-nous, it depends on who you ask. You have heard of Oradour-sur-Glane?'

'Klaus, the more you tell me, the less I realise I know.'

'It was a small village in the southwest of France. There was a massacre there, an awful thing, in retaliation for a resistance attack. The Waffen-SS went in and slaughtered everyone in the town. The men were gunned down with machine guns, and the women and children locked in a church that was then burnt to the ground. Thirteen of the men who committed this atrocity were Malgré-nous, as well as one volunteer. They were all put on trial in Bordeaux about ten years ago and got heavy sentences, and the volunteer was sentenced to death. But the verdict caused a big furore in Alsace, the people there claiming those men were forced to do what they did. Anyone who didn't agree to be conscripted had faced deportation to the camps – not just them either, their whole families – and so it wasn't right to treat them as willing participants. The authorities had to re-examine the convictions, and that led to general amnesty on the Malgré-nous by the National Assembly.'

'And so the Malgré-nous just went home and all was forgiven?'

'Well, they think almost fifty thousand of them were killed, more died in the gulags of Siberia, and the rest came home mostly, broken, invalids, but yes, they came home. That was the fate I assume Berger and Decker were trying to escape when they volunteered ahead of the draft. They both joined the Waffen-SS as corporals, which is surprising – they should have started with the rank of private. But I suppose Berger's social status and German parentage worked in his favour, and he must have insisted on bringing Decker with him. They were definitely close, because Berger saved Decker's life on at least one occasion, and Decker in return saved his.'

Lena sat up straight, alert and listening. 'What happened?'

'Just before Decker was accepted into the Waffen-SS, someone made an anonymous accusation against him, that he was having sexual relations with a Jewish girl named Rebecca Loeb. The claim said the person saw them in a room in the Loebs' house upstairs when the Loeb parents were not there, which was against the law. The Allgemeine SS were responsible for enforcing the Nazis' racial policy, and they arrested Decker. Of course he denied having anything to do with a Jewish girl, but it was his friend Berger who got him off the hook by providing him with an alibi for the night in question, saying they'd been in a brothel in Colmar and bringing a couple of prostitutes to the police station with him to vouch for the truth of it. It seems after a case of exceptionally good Pinot Gris was handed over to sweeten the deal, Decker was released. But Decker never made it into the Death's Head Unit after that, not like Berger. He ended up fighting in Greece, to help the Italians.'

'And Decker saved Berger's life in return?'

'The two men were reunited in the winter of 1944, when the Germans were losing the war. The 19th Army was trying to hold back the Americans, the British and the French from crossing the Rhine – the Colmar pocket was the last bit of occupied territory the Nazis had on the western front. The Russians were coming, unstoppable from the east, the German armies elsewhere bogged down in snow and ice, the Allies driving forwards from Normandy, the Germans grouped together like cornered rats. One night a bunch of the Waffen-SS was busy drowning their sorrows when a group of young maquis ambushed them. Berger was wounded, but a witness account from one survivor says Decker shot and killed the girl who did it – she was only fifteen – then pulled Berger out of there. After that, the trail goes cold – that is, until you told me that they'd ended up in Kilteegan Bridge.'

She pictured the two of them, one near fatally wounded, struggling across Europe among crowds of refugees. 'I don't understand how two German officers could make it all the way to Ireland without being stopped?'

'I imagine they took off their uniforms, got some peasant clothes, reverted to speaking French, got rid of their tattoos and managed to get behind the Allied lines. It was chaos in those days, you see, millions of people displaced and searching, the Germans scattered and terrified, the camps being liberated – it was easy to disappear. They would have spoken fluent French, and though they had Alsatian accents, they would have claimed to be among the few Malgré-nous who had escaped and joined the resistance.'

'That's true, that's what August Berger told his son,' said Lena. 'They lied that they were heroes rather than answer for what they'd done.'

'And they successfully disappeared, until you came to me with their names,' said Klaus. 'After which Pierre was able to pick up the scent again. Berger is dead, of course, as you know, but Pierre thinks his more humble friend Decker is living in Strasbourg.'

'What!' Lena couldn't believe her ears. It was the last thing she'd been expecting to happen, to be told right out where Decker was living now. 'Strasbourg? Where in Strasbourg? Do you have his actual address?' She realised the professor was looking at her in puzzlement. 'I mean, I just wondered...'

Klaus took off his glasses to wipe them with a clean handkerchief. 'Lena, do you have some personal interest in this man, more than that he was the previous occupant of your house? Is there something you know about him?'

She flushed and shifted in her chair. Like Jack, she was a bad liar. 'Not really.'

'Is it to do with Eli?' Klaus knew that Lena's husband was a fellow German, a Jew, and had once even tried to apologise to Eli for having been in the Wehrmacht in France; Eli had waved his apology away like it wasn't needed and said something about the past being over and done with.

'No, it isn't... Well...' She wanted so much to confide in this kindly, fatherly man, but she hadn't even told Jack the truth about Paudie O'Sullivan's death, and that was such an important part of this story. 'Klaus, I will tell you one day why I'm asking this, but right now I can't. I'm so sorry. But it would really help me if you had a proper address for him.'

He settled his glasses back on his nose and looked at her

owlishly. 'If you're planning on dashing off to find this pathetic man, Lena, then I strongly advise against it. He will be afraid and desperate, a shunned member of society, and maybe disposed to act violently.'

She shivered. 'No, I promise I won't do that. I only want to write to him.'

'About...?'

'I'm sorry, Klaus, I can't say.'

For a long time, he looked at her, and then he shrugged, rummaged for a pen and tore the title page out of a battered book. 'You're an intelligent woman, Lena, and your own person. Pierre does not have Decker's actual address, but remember he can also help you with any other questions you might have about other people, on Eli's behalf perhaps.' He scribbled a few lines, then held out the paper to her. 'This is Pierre's address and phone number.'

'Thank you, Klaus, thank you...' She stood to take it, and he also got up and drew her in for a big bear hug, then held her away from him, his hands on her shoulders, looking closely into her face.

'Lena, I am not your father,' he said in his very formal German-accented English, 'but your family has been very welcoming to me, and I think of you almost as a daughter. So for my own selfish sake, I am asking you not to do anything foolish with any information you discover, please, and to come to me for help if you need it. Also, Pierre is a helpful man, so if by any chance you find yourself in Strasbourg, for whatever reason, you must go to him first.'

'I will, Klaus.' Her heart was warmed by his concern. Her mother was too fragile to be reliable, so the nearest thing she'd had to a parent in her life was her godfather, Doc, and he had died five years ago. 'I really will, and I promise I won't do anything stupid.'

'Thank you, my dear.' He handed her the white cloth that had contained the scones, after shaking the crumbs into a wastepaper basket. 'And I'll see you in Kilteegan Bridge soon, so tell your mother to keep baking these little bundles of delight.'

'Oh, she makes them every day when she bakes the bread.' Lena smiled. 'So you just have to get there early enough, because they're gone by halfway through the morning – Jack and Skipper still eat like teenage boys.'

'Then I will certainly have to come for breakfast,' the history professor said solemnly, 'because I think when it comes to your mother's cooking, I can also eat like a teenage boy.'

Lena opened the door to find a shy young woman of about eighteen standing there waiting, and Klaus greeted her enthusiastically. 'Ah, Mary, you should have knocked and come in! Is your essay on the *95 Theses* complete already? I only have a few moments, but I am very much excited to read your analysis.'

As she walked through the corridors and quad on her way out, Lena noticed a lot of the students were women, maybe one in five, and was glad to see how normal it was becoming. She and Jack had had to leave school to work on the farm when Paudie died. Lena had been fifteen, but Jack was only twelve, and the isolation hadn't helped with his shyness during his teenage years. Lena envied her older sister, Emily, who had been able to take her final exams, but she'd never thought about going back into education herself apart from maybe doing a pre-nursing course in Cardiff, and even that had been abandoned when she married Eli and returned to Ireland.

Maybe when Molly and May finished school, they might want to think about college. They were very interested in farming, but you could even go to university for that now. Sarah might want to study something too. Emmet would be going, of course; he was the brightest child in his school. Pádraig, it was still too early to tell; they would have to wait and see.

* * *

BACK AT THE FARM, she left the Morris Minor at the empty end of the turf shed, then ducked under the swinging lines of drying sheets to enter the farmhouse, carrying the heavy brown paper parcel of material for the dresses, which she dropped on the high-backed settle.

Maria, Jack, Skipper and the twins were at the table, tucking into a huge shepherd's pie. Maria jumped up to fetch an extra plate, but Lena took it from her and put it away again.

'Mam, no, I'm not staying. I need to get home. I'm later than I thought I'd be, and I have to let Katie go, and Eli had loads of house calls to make today – there's some virus going around. I don't know if he'll even be back yet, but either way, when he comes, he'll be starving. I left Katie enough for her and the children, but apart from that, there's no food in the house. In fact, Mam, if there's another tray of this going...'

'Of course there is.' Maria was thrilled. She loved it when her children needed her help; it made up for her sadness when she couldn't be there for them.

'But if you give it to Lena, what will me and Skipper eat at midnight?' objected Jack.

'Yeah, Mama, we'll starve...' protested Skipper. The American had taken to calling Maria 'Mama' a while ago as a joke, but gradually it had become the normal thing he called her every day. Skipper's own mother was dead, and his daddy had taken off with a showgirl when Skipper and his brother, Wyatt, were kids, so maybe Maria had become the parent figure in his life, despite her mental illness and frequent absences.

'Don't worry,' Maria fussed happily, 'I'll bake a ginger cake after tea, and there's a joint of boiled ham and fresh tomatoes in the fridge.'

'Mam, we want a midnight feast as well!' chorused Molly and May, and their mother laughed and shook her finger at them.

'If I notice there's iced buns missing from the larder tomorrow, well then...I'll just have to make some more.'

'All right, Mammy!' The twins grinned at each other, delighted to be spoiled as much as their older brother and his friend.

Lena threw a look at Jack, and he shook his head while still smiling, which she knew meant, 'Don't worry, she's not being manic, just making the most of being a normal mother.'

Maria placed the second warm tray of shepherd's pie in a large flat basket and covered it with a red-checked tea towel that she tied underneath, then made up a bag with a loaf of bread, butter and salad leaves. Lena sat waiting on the settle, looking around at the familiar room. Above the mantelpiece, a framed tapestry of JFK had joined the picture of the pope and Michael Collins. It wasn't just Skipper's influence; lots of Cork people had an image of the assassinated American president on their wall these days alongside the pope, although sometimes Michael Collins was replaced by the Virgin Mary or the Sacred Heart.

Jack Kennedy had been the first Irish American Catholic to be president of America, and the whole of Ireland had been so proud when he visited Cork in 1963, just before he was shot. At least 100,000 people had turned out to see him, including her own family – and Skipper, of course. The Lord Mayor, Seán Casey, had conferred Jack Kennedy with the Freedom of the City, telling him, 'President Kennedy, you have reached the highest point in American public life, which any Irish man or any man of Irish descent has ever reached before. In honouring you...we honour our own kith and kin beyond the sea. We honour all those who crossed the Atlantic from this tiny island who made their new homes in the United States and who have contributed so much to that country throughout the years.'

Five months later, in November, Kennedy had been assassinated in Dallas.

Skipper didn't seem to care much about politics – Lena didn't know who he supported – but the death of JFK had affected him badly, and his usual irrepressible grin had vanished for a whole month.

However, it was hard to keep Skipper down for long, and when Maria handed over the basket of food, he jumped up to grab it and insisted on driving Lena home.

* * *

As she let herself into Kilteegan House, after waving goodbye to Skipper, Lena wondered what Eli would think when she told him she'd found Phillippe Decker. Despite what she'd promised Klaus, she felt more and more like just going to Strasbourg to confront the old murdering Nazi, and she hoped her husband would feel the same way.

Eli came to the door of the library as she passed, sniffing the air. 'What is that wonderful smell? Is it manna from heaven? Or better still, could it be Maria's famous shepherd's pie you have in that basket?'

'It is indeed, and if you come with me into the kitchen, we'll both have some. Are the children asleep?'

'They are. Myself and Katie wrestled them into bed and read them a thousand stories each – my vocal cords are exhausted.' He followed her into the kitchen and chatted about his day while she put the tray on the range to warm up again, cut bread and threw a dressing together for the salad.

Eli would never discuss his patients with anyone but her. He knew she wouldn't ever breathe a word of what he told her, and it was good for him to get the burden of some of it off his chest in the evenings. Being from a different culture, she sometimes steered him how best to handle a delicate situation, and he was always grateful for her advice.

'Blackie's mother's bunions are very bad. I've arranged for an operation, though she's saying she doesn't want it. And Katie's cousin who just got married thought she had food poisoning, but she's pregnant, which she's not thrilled about. And Nettie Collins has developed an allergy to dust, which is no good for a librarian, and Twinkle is getting very thin again – I've sent him to Cork for more tests. I'm being very positive with him, but I think the poor man knows it's not going to be good.'

'Oh, that's awful. Poor Twinkle.' She was fond of the publican, whose real name was Gerard Coughlan, and who owned the Donkey's Ears pub. Before his illness, he'd been an enormous man with a mad head of red curly hair, and he'd earned his nickname by punching out a troublesome customer, who when he came round went on and on about seeing lovely twinkly stars. 'Is there hope?'

'Where there's life, there's always hope,' said Eli simply. It was his favourite saying.

She served them both and sat down.

As he tucked in enthusiastically, Lena sat eating slowly, thinking. At last she said, 'Eli, I went to Cork today.'

'I know.' He wiped his plate with a slice of Maria's bread. 'Katie said you'd gone to buy a ton of material for Maria to make wedding dresses or something. All this fancy wedding palaver is getting out of hand, isn't it? I'm glad ours was a simple one – it was perfect.'

She smiled. It had been perfect. Just herself, Eli, his family, a couple of his friends and Doc. And then, during their honeymoon, Clare Winton, the social worker, had arrived with Emmet, and her life was complete.

'There's another thing, Eli. While I was there, I went to see Klaus.'

He looked up over his fork. 'Really? That's nice. How is he?'

'Klaus is fine, but I didn't go to see how he was. I went to get some information he had for me.'

Eli's brown eyes widened. 'He's found Ted?' Eli knew all about Klaus Rizzenburg's search for Maria's long-lost brother; it was an ongoing topic of conversation in the O'Sullivan household.

'No, this is nothing to do with Ted. But he's found someone else for us.'

'For us?' For a moment, the exhaustion of the day drained from his features, and he looked at her with bright, interested eyes. 'What do you mean?'

'I think you've guessed.' It was great he was so pleased; she'd thought he would be ambivalent about her discovery at the very least. Maybe he really was as keen to get hold of Decker as she was.

'Just tell me.' He smiled.

She smiled back. 'Phillippe Decker.'

'Oh, Lena…' His face fell again, and he put his head in his hands. 'Oh, Lena, I thought…'

'Thought what?'

He shook his head and looked up with a strained smile. 'It's fine, never mind. So Phillippe Decker is alive? But we knew that. He's writing to us via his solicitor, from a secret address.'

'But that's just it. Klaus hasn't just found out he's alive – he's found out he's in Strasbourg. He has this historian friend called Pierre

Laroche who lives in Alsace and works with Nazi hunters, and Klaus gave me his address –'

'Lena.' He was looking tired and drawn again. 'What are you expecting to achieve by this, even if we have found a way to contact this man other than through his solicitor?'

'I don't know, Eli, but I think we should discuss it.' It was hurtful and disappointing, the way he kept dismissing her. This was more her business than his. It was her father who was murdered; it was Emmet who was being disinherited. Of course Emmet was Eli's son in the eyes of the law, but this house had belonged to Emmet's grandmother, and great-grandparents, and great-great-grandparents. 'We have to do something. We could go talk to Decker when we find him. We can threaten him with telling everyone in Kilteegan Bridge the truth about him – maybe we can shame him into backing off, maybe –'

'Lena.' Eli pushed away his plate wearily. 'You know what I think, and the answer is behind the clock in the library. A cheque for 4,000 pounds. A clean slate. No more Decker, no more August Berger, no more Malachy. Just us and our three children and our house, which will belong to you and me and the children equally after we are gone.'

She looked down at her own food, barely touched. Of course she shouldn't object to their children sharing the house. But… She looked up at her husband. 'It's not just about the house. It's about the murder too. I would love to live my life as you do, putting all the hurts of the past behind me, and I admire you, I really do, for your ability to do that. But I just can't with this one. We're different like that. I can't just give up.'

Eli had his hand over his eyes, his elbow on the table. 'It's not about giving up. It's about not getting dragged down into the swamp of regrets and recriminations and bitterness.'

'No, Eli. I can't just let him get away with it. I've lost so much because of that man – I can't give him all your savings too. He killed my father. You just don't seem to understand. I want to look him in the face and tell him I know all about him.'

He lowered his hand and a flash of something passed over his face. 'I don't understand?' he repeated, his voice a low rumble.

'No, you don't. You're so good at looking to the future, you never think about the past, and –'

He interrupted her in a grim voice. 'Not think about the past, Lena? Are you serious? Are you forgetting that I was a Jewish child in Berlin? That the Nazis killed my father, my grandparents, my aunts and uncles, cousins, friends, neighbours? Just because I don't talk about it doesn't mean I've forgotten. For pity's sake, Lena. Do you know what I thought when you said Klaus had found someone for us? I thought it might be a relative of mine, maybe my cousin Greta, who had such lovely dark curls and was always laughing, maybe my Aunt Sarah, who taught me my numbers, maybe baby Rosa the sweetest child ever born. You think I've *forgotten* them?'

Lena sat there in shock. She had no words, realising what she had said, how cruel she'd been. She felt awful. Yet the truth was, it was easy to forget Eli's past because he seemed to forget it himself. He'd escaped from Germany as a boy with his mother and his uncle, but he never, ever talked about his life before that. He spoke with a strong Welsh accent, and he never referred to the war; if it came up in company, he either changed the subject or withdrew from the conversation. He'd always given her the impression he'd moved on, shed his past entirely, looked only to the future.

She found her voice. 'I'm sorry, Eli. That was thoughtless and horrible of me.'

'I remember, Lena, believe me, and I haven't forgiven. Do you think for a moment I'd choose to give a member of the Waffen-SS all my savings just to secure this pile of bricks and mortar? It makes me sick to my stomach. But I've learnt to do what is necessary to survive. My mother taught me that we have to survive or there is no reason for anything. We must survive, or they have won. And we will survive, and we will rise, and our children will be happy, and they will live in this house that you love and they love, and no Nazi is going to have power over us ever again.'

His eyes were burning, but then he shuddered deeply and pressed his fingers against his temples and lowered his gaze.

Silence consumed the room. At last, Lena said timidly, 'I wish

someday you'd tell me everything about your lost family, and everything that happened. I want to understand. Maybe then I wouldn't say
such stupid things.'

He shook his head. 'No, Lena. I can't talk about it.'

'Even to me?'

He summoned a weak smile, raising his eyes to hers. 'Not even to
you, and I tell you everything. Lena, don't worry. I thank my lucky
stars every single day that you're my wife and we have three little
ruffians to fill our hearts. And what more would I want to talk to you
about than that?'

CHAPTER 10

The simple inscription read:

HANNAH BERGER née FITZGERALD

1919–1955

Beloved wife and mother

Gone too soon.

Malachy stood awkwardly over the grave, his arms folded. 'Hello, Mam. I've...um...missed you. I'm sorry you were so sad, and that I was away at school when you did what you did. Maybe I could have saved you, but I wasn't there. I so wish you hadn't left me.'

It was the first time he'd visited her resting place since that awful night when his dying father told him that Hannah hadn't died of heart failure, but suicide. Until then, Malachy had always come to this grave with love. Now he felt differently. He still loved his mother...but now that love was mixed with a deep hurt and anger that wouldn't go away.

Eleven years ago, in the apple orchard of Kilteegan House, Malachy's mother had climbed the stepladder used to pick the high fruit, placed a leather halter around the branch and then her neck and kicked the ladder from beneath herself. Nobody alive but himself and Lena, and Phillippe Decker, knew she had committed suicide. Doctor Dolan had lied on her death certificate. The Catholic Church would not have allowed a suicide to be buried in the Kilteegan Bridge cemetery, so he had recorded the cause of death as heart failure.

And heart failure *was* the reason for her death, thought Malachy as he touched the deep letters carved into the stone. She had killed herself for love of Paudie O'Sullivan, Lena's father. It hurt Malachy to his bones that his mother's love for him had not been enough to keep her from suicide. Maybe she'd never loved him at all. All the times she'd played with him in the orchard and stables and taken him riding on his pony, maybe those times were about being with Paudie, who was always working around the grounds, and not with her son after all.

Hannah's name was no longer the last to be carved on the massive headstone of the magnificent Fitzgerald family plot, where her parents and grandparents were also buried.

Underneath was written:

AUGUSTE BERGER
1910–1959
A hero of the French resistance
Fond father to Malachy Auguste Berger.

It was all lies, of course, from beginning to end. Malachy's father's name wasn't Auguste, it was August, and he was no hero of the resistance, nor had he been a fond father. But the will Berger had drawn up with Kieran Devlin had specified the wording for his grave – he'd even paid the local stone mason in advance – and so by the time Malachy had told Devlin the truth about his father's past, the stone had been cut and August Berger continued to tell his lies in death, just as he had done in life.

Malachy pushed his hands into the pockets of his long black cashmere coat. It was June, but there was a cool wind blowing up from the Atlantic, ruffling the fresh green leaves of the chestnut in the corner where Lena's father lay, next to his friend Doctor Dolan. The O'Sullivan family plot was near the Fitzgerald plot, where Lena's grandparents and grandaunts were buried, but perhaps Maria O'Sullivan had not wanted her husband buried next to Hannah; perhaps she knew about Hannah's love for her husband.

Her murdered husband.

As he lay dying, with only Lena and Malachy there, August Berger had croaked out that he'd ordered Decker to kill Paudie O'Sullivan in revenge for his wife's suicide, because Lena's father 'might as well have killed her himself with his own hands'. And then he'd boasted how he'd lied to Malachy, telling him Lena had brought other men and boys to the tack room – Bill Madden, Blackie Crean, Donal Lamkin...

After his father died that night, Malachy had followed Lena home, begging her to abandon her husband, to start again with him in America. But a baby had cried upstairs, and she'd left the room and returned with a toddler in her arms. And the child had looked at Malachy with Hannah's green eyes, and he had dark-red hair curling around his head.

And then Eli had returned, and the child had held out his arms to the other man and cried 'Dada!' And Malachy knew he had lost.

It was easy to blame his father for the wreck of his hopes, and he did, but the truth was he was exactly as Lena described him then: a foolish boy who'd listened to a liar instead of his own instinct, a boy who had abandoned Lena, just as his mother had abandoned him.

Since then, he'd had many girlfriends; there was no shortage of women who wanted to be with him. He knew he was a good-looking man, with thick dark-red hair and green eyes and pale skin, and he was worth a lot of money. He'd used the millions of francs from the sale of his grandparents' wine cellar and chateau to set up his own engineering company, which was now a thriving business. But none of his relationships had lasted more than a few months. Whichever girl he was going out with might be gorgeous, clever, talented... She might be anything, but she was never Lena.

He remembered when he'd first seen how beautiful Lena was, in this very cemetery, at her father's funeral. She'd wandered away from the other mourners, sobbing, and he'd given her a clean handkerchief. They'd talked together over his mother's grave about their parents.

Two years later he'd finally managed to ask her for a dance, at the Lilac, and after that, a brief period of happiness… But then his father destroyed it all.

And now he had to go and see her, and talk to her, and try to act like a normal human being in her presence.

It was strange being back in Kilteegan Bridge after so many years in America spent building up his business, first in Boston and then in California. He'd been back to Ireland once for his father's death but he had left again within twelve hours, too broken-hearted over Lena to stay for the funeral.

Now he drove slowly up the main street in the two-seater sports car he'd hired from Shannon Airport, an Alpine A110, expensive to hire but pleasant to drive. He passed the Donkey's Ears pub, where Twinkle the landlord was outside watering the flower boxes, looking surprisingly thin, and then Maureen's Fashions, where the cardigans were still pastel and the skirts long and sensible. It used to drive Lena mad that she couldn't buy an outfit in there that didn't make her look like 'an off-duty nun', as she called it.

Next was Crean's Hardware, which unlike Maureen's Fashions looked completely different from how he remembered it. The big picture windows were bright and colourful and spotlessly clean. They had dinner sets, oilcloth and copper kettles instead of sacks of sheep nuts and bundles of fence posts. Of course it was Lena's sister Emily who was married to Blackie Crean. *She must have some of Lena's energy and creativity.*

The whole town had been astonished that Blackie Crean, son of the horrific Dick Crean and brother of the equally dreadful Jingo, had managed to convince Emily O'Sullivan to marry him, but he did, and it seemed to be working out.

The town library was looking brighter too, with a huge poster in the window advertising an author called Roald Dahl, who had just written a book called *Charlie and the Chocolate Factory*. He would love to buy some books for Emmet, but he suspected Lena wouldn't allow it.

Opposite was Doctor Dolan's old house, where Lena had been

living the last time he saw her. As well as the doctor's sign by the door – 'Eli Kogan, MD' – there were brass plates advertising the services of a physiotherapist, a dentist and an optician. Malachy's mouth tightened. Eli Kogan had done well out of the gift of Kilteegan House, but he must try not to resent it. Lena deserved to live there, and so did Emmet, and they could hardly live there without Eli Kogan, husband and 'father'. Or was he a real father now? Were there other children, younger siblings for Emmet?

He passed the red and white windows of the butcher's; the butcher was pulling down the shutters now because it was past five o'clock on a Saturday. Devlin's office, where he'd been earlier, was also closed.

He drove on out of town towards Kilteegan House. He hadn't called in advance, but surely she would be there. He would be polite and formal, and accept a cup of tea or a small whiskey, and tell her that he was planning to crush the second will. He'd already asked Devlin to write to the solicitors in Dublin, telling them that he wouldn't accept it, and now he was going to prepare a legal challenge.

Devlin was against it. He'd said Malachy was unlikely to win, and either way it would cost him a fortune, but he had deep pockets and was damned if Phillippe Decker, the man he had always thought of as his father's servant, was going to push him around.

The expensive car purred up the hill to Kilteegan House.

* * *

LENA OPENED the door with a smile, expecting Eli with the children and Katie. It was Saturday and a bank holiday weekend, so her husband had taken the afternoon off to bring them to the beach. He was picking Katie up on his way home because she loved helping the children groom their ponies and plait their manes.

The man on the step was shorter than Eli, and much more fashionably dressed, in a black cashmere coat and with a blue silk scarf patterned with red horseshoes around his neck. His dark-red hair flopped low over his forehead, and his green eyes met hers, creased at the corners by a hesitant smile. 'Hello, Lena,' he said. He sounded like he came from a posh area of Dublin, though there was the hint of an American accent.

'Malachy! Goodness!' How had it taken her so long to recognise him? She'd thought she would never forget his face, and yet... Perhaps because his cheeks were thinner, his cheekbones more prominent. He still had Hannah's colouring, but his father's bone structure was creeping through the softness of youth. 'I'm sorry, I didn't... You look so much older, so much less like a boy.'

'And you look exactly the same,' said Malachy, still with that slight smile, his eyes drifting over her.

She fought back a blush, and then felt a rush of annoyance that he could still make her blush. For a moment she was tempted to tell him to go away, but that would be mad. She could hardly not invite him into what had been his own family home and that now belonged to his son. Their son. 'Come in. Eli isn't here. He's at the beach – it's such a beautiful day – but he'll be back with the children any minute.'

'Children?' He seemed surprised.

'Yes, didn't you know? Well, I suppose there's no reason you should. Emmet has a younger sister, Sarah, and a baby brother called Pádraig. Anyway, please...come in.'

'Thank you.' He was grinning at her now, clearly amused at how flustered she was by his presence. As she led him across the large hallway, he gazed around in surprise. 'The place looks so different, Lena. I see you got rid of the stand and the big round table.'

She turned to face him from the kitchen doorway, feeling oddly guilty. 'Yes, I was trying to make it more of a home for the children.'

The enormous teak hallstand, dwarfed by coats nobody wore and umbrellas unopened for years, had been one of the first things she'd thrown out. The ugly round table, which had forced them to walk either to the left or the right when they entered the hallway, had been banished to the attic.

'And you've repainted the stairs.'

'Yes, they were very gloomy, I thought.' They'd been dark-brown with an old green carpet but were now painted cream and had a royal-blue runner complete with brass carpet bars. The floor of the hall was sanded and varnished, a lovely honey pine, and the walls painted eau de nil. She thought it looked beautiful, but now she was worried that he'd be offended, that it was disrespectful to his mother, who had probably liked the house the way it was. 'I hope you don't mind. I didn't mean...'

'Lena, it's fine. It's bright and airy and beautiful. Now show me what you've done to the kitchen.'

Relieved, she pointed out to him how they'd knocked an archway through from the kitchen into the former dining room, which now was home to the long pine dining table with crayons and picture books strewn across it. 'I'm afraid the whole place has been taken over by the children.'

He nodded. 'As it should be. I like what you've done. When I was a boy, the dining room was a formal place of silent meals and my mother creeping around my father as he sat in his wheelchair rustling the newspaper and talking to Phillippe in French.'

Lena was beginning to relax. The last time she'd met him, Malachy was an impetuous boy who had begged her to leave Eli and come with him to America. It looked like he'd been finally replaced with an adult man, sensible and polite, the sort of man even Eli might come to like.

'Take a seat at the table, and I'll make us some tea.' She got down the teapot and two cups, made a pot of tea and took some apple tart from a tin in the larder. 'So did you just get here today?' she asked, setting the cake down in front of him.

'Yes, I flew into Shannon and hired a car. I have an engineering conference in Dublin I wanted to go to, and I thought I'd swing by to see Devlin first and pay a visit to Mam, you know.'

She noticed he didn't mention visiting his father, even though August Berger was buried in the same grave. She pulled up a chair and sat opposite him. He was tucking into the tart, which he'd covered with thick cream from the jug, his red hair falling down into his eyes, longer than it used to be. Why was he here? She assumed it was something to do with the house, but he seemed in no hurry to tell her.

The last thing she wanted was for Eli to come home to this cosy scene, so she had to try to wrap it up as quickly as she could within the boundaries of politeness.

'Malachy...'

He beamed at her. 'Lena, you have no idea how good it is to eat Irish food again, all local and fresh. In the States, I've been living out of tins and packets. I should probably learn to cook, but I'm so busy, I can't be bothered. And they can't make proper tea – it's like dishwater. They all drink coffee.'

'Malachy...'

'And this house, you've done an amazing job. My mother would love it.'

'Malachy, I'm not saying you're not welcome to visit any time, but, you know, is there something you have to tell me about the house?'

He nodded, raised his finger as if to say, 'Hang on just a moment,' took another sip of tea and wiped his mouth on the napkin she'd given him. 'Yes. I'm here to tell you that I'm going ahead with a full legal challenge to the will. Devlin's going to do it for me. With his help, we'll kick that murdering Phillippe Decker where it hurts, and we won't stop until he crawls back into the hole he came from.'

She was delighted but remembered what Kieran Devlin had said. 'Are you sure? Kieran said a legal challenge could cost you a fortune and you'd probably lose. Has he changed his mind?'

'No, but I've very deep pockets these days. I'm a rich man, Lena, thanks to my grandparents and some wise investment in an engineering company, so I'm willing to go as far as we need to. He'll run out of money before I do – that's where these things normally go. So don't worry. I'll sort this out for you, and for Emmet.'

'Then that's wonderful! I'm so happy.' She beamed at him, reaching out to touch his hand.

'Are you going to introduce me to our visitor, Lena?'

Lena looked up with a start. She'd been so engrossed in what Malachy was saying that she hadn't heard her husband come in, but there he was, standing in the open doorway, looking in surprise at Malachy, who was sitting with his back to him.

Malachy immediately stood and turned to face him fully, holding out his hand. 'I'm Malachy Berger,' he said pleasantly. 'And you're Lena's husband. We met in this house once before.'

'Mr Berger,' said Eli, his face suddenly expressionless and his hands remaining in his pockets.

'Eli, come and sit down. Malachy came to tell us his plans for Decker.' Lena tried to sound cheerful, but she hated the way Eli was making her feel guilty just for sitting across the kitchen table from Malachy Berger.

Emmet appeared behind Eli, his dark-red hair standing on end, still wet and sandy from the beach. His green eyes fixed on the stranger at the table.

'Emmet, go upstairs with your sister and brother and Katie,' said Eli calmly, without even looking over his shoulder, 'and get washed and changed before Katie takes you all to groom the ponies.'

'Do you own the Alpine A110 parked outside?' asked the boy, totally ignoring Eli's order and staring boldly at Malachy with round green eyes.

Malachy winked at him. 'It's only rented, I'm afraid, but I have a Pontiac Firebird back in San Francisco, and a little soft-topped Corvette for the weekends.'

'Emmet, I said go and get changed.'

'Is it a Chevrolet Corvette?'

'Actually, it –'

'Emmet. Upstairs. Now.'

'But Dad, I want to hear what –'

'Now!'

'Oh, all right.' Sulkily, Emmet retreated into the hall.

Malachy stared after him until Eli closed the door, then he turned to Lena. 'Your son certainly knows his cars – I'm impressed. And you can tell him from me, it is a Chevrolet.'

She couldn't help smiling, happy to hear Emmet praised. 'He knows lots of things. He's very clever. Although...' – she glanced at Eli, who was stony-faced – 'of course, he does need to do what he's told without us having to say it a second time.'

'Sure, I was like that when I was –'

'So what is it you came here to tell us, Mr Berger?' asked Eli coolly.

'Call me Malachy, please.'

'I prefer surnames until I get to know someone better.'

'Of course. I'm being too American. So, Mr Kogan...' Malachy was still standing, but he had to look up at Eli because Lena's husband was several inches taller than he was. 'I came to tell Lena that I'm going to challenge this second will.'

Eli looked past him at Lena without smiling. 'I assume you've told Mr Berger the problem is taken care of because I've raised enough money to buy the house?' he asked coolly.

Again Lena felt like he was accusing her of something and hated it. 'No, not yet, I –'

'There's really no need to buy the house, Mr Kogan,' said Malachy smoothly. 'And it's not advisable, as it recognises Decker's claim to the property. Suppose he then decides he wants to return here instead of selling to you and Lena? This is a poisonous man who may hold a personal grudge against you.'

'He's right, Eli,' said Lena. She hated seeming to side against her husband, but the idea of Phillippe Decker being around Kilteegan Bridge was too much for her to bear. 'Supposing he comes back?'

'Lena, I guarantee that after I buy the house, we will never hear from him again. We'll make it a term of the deal.'

'But respectfully, Mr Kogan, that's not how we're going to do this.' Malachy's voice was cold. 'I am challenging this will on behalf of Emmet, in order to assert his full rights to this property, my family's home.'

Eli flushed angrily. '*My* son's rights are already taken care of. When the house is bought, he will inherit it along with his siblings.'

Lena wished the two men would stop glaring at each other and come to a sensible compromise. 'Can't we talk about this calmly? Maybe we can try Malachy's way first, Eli, and then if it doesn't work –'

'His way and *then* mine?' Eli's words were fused with hurt and frustration.

'Surely the person that matters most here is Emmet?' Lena pleaded.

'I agree,' said Malachy quickly, 'and that's why I'm challenging the will, for my son.'

Eli's brown eyes flashed angrily. 'Emmet is *not* your son.'

Malachy raised his hands, palms out, as if to say no offence. 'I'm not trying to deny the obvious fact that you have raised him as if he were –'

'As if?' Eli spluttered in fury; Lena had never seen him so angry.

Lena stood. She was afraid if she didn't intervene, this was going to develop into a shouting match, even a physical fight. 'Eli, wait... Malachy, there's no "as if" about any of this. Eli didn't just raise Emmet – he's Emmet's father.'

'Lena, stop saying that. As soon as you brought him downstairs in your arms that night when I followed you home, I knew, and you knew that I knew.'

'You can't say those things in this house!' She was getting angry herself now.

'Do you remember that photo of your father helping me down from the apple tree? It could be Emmet in that picture. Don't you see me every time you look at him?'

'No, I do not.'

'You must do –'

'Malachy, *stop it!*'

'Get out of my house,' growled Eli through clenched teeth.

'Eli, no...'

'*Your* house?' sneered Malachy, suddenly sounding as arrogant as his own father.

'Yes, mine, or it soon will be. We shouldn't have allowed you to leave it to Emmet in the first place, but we did, and now it turns out it wasn't yours to give, so I'm going to buy it from the legal owner for *my* family.'

'And I'm telling you, this house belongs to Emmet, and you signed a document obliging you to hold it in trust for him, not to buy it off him without him even knowing it belongs to him, and then to give two thirds of it away to your own children –'

'Stop it, stop it, both of you!' snapped Lena, banging her fist on the table.

'*Both* of us?' Eli turned white with fury.

'Yes, both of you! You're as bad as each other!'

'Mammy?'

'Emmet!' Horrified, Lena rushed to her son, where he stood with his hand on the half-open door, and led him out into the hall, slamming the door shut behind her. *Let them fight if they want*, she thought furiously. She didn't care any more; all she wanted was for her son to be happy. 'Darling, I thought you'd gone with Katie to groom the ponies?'

'I came back to see if you were all right, Mammy. I thought I heard shouting. Who is that man, Mammy? What does he mean, this house belongs to me? Why are him and Daddy fighting?'

'Oh, he was talking about a different Emmet, and he and Daddy aren't fighting – they're just having a disagreement about a bill. It's not important.' She hurried him across the hall towards the open front door.

'When they stop having a disagreement, can I have a spin in his car?' he asked, trotting along beside her.

'No, I'm afraid he's going in a minute.'

'But can I ask him?'

'No, darling, I want you to bring me to the ponies. I want to see you jump Ollie over that log again.'

'Oh, all right.' He slipped his hand from hers, skipped down the front steps, paused to look longingly at the two-seater sports car, then raced off around the corner towards the stables.

Lena followed more slowly, her heart still pounding with the shock of seeing her son listening in the kitchen doorway. As she turned the corner, a motor started up. She peered back through the wisteria to see Malachy driving fast away down the avenue, gravel spurting from under his wheels. *Good.* Then Eli appeared on the step, and she ducked back out of sight because she felt too angry to see her husband. She was furious with both him and Malachy.

Both men went on about caring so much about Emmet, but she suspected it was all male pride. Malachy wanted to assert his right to Emmet as much as his son's right to the house. Then Eli wanted to pay Phillippe Decker off. She knew he hated the idea of it, giving all his savings to a Nazi murderer, so it was ridiculous he was insisting on it just because he wanted nothing to do with Malachy.

She felt like knocking their heads together. It was she and Emmet who were in the middle of this mess, and it was she and Emmet who were going to suffer if this dragged on. Suddenly it came to Lena as clear as a blue sky. She knew what she had to do.

CHAPTER 11

*L*ena barely tuned into Blackie as he drove her to the station. There was a pause, so he must have asked her a question.

'Sorry, Blackie, I missed that. What did you say?'

'Ah, nothing, only how Em was a bit down because she heard that young Olivia Quinn is pregnant and saying how she's sick of babies. My Em would have loved more, and God knows we tried, but she lost so many. I know she doesn't talk about it much, but she has a rose bush planted for each one in my mother's garden. Sometimes I wish we had a bit of ground of our own, but living over the shop…'

Lena's heart went out to her brother-in-law. She knew the heartache the many miscarriages had brought, not just to Emily but to him too, getting their hopes up time and again, only to have them dashed. Eli had sent them both for tests and everything, but it was inconclusive, just one of those things.

'You and Em have made a wonderful life, Blackie, and Nellie is a little dote. And I know cousins aren't the same, but she and Emmet are so close, even though they have the odd squabble.'

'Ah, sure I know it, and you know so much of our success is because of yourself and Eli letting us use the barns above at your place. Emily is so excited about opening new shops, and it really takes her mind off us only having the one child. If we didn't have that, I don't know what we'd do.'

Lena knew Emily hadn't mentioned the risk to their business the Decker situation posed. Blackie was distracted these days, and Emily didn't want to worry him further. His brother, Jingo, was up in court on burglary charges; he'd been caught in possession of stolen property from the Lamkins' place, and though he swore he had no idea how the items got to be in his mother's shed, nobody doubted he was the culprit. Blackie lived his whole life mortified by the carry-on of his father and brother, who were thieving, conniving and thoroughly unlikeable men.

It made Lena even more determined than ever to sort it out her way. If she couldn't fix this situation, then Blackie and Emily stood to lose a lot. They'd borrowed for the new shops, she knew, and if they lost the storage units, then things would be very bad.

She still had the 4,000 pounds in reserve, but she did agree with Malachy that the house was his, and now Emmet's, and Decker should not benefit financially from his criminal past.

She was going to catch the train from Cork to Dublin, but she asked Blackie to drop her off in the city centre, telling him she had an appointment. That way, if Eli questioned him, he wouldn't be able to say where she went. Blackie was too polite and respectful to pry as to the nature of the appointment.

* * *

IN DUBLIN, Lena took a taxi from Kingsbridge station to Anthea O'Halloran's address, which she read out to the driver from the card the woman had given her in the graveyard. She hadn't had a chance to write and ask permission to stay with her, so hopefully Mrs O'Halloran wouldn't turn her away.

Well, Lena thought, *if she's not there, I'll just go to a hotel.* The only money she'd brought was the small amount she kept in her desk for housekeeping and paying bills, but hopefully it would be enough. Today was a bank holiday Monday, but she could get more on Tuesday if she needed it. Eli and she shared a bank account, something that the stern balding bank manager in Bandon had deemed the most extraordinary suggestion he'd ever heard. Eli had been insistent, though, and so they each had a chequebook.

Her plan, loose and possibly foolish, was to go first to the offices of Hayes, Kilgallan and Moran, ask to speak to Mr Ignatius Hayes and hope they weren't too snobby to turn her away because of her being only a young woman with a country accent who wasn't a doctor or a lawyer or a teacher. If he did agree to see her, she'd just ask him straight out for Phillippe Decker's actual address, and if he gave it to her, well, then she could write to Decker, threaten him with exposure.

Or maybe just go and confront him in Strasbourg. As to how exactly that would all go, or how the Frenchman would react, she had yet to consider. Probably it was the height of foolishness, but she had to do something.

For the millionth time, she wished Eli was with her and on her side. He was a doctor, so Hayes might speak to him as a fellow professional. But last night they'd had another horrible row. She clenched her fists in her lap, reliving that awful fight. How had her marriage come to this?

Eli had been so pleased to see her when she came back into the house with Emmet, but then she realised it was because he thought she might have gone off in the car with Malachy, taking their son with her.

She was deeply hurt. And also furious.

Then, when things had calmed down and Eli had sort of apologised – he could charm the birds off the trees – she started telling him her plans. He'd reared up again and actually ordered her not to go anywhere near Dublin to see Hayes, because that's where Malachy had gone.

In the taxi, Lena felt close to tears of rage. How dare her husband imply that her motivation was something to do with Malachy Berger!

As if that was what was at the heart of her problem and not the need to confront the man who had killed her father.

Eli had even tried to stop her from going by going away himself. He rang Margaret, the woman he had hired as his receptionist, to tell her he was going to Wales to see his mother and Charlie, to book him the next ferry from Rosslare and to arrange locum cover for a few days. It was clearly done to stop Lena leaving Kilteegan Bridge, because the children would need her, but he was taking on the wrong woman. Lena loved Eli with all of her heart, but she would not be dictated to by anyone, even her beloved husband. She knew well there were women who thought differently, who took the whole 'love, honour and obey' business seriously, but she was not one of those women.

So she'd told Katie and Mrs and Mr Shanahan that Eli had been called home unexpectedly, but that nothing was wrong, only she had plans herself she couldn't change. She asked the Shanahans to keep an eye on the house. The children were going to have to stay up at the farm, so she asked if Katie would please move in there to help take care of them. She might not have asked Katie at all, but when she was last up at the farm, Maria had been so... Well, there was that euphemism 'happy' again. Jack thought their mother was still steady, but Lena wasn't sure. She might be steady enough to care for Jack and Skipper, and even the twins who had an escape route with the Maddens across the fields, but she would have to be very steady indeed to be looking after Emmet, Sarah and Pádraig. And when Maria got overly enthusiastic, there was no knowing what she might do. She might just make the children all wonderful costumes of their favourite comic characters, but then again she might take them walking across the fields to the sea and then not watch them properly.

The taxi pulled up outside a beautiful house, too big to be a private home but not on the scale of a hospital. It was a large Victorian place with two storeys covered in Virginia creeper and Boston ivy. The front door was magenta, with a huge brass knocker and an elaborate fanlight.

The taxi let her out and turned in the expanse of gravel driveway.

There seemed to be several buildings on the campus, but it didn't feel like a hospital. The day was warm enough for some people to sit out, and dotted around the manicured grounds were three or four small groups, a few with a person in a wheelchair.

The door was slightly ajar, and so she pushed it in. It opened into a rotunda with terracotta and black tiles on the floor and whitewashed walls adorned with cheery prints and paintings. A youngish woman in a nurse's uniform, carrying folders, came through from one side and stopped.

'Can I help you?' She was smiling and efficient; clearly she had somewhere else to be.

'I was looking for Doctor O'Halloran.'

'Doctor Anthea or Doctor Mike?'

Lena was surprised. She was sure Mrs O'Halloran had said her husband, Michael, had died. 'Doctor Anthea, please.'

'Patient or a patient's relative?'

Lena smiled and shook her head. 'Oh, neither, a sort of friend. I'm sorry, she wasn't expecting me...'

The nurse checked the fob watch on her uniform. 'The prof won't be in here for an hour or so. Check the Res – that's where she'll be most likely.'

'I'm sorry, the Res?' Lena was confused. And did the nurse just call Doc's friend 'the Prof'?

'The Residence. Round the back, gate to the left, open that and go up the path and knock. If she's there and she wants to talk to you, she'll answer. But she might not. She gets a lot of visitors, journalists and medical students and researchers and such like. She can't make time for you all.' And the nurse swept off with her folders in her arms.

Lena nearly left then and there, but she was here now, and Anthea had been really friendly when she'd met her in the grave-yard, so she figured she might as well say hello at least. She followed the nurse's directions. At the back of the large building was a series of others, with various signs directing people to X-ray and pathol-ogy, the rehab clinic and the administration building. To the right was a pretty red-bricked house, a neat two-storey, almost a miniature of the main house, with a sign on the gate that said 'The Residence'.

She opened the gate and entered the garden. A profusion of pinks, nasturtiums and sweet peas lined the path to the teak front door. Before she could knock, a muscular young man with longish brown hair came around the corner, pushing another man in a wheelchair.

'Hello.' The man in the wheelchair looked to be in his mid-twenties, stocky with a red beard streaked with silver and twinkling blue eyes. He wore a purple shirt and light-blue trousers. In a world where men seemed to dress in monochrome, he looked quite eccentric.

'Oh, hello.' Lena coloured – she didn't know whether to make eye contact with the man pushing the chair or the man in it.

'Can I help?' the bearded man asked.

'I was looking for Doctor O'Halloran?'

The man laughed. 'You've found him.'

'Oh, then you're Doctor Michael...' Lena blushed again, confused. Surely this man was too young to be Anthea's husband, who'd trained with Doc.

'Except I'm Mike, not Michael – he was my father. I'm Anthea's son. And who might you be?'

'I'm Lena Kogan, Doctor Dolan's goddaughter. I don't know if you know –'

His face creased into an enormous smile. 'Ah, Paddy, push me out there till I greet Emmet's goddaughter properly.' The other man drove the wheelchair towards Lena. Mike thrust out his hand and she took it. 'Your godfather was also my godfather, Lena. I knew him all my life. He visited often, and he felt like a second father to me. We were bereft when he died. I would have gone to his funeral but...' – he indicated the wheelchair – 'travelling isn't easy for me, I'm afraid, especially on our terrible Irish trains. And my father was very ill at the time and couldn't be left.'

Lena hardly knew what to say to all this. Meeting Anthea had felt mysterious enough, but here was another secret – Doc had a godson, and he'd never said a word about him. It was like suddenly finding out she had a secret brother. 'I'm... Well, I'm so happy to meet you.' She put on her best smile. 'I met your mother at Doc's grave. She was leaving an orchid on it and I spoke to her, and we had such a lovely chat. She said to come and see her any time, and here I am, landing in on top of you without any warning. And you're all so busy – I'm intruding...' She glanced down at her overnight bag and realised how presumptuous she must look. In rural Ireland, people dropped in on each other unannounced all the time and stayed for hours, and even the night if they'd come a long way, but this was Dublin.

'Not at all. You're very welcome, and we've plenty of room to put you up. My mother's meeting with someone interested in her research at the moment, but she won't be long. Cup of tea? Something stronger?' He winked and Lena warmed to him.

'Tea would be lovely.' She followed him and Paddy into the house.

It was a lovely home, adapted for Mike's wheelchair by having wider doors and no steps. Lena suddenly remembered the last man in a wheelchair she'd encountered; it sent a shiver down her spine. The evil grin, the hollow cheeks, that *sangfroid*, as the French called it. But Mike O'Halloran was nothing like August Berger, not one bit. In fact he reminded her of someone else from Kilteegan Bridge, but she couldn't think who.

The house was messy, books and papers and dirty cups every-where, which surprised Lena for some reason. Anthea was so glam-orous and well put together, and well, she was a *woman*. She had assumed Anthea's home would be as neat and elegant as its owner. It seemed the opposite was true.

'Aha, I see by your face you've noticed.' Mike chuckled. 'My mother is a brilliant doctor, but the poor dear can't boil an egg or sweep a floor. And quite rightly, you might point out, if you weren't so polite, that the top half of me works, so why couldn't I do it? Why couldn't I indeed? But I don't, she won't, and so here we have it.' He guffawed, and Lena couldn't help but laugh. 'It drives Paddy daft enough sometimes that he tries, but it's like shovelling snow when it's still snowing, isn't that right, Paddy?'

'It is, and I haven't tried for a while now.' The young man had the soft accent of the north, Donegal maybe. 'Waste of time. You two are like a pair of magpies with the hoarding.' He grinned. 'Right, I'll leave you to it. I'll be back later.'

'See you, Paddy, and come here to me.' Michael reached into his own shirt pocket and handed the younger man a banknote. 'A pound on Lily's Fancy in the three o'clock at the Curragh.'

'Mike, you know...' Paddy seemed to protest.

'Blah, blah.' Mike dismissed him with a wave of his hand. 'Not a word or I'll tell her about your plans for the weekend.'

'You do that and see how you like being stuck in here seven days a week with no one to take you out. See how you like that.' Paddy laughed, took the money and left.

Mike seemed able to get around on the smooth floor of the kitchen just fine, spinning himself along with his hands on the wheels, and he refused Lena's help to make a pot of tea. 'Sit down, sit down. I don't need pushing around all the time – I'm perfectly capable of rolling myself,' he said as he found a packet of biscuits under a newspaper and a scarf. 'It's just that Paddy is an inmate here, his family has sort of abandoned him, and he's taken it on himself to shove me around for the company. He's got cancer, the poor lad. But he's going away to the west of Ireland for a weekend with some of his friends on Friday. He's not supposed to drink or smoke with the stuff they have him on, but he's going anyway.'

'Oh...is that not dangerous for him?' Lena asked, taking the cup of tea he offered and moving some medical journals off a chair.

Mike sighed. 'No more dangerous than the damned cancer that's killing him anyway. He might as well, I suppose.'

'But you think your mother wouldn't agree?'

He smiled, and a soft look came over his face. 'Anthea treats every patient as if they were family. Worries about them, badgers them to do the right thing. She's a wonderful doctor and a wonderful woman. If he overdoes it this weekend, he'll get very sick, and she doesn't want that for him. Neither do I. But he has to cram a lot of living into the time that's left to him.'

Lena found it hard to believe Paddy was so ill; he'd looked so young and strong. 'That's dreadful. But maybe he could go and not drink or smoke?' Lena now was worried for him too.

Mike shook his head. 'He'll be all right, or he won't. I know you're probably shocked by that, but my own situation gives me an outlook on life not everyone shares. I dove into the sea six years ago and broke my back, and I don't think I'll ever walk again despite all the new treatments, which is why you find me living at home with my mother. But I still don't really believe that fearing consequences should stop you doing what you want, provided it's legal and moral of course.' He winked again, then ate a chocolate biscuit in two bites. 'We only get one go at this, so no regrets – that's my motto. I'm trained as a doctor myself, but I don't believe in wrapping people in cotton wool. Anyway, to happier things. How are you and your family?'

'I'm all right. We're all all right,' Lena lied, sipping her own tea.

'My mother told me she met you down in Cork when she went to Emmet's grave to visit him. It's a strange idea, isn't it, visiting the dead in their graves, like they're a patient lying in a bed? I don't believe my godfather is there, or anywhere actually, but that's my own thing and I hope you don't mind me saying it.'

'I don't mind at all, but it's still a comfort to me to talk to him, and to believe he's there listening. I miss him so much.'

'And so do I,' said Mike kindly. 'He spoke about you all the time. He really saw you as his daughter.'

Lena felt her eyes sting. Though Doc was dead five years, it still hurt. 'He was very special to me.'

'I remember the night he came here with a bottle of champagne to celebrate you getting your little boy back. I'd never seen him so happy. That whole time, when you were in Wales and having to give him up, it tore at him in a way. You marrying your Welshman and becoming a proper family gave him such comfort. He was never sure he'd done the right thing, you see.'

'It was the right thing at the time, undoubtedly.' Lena liked this man but she'd only just met him, and a stranger knowing the intimate details of her life was a bit unsettling. And it was also unsettling that she knew nothing about Mike at all, even though he was Doc's other godchild. It was so strange that Doc had said nothing about it. He was always saying how if being a country doctor had taught him anything, it was that there were no big secrets that could be kept without causing disruption and pain. She could remember him saying, 'Honesty is always best, because a lie only festers with time and the truth always comes out in the end.'

Picking up on her discomfort, Mike changed the subject. 'So apart from a very welcome visit, what brings you to see us?' He sipped his tea.

He'd been so open with her that she didn't hesitate. 'I've come to talk to a solicitor called Ignatius Hayes. He has some information I need.'

'And what information is that? Sorry, I'm incorrigibly nosy. Just tell me to stop.'

'It's fine. It's just an address of one of his clients. I need to get in touch with him. Though I'm worried Mr Hayes won't see me because, you know, I'm not a teacher or anything professional like that...'

'Tell me about this man you need to know about,' Mike instructed, and she filled him in on as much as she knew. When she finished, he smiled.

'All right, let's see what we can do.' He pushed himself over to another small table and picked up a telephone that she'd not noticed at first because of all the detritus around it. 'Hello, Pat, can you put me through to Hayes, Kilgallen and Moran please?'

Lena's heart missed a beat. Would it be this easy?

'Hello, Dr Michael O'Halloran speaking. Could I speak to Iggy Hayes please?' A pause. 'Certainly, I will, thank you.'

He waited a few moments, then spoke again, this time in a booming, friendly voice. 'Iggy, Mike O'Halloran. How are you? Good, good. And Celine and the boys? I saw your middle lad was in the first fifteen at Lansdowne Road last Sunday, fair play – he's a flyer. My mother's great, thanks, busy, you know yourself.'

He waited for another second and then winked at Lena. 'Listen, Iggy, you're representing a French man, name of Phillippe Decker? It's a messy old thing involving a house in West Cork. Don't know anything about it or care less to be honest, but I knew Phillippe a few years ago. He and his friend Berger used to fish with myself and my father and a few others out Glendalough way. Anyway, long story short, I heard his name come up at a medical dinner – the house is something to do with a local GP down in Cork – but anyway, I'd love to get in touch with him. The truth is I owe him some money, and a gentleman's debt unpaid and all of that. You wouldn't have an address for him, would you? I know he lived in Alsace somewhere?'

Mike nodded, then miraculously found a pen among the debris and scribbled something on the back of an envelope. 'Marvellous, Iggy, thanks a million. Love to Celine and the boys and tell…Maurice, isn't it? Yes, good, tell him we'll see him in the green jersey yet.'

Mike hung up and wheeled over, handing her the envelope.

BP 1538, 23 Rue de Glaciers, Strasbourg, 34538.

'There you go. I'm afraid it's only a post office box number – that's where Phillippe Decker goes to pick up his mail. But you can write to him there anyway.'

Lena stared at the address and felt a cold sense of disappointment. This was all she needed. She'd only been going to write to Decker – she'd promised as much to Klaus – so why would it matter that it was only a postbox address? Yet it felt like a letdown. 'Thank you so much, Mike.'

'Ah, would you stop it,' he admonished her with a kind smile. 'No thanks needed. I'm your godbrother, aren't I?'

'Godbrother? What are you talking about?' Anthea's clear voice made Lena turn as she entered. 'Oh goodness, look who it is.' She bent over Lena's chair to give her a hug. 'Lena, welcome. So you've met my son?'

'I have.' Lena smiled. 'He made me a cup of tea and everything.'

'Astonishing. He might make his hard-working mother one too then?' She raised an eyebrow as she cleared a seat of letters and magazines, and Mike rolled away and busied himself with the kettle. 'So what brings you to Dublin, Lena? I hope you're staying with us for a few days.'

'Just one night, I think, if that's OK, Mrs O'Halloran... I mean, Doctor...'

'Anthea, I told you, please. I'm not your doctor, I'm your friend, and Mrs O'Halloran was a cranky old crone who gave my husband dog's abuse for marrying an opinionated woman with her own career. She died ten years ago, and it was the only compliant or decent thing she ever did. To misquote Shakespeare, "How sharper than a serpent's tooth it is to have a vicious mother-in-law."'

Lena smiled, a bit taken aback by how open and chatty this woman was when she'd hardly met her before; she was just like her son. But Doc was a wonderful judge of character, and if he liked Anthea, then she should too.

'Not that I'm wild about the name Anthea either,' continued the elegant, untidy woman, 'but it could be worse. My parents were bullied into naming me for my grandfather Anthony but decided it was too cruel on a little girl to be saddled with such a name, so they called me Anthea. I didn't find out I was Anthony on my birth certificate until I needed my first passport. Anyway, what brings you up to Dublin?'

'Mike just saved me a lot of trouble by helping me get an address I was looking for, but there's no train back to Cork until tomorrow...' Her voice trailed off, and Anthea looked at her sharply.

'And you don't want to go home tomorrow?' The doctor's intelligent hazel eyes rested on Lena's; she was clearly very astute.

Lena blushed. She didn't want to be disloyal to Eli by telling these two people she'd barely met how she'd had an awful row with her husband, but she was feeling so low again after the matter of the address.

'Lena, what's the matter?'

'I...'

Mike rolled over to them and handed a cup of tea to his mother and a fresh one to Lena, then tipped out the rest of the chocolate biscuits onto a plate. Then he headed towards the door, saying over his shoulder that if they didn't mind, he was going to watch rugby on television and he'd be back to cook dinner for them in a couple of hours.

'You can cook?' Lena sounded astonished and realised how rude that was immediately. 'I don't mean because... I just mean men usually...'

'Ah, Lena, have you not noticed by now? I'm not like most men.' He laughed. 'I live life my way, and cooking makes me happy. Anyway, aren't all the best chefs men?'

'Because the professional world is a man's world,' grumbled Anthea, shaking her finger at him. 'Any job that's well paid, a man will get it.'

'Yes, of course, *Doctor* O'Halloran,' he teased. 'Now I'll leave you two girls to gossip about trivia.'

'Oh, get out of here.' Anthea laughed as she threw a rolled-up newspaper at him, which he ducked expertly as he scooted out of the room. After he'd left, she stopped laughing and looked a bit sad. 'He's being discreet by leaving us to it, but I know he does want to watch the match. Mike was such a wonderful rugby player before his accident. He played for Blackrock College, then Leinster. I'm amazed how he can bear to even watch the game now, but he's got such an amazing spirit.'

'I can see that. Doc loved rugby as well. He played for one of the teams in Cork when he was young. He must have been very proud of Mike.'

'Yes, he was.' She moved a pile of what looked like tory tops off the table to make more room for the cup Mike had handed her. The dried pinecones fell to the floor, and she absentmindedly kicked them under the table with her leather-booted foot. 'He was very proud of Mike indeed.'

A silence hung between them. Anthea met Lena's eyes. 'Emmet didn't tell you about Mike, did he, Lena?'

It seemed cruel to say no, but it was too obvious that it was the truth. 'No, he didn't. And it seems really strange, because it was not like him to keep secrets.'

'Yes, but this secret wasn't his to tell. It was mine, and my husband's.'

'That Doc was Mike's godfather? I don't understand...'

'That he was Mike's father.'

'Oh!' Suddenly everything fell into place, especially the way Mike reminded her of someone in Kilteegan Bridge. Mike had Anthea's hair and mad chattiness, but his kind eyes were Doc's, his smiling mouth, his long nose... Of course! Now that she knew the truth, she couldn't not see it; it just seemed so obvious. 'But then why...' She couldn't, *wouldn't*, believe Doc was like Malachy. Surely he wouldn't abandon a girl who was in love with him enough to sleep with him?

Anthea smiled. 'Because I was already married.'

Lena tried not to look shocked. Had Doc been carrying on with a married woman all these years?

Anthea went on gently. 'I think I'd better explain, hadn't I? I don't want you thinking badly of your godfather. So this is the story. Michael, my husband, and Emmet and I all trained together. I actually went out with your godfather first, but then he went home to Kilteegan Bridge, letting me down gently that he wasn't the settling-down type. So Michael and I got together and later we married, once we qualified.'

Lena really didn't know what to say. So Anthea was unfaithful to her husband with Doc later on?

'Michael was a wonderful man, a brilliant mind, and I adored him. Emmet and the two of us stayed close all the years. He visited us often, and we would have wonderful conversations about all sorts of things.'

Lena was confused. Anthea had implied she and Doc became lovers, hadn't she?

'Year after year went by, and there were no children, which was a source of great sadness to both of us. Michael felt even worse about it than I did, I think, because it turned out he was the infertile one. He'd had mumps when he was younger, and it can have that effect. He even suggested I leave him and settle down with Emmet. He knew we still had feelings for each other – not "get married and settle down" feelings, but certainly those between a man and a woman.'

'Oh.' The idea of wanting to sleep with more than one man at a time was quite shocking to Lena. She'd had complicated feelings for Malachy even after marrying Eli, but it never crossed her mind to do anything like that – it was unthinkable.

Anthea smiled at her obvious dismay. 'Don't worry. I was married to Michael and he was my true love, so there was no way I'd ever leave him. Still, it gave me an idea, and Michael and Emmet agreed, and... Well, I suppose you can guess what my idea was.'

Lena blushed furiously. 'I suppose... I mean...'

'Yes. We asked Emmet to father our child. And now Emmet and my husband are dead, and nobody knows except my son, Mike, and me, and now you.'

'You told Mike?' She was fascinated.

'Yes. We didn't have to, but as doctors, we were aware that a new science of genetics was coming down the line and that soon it was going to be wrong for children not to know who their biological parents were, because it would make a difference to their health.'

'And Mike didn't mind when he found out?'

'No. It was a shock at first, but he knew who his real father was, and that was my husband, Michael. Emmet was wonderful, of course. He was always concerned and interested in little Mike, but he never tried to intervene in the way we brought him up, and so to Mike, he just remained his beloved godfather. We miss him so much, both of us.'

'And your husband really didn't mind?' Lena couldn't imagine Eli agreeing to her sharing her bed with another man, no matter what the circumstances.

'No, he didn't. I know he wished it were different, but he was an unusual, freethinking man. Emmet was like a brother to him, and he wanted me to be happy, and so as far as Michael was concerned, it was a perfect solution – he would be raising his best friend's child.'

'And Doc thought it was a good idea?' Doc was always tolerant and forgiving but lived very much in the real world. He was the one who told her that having a baby without a husband would be a living hell for a girl, and for the child, and arranged for her to go to Wales to stay with friends of his. So he wasn't a bohemian who cared nothing for the rules by any stretch of the imagination.

'He took some convincing.' Anthea laughed. 'Not by me, I hasten to add. A lady should never have to talk a man into sleeping with her. But Michael persuaded him.'

'Really?' Lena had never met anyone so forthright and open about something so deeply personal and potentially scandalous, but it helped her understand why Doc had talked so freely to the O'Hallorans about little Emmet. 'I…I mean… Well, I suppose… I mean, of course as you know, my oldest child, well…' She felt her eyes fill with tears. 'And now… Oh dear.'

Anthea had stopped smiling and was looking concerned. 'Something's wrong, isn't it, Lena?' she asked gently.

'I can't…'

'You can tell me, I know I can talk for Ireland about my own concerns, but I'm also a doctor and know how to keep a secret. So if you're in trouble, please tell me.'

'Ah I'm fine, it's just…'

But Anthea's warm motherly smile was too hard to resist. Lena had never had a female role model she could rely on. Emily had done her best, but she was only two years older than Lena. And Doc had been wonderful, but he wasn't a mother. And so the story all came out, about Decker and the murder and Malachy and Saturday's awful argument.

'Eli is so upset. Every time I say I don't want him to pay any money to Decker, he thinks it's because I've still got some kind of attachment to Malachy and that's why I want Emmet to have the house free and clear, because somehow he's my favourite child.'

'And the real reason?'

'I can't stomach giving my father's murderer any money.'

'And you can't get Eli to listen?'

Lena shook her head sadly. 'He won't. I've tried. He's Jewish, you see, and escaped Germany as a child. Most of his family were murdered, and he's dealt with that by closing the door on it and only moving forwards. He refuses to give them any more of his time or thoughts or energy. And that's his prerogative to deal with that horror whatever way works for him, but this man, this Phillippe Decker... He just got away with it, and now...this feels like such a kick in the face.'

'One could think Eli would have more reason to hate an ex-Nazi than you, though?'

'Normally I suppose that's right, but the way he has coped is to refuse to acknowledge them. He kind of defies the memory by simply ignoring it.'

'It's hard for us to understand,' said Anthea. 'But then we didn't live through it. We never saw what he saw, or lost loved ones to the same degree. We all do what we must to survive.' She put her cup down. 'So enough of Eli. What is it you want to do, Lena?'

'I suppose I'll write a letter to Phillippe Decker at this postbox number, threatening to expose him, and hope he backs off.'

'You don't sound very happy.'

'I'm not, to be honest. It just seems childish when I think about it.' She took a deep breath. 'I think what I really want is for me and Eli to go over there to Strasbourg and confront him and *make* him go away. I don't mean hurt him or anything. I just mean make him understand what he's done, look him in his eyes, make him admit his guilt, confess everything, stop acting like this is OK.'

'And why are you waiting for Eli to come with you? If you're nervous about facing Decker alone, you can always ask this Pierre to come with you to see him, or some Nazi hunter friend of his. Why not go and do that, and not tell Eli what you're doing?'

Lena was shocked again. 'I've never lied to my husband – I couldn't start now.' But then she blushed, because a little voice in the back of her head piped up to remind her that she'd kept Malachy's card in the secret drawer of her desk, and while she hadn't actually lied, she certainly hadn't told Eli until she'd had to.

'I think lies are underrated,' Anthea said calmly.

Lena stared at her. 'You think they're...*good*?'

'Sometimes. People are too quick to judge. There are such things as kind untruths, you know? I tell lies all the time, working as I do in the hospice. I tell patients who are dying that it will be all right, that it won't be painful. I tell their spouses and children that they were peaceful in the end when it was anything but. I've even told people their loved one mentioned their name in the time before their death if it brings them comfort. I lied to my family and friends about Emmet and Mike, or lied by omission at any rate, and Emmet lied to you about the nature of our relationship. I told Michael I didn't enjoy sleeping with Emmet, but I did. All I'm saying is if a lie is intended to ease hurt and not cause it, then it's not the most awful thing.'

Time after time, this bold woman took Lena's breath away.

'I'm not suggesting you never tell Eli, but perhaps you should just go ahead and do what you want and tell him later.'

'But I'll be going behind his back.'

'Lena, it's 1966. You are an independent woman, and you can do as you please. This is your business, and you want to seek some clarity. You don't need to run every single thing past your husband. I'm sure he doesn't tell you everything he does, every conversation he has? Yes, you're married, but you are the master of your own destiny. Do what's in your heart – it never lets you down. Your heart, instinct, intuition, whatever you want to call it, is yours alone. Not Eli's, not some man's in France, not Malachy's – yours. So have a think, and ask yourself the question, "What do I really want?" Then go and make it happen.'

'Is it that simple, though, really?'

Anthea shrugged. 'Nothing worth doing is ever simple. All I will say is that I got some great advice as a young female doctor competing in a man's world. Don't start a fight unless it's one you at least stand a chance of winning, but once it's started, make sure you take it all the way.'

Lena shivered. Did she really want to pick this fight? What if he killed her too? But she had to try, for her own sake and Emmet's sake. And all their sakes.

'Oh Judas!' Anthea was checking her watch. 'I should have been on rounds ten minutes ago, especially if I'm going to be back in time for dinner. Lena, we'll finish discussing this later. Now, the spare room is facing you as you go up the stairs. I'm afraid Mike can't show you up, but you should find it all right. Hopefully it's slightly less messy than the rest of the house, because that's where my mother stays when she's here – she loves cleaning and tidying. We adore each other, but we don't understand each other at all. And there's a bathroom to the left of it, so have a good soak and a think about how you want to do this. Use the Epsom salts. I do some of my best thinking in a bath of Epsom salts.'

And with that, this extraordinary woman swept out of the house, leaving Lena feeling utterly stunned, as if in the last hour, every thought she'd ever had had been given a good shake, and some of them even put back into her head upside down.

CHAPTER 12

The Aer Lingus office on O'Connell Street, Dublin's main street, was very intimidating. Lena had no idea how much an aeroplane ticket might be, but it was no harm to ask, she supposed. She'd never been on a plane, and while it was something she would have been looking forward to normally, she always envisaged taking her first flight with Eli and her family, not alone and without his blessing.

Up until yesterday evening, she'd been planning on taking the ferry, but according to Anthea and Mike, that would add two days to her journey – actually even more than that, because it would leave her stranded miles from where she wanted to be. So she'd decided to at least see if she could get a flight direct to Strasbourg.

On the way to the office, she'd stopped at a telephone booth and rang the farm. Katie had answered and all was well. Lena had casually enquired if Dr Kogan had been in touch. Katie told her that he'd telephoned and spoken to the children but hadn't mentioned when he'd be back. Lena's heart sank. She said goodbye to Katie and hung up, pulling herself together.

She needed to be strong and decisive for the task ahead, so she strode purposefully up the street with her head high and chin jutting out. She was doing something that mattered to her. Anthea was right – she was a woman, not a child. And if Eli couldn't understand that, or thought she should just bow down to his will simply because he was a man, then he could take a running jump for himself. The anger bubbled up again, dispelling her terror, as she arrived at the Aer Lingus office.

The glass-fronted office was very swanky, she thought, and she braced herself once more as she grabbed the handle and pushed the door inwards. The lady behind the counter was dressed in the beautiful and iconic Aer Lingus suit designed by none other than the famous Irene Gilbert from Tipperary, whose name regularly appeared in magazines featuring the rich and famous. Lena had recently read an article about how Gilbert had even designed outfits for Princess Grace of Monaco. The woman behind the polished wood desk wore the elegant green tweed suit, with tiny flecks of orange, a jacket and calf-length skirt, with poise and sophistication. The lemon-coloured blouse and matching gloves completed the outfit. She had a jaunty little hat perched on her perfectly coiffed strawberry-blond hair. Lena thought she was like an advertisement for Ireland.

'Good afternoon, may I be of assistance?' the woman asked imperiously.

Lena swallowed. 'I need to get to Strasbourg as soon as possible...' she began, her voice hoarse with nerves. She wished she'd worn gloves; this felt like the kind of place women were expected to wear gloves. Luckily she had dressed conservatively in a maroon dress and jacket, and she had a hat and wore her hair neatly pinned back. 'In France,' she added, then realised that was unnecessary. Of course this urbane woman would know where Strasbourg was.

The woman smiled, but it never reached her lightly made-up eyes. 'And you wish to fly there?'

No, Lena thought to herself. *I want to cycle – I thought it would be quicker.* She bit her tongue. 'Yes, I do.' She refused to let this woman intimidate her.

The lady consulted a map and ran her finger down a ledger of some kind, then consulted another log table and finally looked up.

'You could purchase a seat on the DC-3 going to Le Bourget. It's the Starflight so a little less expensive...' She ran a gloved finger down what looked like a pricelist now. 'It would be twenty-six pounds return.'

Lena didn't understand a word and her face must have betrayed that, because the woman sighed and explained very clearly and slowly, as if Lena were both deaf and mentally challenged. 'The aeroplane we fly to Paris, it's a DC-3, and it lands at the most central airport in Paris, which is called Le Bourget. And the Starflight is the last one tonight, and because it arrives at one in the morning, it's a bit less expensive.'

'How long does the journey take?' Lena asked nervously.

'Three hours and fifteen minutes.'

She hated looking vulnerable to this know-it-all, but she had no choice. 'And how do I get from Paris to Strasbourg? Is it very far?'

The woman smiled again, a saccharin effort. 'Madam, this is an airline, not a tourist information office.'

The door behind her opened, and a man emerged. He was almost six feet tall, with a stocky build. He looked like a glamorous movie star, with his dark suit with gold-striped braiding on the cuffs. An immaculate white shirt, a dark tie and a braided hat with a peak finished the outfit.

'Marjorie, could you please see these get in the post?' He glanced at Lena, then took a slower second look. He gave her a smile that oozed charm. 'Good morning, madam. I'm Captain Andrew Ahearne. I hope we've been able to help you?'

Lena was amused. It wasn't every day of the week a handsome pilot flirted with her. 'Well, yes, I think so. I'm trying to get to Strasbourg, but...'

Marjorie looked like a bulldog chewing a wasp. Lena suppressed a smile to see her so put out. Clearly Marjorie thought Lena was a right hussy for speaking to someone of such exalted rank.

'I've been trying to help, Mrs...Mrs...' Marjorie cast a pointed look at Lena's wedding ring, perhaps for the captain's benefit.

'Kogan, Mrs Lena Kogan. But you just said you weren't a tourist office?'

'Well, we're not really...' Two pink spots of indignation appeared on Marjorie's cheeks at Lena's temerity in exposing her.

The captain looked crossly at the receptionist. 'Nonsense, Marjorie. We are here to do our best for all our customers. Where was it you wished to go, Mrs Kogan?'

'Strasbourg?' She hoped she didn't sound too nervous and inexperienced. 'I was going to take the Starflight...'

'Perfect. I'm actually flying the Starflight to Paris tonight. I'd be happy to have you aboard. Once you land, it will be late, mind you, so I can recommend some very nice Parisienne hotels, and tomorrow morning you just need to take the train to Strasbourg.'

Lena's face must have betrayed her dismay at the reality of her new situation, flying alone, staying in a hotel in Paris, taking a train in a foreign country, because Captain Ahearne became very warm and reassuring.

'Don't feel overwhelmed, Mrs Kogan. I'll look after you. My crew always stays at the Cheval Blanc. It's in the tenth *arrondissement*, so it's near the Gare de l'Est, where you'd catch the train to Strasbourg. We could book you a room there, and you could share a taxi with me and the crew once we land if you like? Actually, we could book you a room in Strasbourg too if you wanted, couldn't we, Marjorie? Send her to the place by the Jardin d'Orangeries – La Belle Étoile is the one we use, isn't it?'

'Well, yes...' Marjorie didn't dare contradict him, and Lena found herself struggling not to smile. She deserved it, the snooty old cow.

'Marvellous. Thank you, Marjorie.'

'Yes, thank you, Marjorie,' said Lena sweetly. 'I've never flown before and I've never been to France either, so I need all the help I can get.' She might as well be honest.

'First time for everything.' The captain smiled. 'Marjorie will book your seat and the hotel rooms for you. Don't worry, Mrs Kogan, we'll take care of you.'

'Thank you, Captain Ahearne.'

'My pleasure.' He winked and retreated back to his office.

Marjorie was clearly livid. 'A double room, Mrs Kogan?' she asked rudely, trying hard to imply Lena might not be spending the night alone.

'No, a single, thank you. My husband couldn't travel with me this time,' said Lena, making an effort to stay polite. The pilot was just trying to help her, but Marjorie obviously thought Lena was either a harlot or a complete imbecile up from the country who didn't know how to control herself when a man flirted with her, however mildly.

Marjorie filled out several pieces of paper, accepted Lena's cheque and handed her an envelope full of information. 'Please be at the airport half an hour in advance of your flight to check in,' she said sourly.

'Thank you.' Lena took the envelope and left.

Out in the sunshine once more, she wondered what she should do. She stood for a while on the steps of the GPO, where in 1916 Irish independence from Britain had been proclaimed, thinking about that great moment in history. Across the road was Clerys department store, and the big clock outside told her it was ten past four. She decided she had time to go shopping before going back to the O'Hallorans' to pack. Anthea had warned her the weather would be a lot warmer in France, so she crossed the road and then spent almost an hour in Clerys, overwhelmed by the huge selection of women's clothes on offer. It was a far cry from Maureen's Fashions in Kilteegan Bridge, with its ever-sensible display of long skirts and cardigans. In the end she selected three white blouses with floppy necklines that she thought would go with anything; two printed skirts, one black with white flowers and one blue and with red flowers, both rather short; a dainty red cardigan; and strappy sandals. She hoped she would look fashionable enough for Paris.

The green double-decker bus going back to the hospital was full of students, carefree young people in college scarves, all in high spirits chatting about some rugby team. It made her think of Mike, and all he had lost by breaking his back.

Though she wasn't much older than them, sometimes she felt

around sixty. She and Eli had a great life together, normally anyway, but she was a mother, a wife, a homemaker. She could not remember the last time she'd even had one day to herself.

She got off the bus at the hospital and heard someone call her name as she walked through the gates. She turned, and it was Anthea. 'Come and tell me how you got on,' Anthea said, beckoning her over to a pair of wicker chairs on the lawn. 'Did you get your plane ticket? Did you go shopping? Oh look, these are lovely…'

While Anthea admired Lena's purchases, Lena told her all about Marjorie and Captain Andrew Ahearne and how she planned to get to Strasbourg. 'And, Anthea, can I leave my flight plans and contact details for Paris and Strasbourg with you, just in case?' she asked. 'I left Eli without explanation but felt awful so I sent a telegram with your address, but he doesn't know where I'm going after seeing you, and he might worry about me seeing Decker…' Her voice cracked.

'Are you worried as well, Lena?' asked Anthea calmly. 'Are you frightened of Decker?'

Lena nearly said no, but then she realised the older woman wasn't being overprotective. She wasn't about to jump in and talk Lena out of it like Eli would have done; she just seemed to want to know what Lena was thinking.

'I am frightened of him, to be honest. Klaus, the history professor who helped me find him, thinks he could turn violent if he's confronted. But I can't let it stop me. I've got Pierre's address, and I'll see if he can help, though I'm not sure it's even right to drag someone else into this. Decker's a dangerous person, Anthea. He's killed before, at least once.'

'But you still want to do this.'

Lena nodded. 'I've come this far – I have to go on. I could go back home, wait for Eli, tell him I've forgotten it, maybe let him buy the house or move to another house he picked for us, but my life would be a lie. No, I'm going, get it over with, confront this criminal face to face and see what he has to say for himself. I don't think I can get beyond it otherwise. Even if it means risking my marriage.'

'And you fly tonight?'

Lena nodded, suddenly more petrified than ever.

'Wait here, I'll be back.' Anthea stood and strode off.

Holding her handbag in her lap, Lena attempted to take her mind off things by watching as people visited with their families. They were all smiling and chatting with each other, though she wondered how many, like poor young Paddy, were terminally ill. It was difficult to tell. They seemed relaxed and happy in the warm sun, enjoying the day. She tried to imagine what it was like, to know the end was nigh. Everyone knew that ultimately it was the fate that awaited us all, but nobody liked to think about it. Here, though, one had little choice.

For the millionth time, she longed for Eli. Perhaps she should telephone Wales? She'd noticed a few pay telephones on a wall of the rotunda, presumably for the use of patients. She glanced at her watch. The children would be at school and Eli's parents, Charlie and Sarah, would be at work, so Eli might be there by himself. Would he speak to her, though? Yes, he would. She was still cross with him, but she wanted to talk to him. And he was probably still cross with her, but he must want to know she was all right. She would call him, she decided. Even if he was offhand with her, the sound of his voice would make her feel better. Though whether she'd tell him what she was doing and where she was going, she wasn't sure. It would depend on how he seemed with her, she decided.

Anthea returned holding a small black leather pouch. 'I've a question for you, Lena. Do you want me to come to France with you?'

'What?' Lena couldn't believe her ears. 'But you're so busy…'

'Still, I can come, for a few days, moral support kind of thing. Emmet – Doc – wouldn't want you going into the lion's den alone, and he'd never forgive me if anything happened to you. So for his sake, if you want me to, we'll face this man together.'

'I can't ask you to do that.'

'You didn't.' Anthea smiled. She stayed standing instead of sitting down.

Lena thought seriously about it, but not for long. The company of an older, much wiser woman would be a comfort, but she was a big girl and this was her fight – hers alone. Simply being around this remarkable female doctor had strengthened her resolve and independence, and although she was frightened, she didn't want to cling to her like a dependent child.

'Thanks, Anthea, but I'll go on my own. I really appreciate it, though.'

'Well done.' The woman patted Lena's hand and didn't try to convince her. 'Then take this with you.' She held out the black leather pouch.

'What is it?' Lena asked, accepting it.

'It's a vial of this new drug called Librium. It's a kind of sedative, works fairly fast. Ideally it should go in a vein, but it can be delivered into a muscle as well. Just mix the solution before you meet him, and fill the syringe like this.' Anthea demonstrated. 'And if he gives you any trouble, just stick it in him and squeeze. It will make him instantly dizzy and disoriented, and you'll be able to get away. The effects will wear off in a few hours.'

'Are you serious?' Lena was stunned.

'Deadly.' Anthea confirmed. 'Now let's go and have dinner – Mike will be waiting.'

Lena stood and gathered her bag. 'I'll follow you in a minute. I'm just going to use the phone.'

'To check on the children?' Anthea asked.

'No, I already did that.'

'To talk to Eli?' The older woman put her head to one side, a smile hovering on her beautiful lips.

'Yes. Do you think I'm being weak?'

'Of course I don't think you're being weak. There's nothing weak about love. And I know you love Eli, and I'm sure he loves you.'

'But I am being weak in a way. I feel so scared about everything. I'm even scared he'll leave me if I go ahead with this.'

'Lena, if there was something fundamental to his happiness or peace of mind that he just had to do, even if you didn't agree with him, would you leave him over it?'

'No,' Lena answered unequivocally.

'Then in that case, he won't leave you either. In my experience, there are few conflicts that don't benefit from a little time and space being put between the incident and the resolution. Maybe he's annoyed and upset you won't bend to his will. Men get like that, dear, and the only way to train them to realise that you're not a pliable little scrap willing to kowtow to their wishes on every little thing is to be defiant and brave. Stand up for yourself and do your own thing. Trust me, he'll admire you all the more for it in the end.' She laughed at Lena's incredulous expression. 'It's not their fault, Lena. They're raised to believe they are the dominant gender, that they know best, that women should be subordinate to them. But they must be retrained.'

'Did you retrain your husband?' Lena asked, both amused and scandalised, even though she was beginning to get used to Anthea and her unusual ideas.

'I certainly trained him not to think of women as inferior.'

'Eli doesn't see me as inferior.' Lena was quick to defend her husband.

'I'm not saying he does, Lena. I'm saying you cannot bend your own will out of shape to please him, that's all.' And off Anthea went, sweeping across the emerald lawn, nodding to her patients, both the dying and the disabled, greeting them all with true affection as the wonderful, independent human beings they really were.

Lena made her way across the grass towards the large front door. Standing at one of the phones in the rotunda, she pulled her red address book out of her bag and dialled the operator, then requested the number of Eli's parents' house in Cardiff. Thankfully she had enough coins, and it wasn't long before she was connected.

The butterflies danced in her stomach as she waited for Eli to answer. An older woman who was clearly hard of hearing was shouting answers into the telephone beside her, and she hoped she'd be able to hear him speak.

After several rings, the phone was picked up. 'Hello?' It wasn't Eli. It was a woman's voice. Eli's mother.

'Hello, Sarah. It's Lena.'

'Ooh, Lena! Hello, lovie, how are you?' Sarah had a hybrid

German-Welsh accent that instantly transported Lena back to Cardiff, when she'd been a terrified, unmarried, pregnant girl and that voice had given her comfort and made her feel that everything would be all right.

'I'm fine, thanks.' Lena tried to keep her voice light and cheery, just as it would normally be when talking to her mother-in-law. 'And you and Charlie, and the children?' She couldn't reasonably ask for Eli until she'd heard all the family gossip.

'Oh, we're very well. Rhys's team won the county yesterday. He was scrum half, and so he's been on air since. I don't know who is happier, him or his dad.'

'Oh, that's marvellous. Tell him I'm very proud. I knew it was on – Eli mentioned it.'

'Talking of Eli, what's up with that boy? He swoops in on Sunday, spends an evening talking to Charlie in the pub and is gone first thing in the morning. Charlie said he was off to a conference in London or something? You know what Charlie's like – he's hopeless at details.'

Lena stared at the receiver. Blood pounded in her ears. Eli had gone to London without telling her? She tried to focus her mind.

'Lena?'

'It's an important conference...' she managed.

'I assumed it had to be to take him away from his beloved family for so long. And how are the little ones? I was hoping you could all come over for Charlie's birthday. He'll be fifty next month and we're going to have a little party. Do you think you'd be able to drag Eli away for a week or two?'

'Of course we will,' she said. 'I'll get Margaret to book a locum now, in plenty of time.'

'Wonderful. Just do it and tell him afterwards, best plan.' Sarah chuckled. 'It's the only way to get men to do what we want them to. Now tell me about my grandchildren.'

Somehow Lena managed to chat about her children for a few minutes, and with more promises to get Eli to call, she finally hung up.

'Where are you, Eli?' she asked under her breath. 'And what are you doing?'

Why would he go to London? Who was he seeing there? A dark thought entered her mind. Was it a lawyer? Divorce was illegal in Ireland, but she and Eli had been married in the UK and so Eli could file for divorce there if he wanted.

Was she to be one of those women, abandoned by her man?

No, no. Eli Kogan would never leave his children, even if he wanted to leave her. Oh God, would he try to take the children from her? Would she become a source of pity, scorn and judgement? And once it became known why he left her, because of his suspicions about Malachy – and she was under no illusion that such a thing would remain a secret in Kilteegan Bridge – would she be a woman left with no husband, no family, no home, no reputation?

Stop it. She was being silly, she knew. Eli would never do that. He *wouldn't.*

But she could feel her heart thumping. She was about to get on an aeroplane, on her own, fly to Paris, stay in a hotel, then go to Strasbourg to confront a murderer, and she had absolutely no idea where her husband was or what he was planning. Suddenly she felt like she was suffocating. She didn't know what was happening to her. She felt like it was hard to breathe, like she couldn't get enough air into her lungs.

There was a seat beside the telephones, so she sat and tried to compose herself. She willed her breath to normalise, but she couldn't help it coming in great gasps. The black and terracotta tiles on the floor were growing blurry, turning grey...

A firm female voice addressed her. 'In through the nose, out through the mouth. Big, calm, slow breaths. Good girl. Just breathe, concentrate on that, forget about everything else. Just breathe.'

She tried to do as the voice said, calming her breathing, focusing on the in and out, but it was difficult.

'There you go now. Slowly, slowly... Inhale and exhale. There you have it now.'

Lena's vision cleared, and she saw that the brisk nurse she'd met yesterday was standing over her. 'I'm sorry, I don't know what happened...'

'Just a panic attack. Nothing to worry about. You're all right now.' The ever-busy nurse quickly checked Lena's pulse against her fob watch, nodded and hurried away to deal with her next crisis.

CHAPTER 13

*P*hillippe had read the newspaper clipping so often, he no longer needed the page in front of him to see the house with its smug little family standing on its front steps. The image was emblazoned on his mind. He owned it, that house.

And to hell with the latest letter from Hayes, informing him that Malachy Berger was mounting a challenge to the will and suggesting that Decker might need to pay even more to countersue, as August's son was very, very rich. Of course he was. He had all the Berger money, the proceeds of the *manoir* outside Eguisheim, the sale of the contents of the cellar, even the private vault. He knew to the last centime, as it was he who did the dealings on August's behalf. And the spoiled brat hadn't lifted a finger to get it either.

To hell with Malachy. To hell with all the Irish.

Maybe he'd actually go back to Kilteegan Bridge, see if they dared bully him then, when he came to claim his inheritance, the copy of the will in his hand. Who needed a greedy Dublin solicitor? He could manage this himself.

The Kogans might be upset at having to find a place of their own, but why should they benefit from his loyalty to August Berger?

He'd only ever been loyal, only ever done what he was asked to do.

Nothing that had happened to him was his fault. He'd never asked to hear the name Adolf Hitler, and it had been August's idea, not his, to put a German uniform on his back. If the world had left him alone, he would have married Rebecca and had children with her and lived happily ever after.

Fury at how things turned out caused him to punch the wall in temper.

That summer of 1938 had been the best of his life. He was working in August's family's business and on the vineyards, he was powerfully strong as a boy, and he was in love with Rebecca, who seemed miraculously to return his affection. He would rise early to help his father in the bakery, then he would go to Chateau de Marin and tend to the vines. He had a knack for it, despite not coming from a *vignoble* family. He knew when to pick, and he could spot flies and parasites before they became a problem. After work he would call on Rebecca and they'd walk, or if the evening was cold, her mother would allow them to sit in the parlour and play records on the gramophone. Sometimes they would dance, and her mother would turn a blind eye as they held each other close. Her father was kind too but much more proper, yet Madame Loeb was an incurable romantic.

When the Germans invaded Poland, the happy times were interrupted. The French government evacuated the whole region because it was so close to the Maginot Line. People were sent from Alsace to the Périgord, the Haute-Vienne, far away in southwest France.

Phillippe recalled his father mutinously shutting up the bakery, loudly complaining to anyone who'd listen how it was ridiculous. They went to stay with cousins outside Paris, a farm on the edge of the Bois de Boulogne. The Loebs and others had been as reluctant as anyone else to go, but they'd had to do it. They were evacuated to a little town called Magnac-Laval in the Haute-Vienne, between Poitiers and Limoges in the southwest of France. As far as Phillippe and Rebecca were concerned, it might as well have been the moon.

Any Jews who had remained were thrown out of their homes and forced to go to Vichy-controlled areas. Jean Claude, a man Phillippe worked with in the vineyard, had had cuts on his hands a few days before, and when Phillippe questioned how he received them, he was told laughingly that they were got by beating a Jew. The other men laughed and smoked their cigarettes as Jean Claude, a huge bruiser of a man, told them how an old Jewish man who lived in one of the nicest houses in the town – he was a banker in Strasbourg and filthy rich according to Jean Claude – didn't leave Ribeauvillé and so was dragged from his house and beaten half to death.

By July 1940, the Germans had declared Alsace *judenrein* – free of Jews – and the Jew hatred that had been muttered under people's breath before in Alsace was now spoken loud and clear.

Phillippe and his family had returned to Alsace by then. The worst had happened – France had fallen – so they thought they might as well go home. August had also returned from Dublin, where he had romanced and married Hannah Fitzgerald. Phillippe took the risk of writing to Rebecca, telling her to stay away, that it wasn't safe.

But stubborn Monsieur Loeb didn't want to give up his business and defiantly returned to Eguisheim. When Phillippe heard they were back, he immediately bolted across the road to see Rebecca, and she ran to him, and even in front of her foolish father, hugged him tightly.

He was torn between delight at being reunited and terror at the danger her family had placed her in, bringing her back to that place. And for that matter, the danger they had placed him in as well, because it was forbidden to associate with Jews let alone have a relationship with one.

'My love, I'm so happy to see you,' he whispered to her. 'But you should not have come back. Things are different now. It's not safe.'

She'd smiled sweetly. 'Papa knows what's been happening, but we are not like others, Phillippe, you know that, in big cities where the Jews all stuck together, not integrating. We are here in this little village, our neighbours are our friends, and we've all known each other for years. Papa isn't worried, and he says Mama and I should not be either.'

That evening, he sat gloomily in their parlour, eating a day-old baguette toasted on the fire and slathered with a pot of last year's strawberry jam he'd lifted from his mother's store cupboard.

The Loeb parents were so tired after their long journey, and they went to bed early.

'Phillippe is just going, Mama,' Rebecca promised as her mother kissed her goodnight, then followed her husband up the stairs. But he didn't go. That night, in front of the fire, he kissed Rebecca Loeb properly for the first time. They'd stolen kisses here and there, always afraid of being caught, but this was a proper kiss, and he thought he'd died and gone to heaven.

On and on they kissed, and he was horrified to feel his body react to her. He desperately pulled himself away from her while continuing to kiss her, but she moved closer to him; his excitement didn't upset her, it would seem. Even now, all these years later, he could remember that sensation. Innocence, youth, passion, love.

A night of pure happiness.

As dawn broke, he'd crept out of the house and gone straight to the vineyard, where he worked all day. When he came home that evening, exhausted, his mother told him that the Germans had come and taken Rebecca and her parents. Nobody seemed to know where. They had been quickly and brutally removed, and nobody, including his own parents who watched from their *patisserie* across the road, had lifted a finger to stop them.

Not that he could have done anything for her – interfering in Nazi business would have meant instant death. Even just spending that night with her nearly got him shot. He'd had to swear blind to the Allgemeine SS that it wasn't him seen coming out of her house that morning, and he was really only saved by August swanning into the police station with a case of exceptionally good Pinot Gris and two prostitutes from a brothel in Colmar who insisted both August and Phillippe had been with them.

He snapped back to the present time. The letter. What nonsense. He had a legal right to that house, and if he wanted to sell it and go and live in South America like so many of his former brothers-in-arms, then that was what he would do.

Or maybe he could even live in Ireland, where nobody had any ideas about him or his past. As far as the people of Kilteegan Bridge were concerned, he was the French manservant of 'Auguste' Berger, and although that nosy country doctor had flinched at the sight of the scar on August's upper arm, nothing had been said afterwards, no rumours had flown around, no one started looking at him with suspicion. And the doctor was dead now, so no risk there.

Ignatius Hayes had made no mention of knowing who he was, even though the Dublin solicitor had been in touch with Kieran Devlin. So clearly his secret was still safe in Kilteegan Bridge.

Whatever August said on his deathbed, even if he'd told Lena and Malachy the truth about Hannah's death and Lena's father's murder, nobody could blame Phillippe Decker. He'd just done what he was told. He was a loyal servant, and he deserved to be paid for it. He could not continue like this, living as a poor church mouse.

Yes, he wanted a home, a place to finally settle and rest his weary bones, and it suddenly seemed to him that Ireland was the best option he had. He'd been content there. It was a quiet, calm, peaceful place where people went about their business, and if you didn't bother with them, they didn't bother with you. He would go there, move into that big house. He only needed a few rooms, so perhaps he could take in a lodger or two, live off the land, farm it a bit maybe, make enough to buy a few groceries, maybe an odd nice bottle of wine – not that the Irish would know a nice wine from a bucket of pig slop, but still. He'd wait there for death, dreaming of the golden past among the trees and green pastures of Ireland.

And once he was settled, maybe he could hire a private detective to go searching for Rebecca, and she would forgive him and understand and come to live with him in Ireland.

CHAPTER 14

*D*espite it being late summer, the night wind whipping through Lena's coat was cold and she had to hold her hat on her head as she was directed to the steps of the DC-3. The bright lights of the airport meant she didn't stumble, but the steps of the plane were slippery, wet with the falling mist.

The plane was smaller inside than she'd imagined. She counted ten green upholstered chairs on each side, only four of them taken – one by a nun, two by a very fashionable-looking woman and her small but equally fashionable-looking daughter and the fourth by a businessman in a pinstriped suit who had already put his seat into the reclining position and had his handkerchief spread over his face, clearly asleep. As she took her seat, Captain Andrew Ahearne came out to greet her.

'Ah, Mrs Kogan, you made it! Welcome aboard. It's rather snug, I'm afraid. These are the workhorses since the war, but we've just contracted for a load of Viscounts, and once they are here, it will be much more commodious, I assure you.'

'It's all wonderful,' Lena said, meaning it.

She, Mike and Anthea had enjoyed a delicious meal he called lamb tagine. She'd never tasted anything like it, but it was divine, with tender meat and apricots with rice and spices. She'd taken a taxi to the airport afterwards and reluctantly left their care. She was on her own now.

She still didn't know what Eli was doing, but he was the most level-headed person she knew; he wouldn't do anything rash or foolish. But he did need time to think things through, and she was sure that was all he was doing. It was his way. And Anthea was right – this was her story, her journey, and Eli, as much as she loved him, would have to understand that.

The propellers started, and the little plane taxied along the runway and then started to pick up speed. As it rose into the air and the lights on the ground dwindled, Lena's ears hurt and she yawned frantically until they popped, as Anthea had instructed her to do.

Her ears stopped throbbing when the plane levelled out, but the flight was nerve-wracking and bumpy, and she tried to hide her panic as the little aircraft bounced along in the inky skies. Somehow she'd imagined flying would be smooth, like a boat trip on a river – birds made it look so graceful – but this was more like being in a tiny rowboat in the middle of the ocean. Every so often, the plane seemed to drop for a hundred feet, and each time it did, Lena's stomach threatened to get rid of the lamb tagine and the little girl further down the plane shrieked shrilly.

Her only consolation was that the hostess was completely calm, her elegant tweed suit and lemon-yellow blouse unruffled. She assured Lena it was just something called turbulence and offered her a glass of champagne, 'compliments of the captain', but Lena refused. She just couldn't wait to get on terra firma again.

After a terrifying two hours, things became smoother and her eyes began to close, and when the aeroplane touched down with a jolt, she nearly had a heart attack. She must have nodded off despite her terror. There was a lurch, several bumps and finally a prolonged judder, and at last the journey was over.

On legs that felt like jelly, she descended the steps into the night, which was so warm she started sweating in her woollen coat. She stopped to take it off and fold it over her arm. The hostess descended behind her and pointed out the way to the terminal, a low, dimly lit building, and as she entered through the glass doors, the handsome captain fell into step beside her and took her case.

'We'll take a taxi to the hotel,' he said. And she was so tired and overwhelmed, she allowed herself to be shepherded along by him through the almost deserted terminal. He waited for her while she stood with the few other passengers to have her passport stamped by a solitary bored-looking man in uniform – '*Merci, madame*' – and then he led her out into the warm night again, on the far side of the building.

There were several taxis waiting, and Captain Ahearne flagged down two of them. The air hostess from the plane climbed into one, along with another hostess in a red and blue suit and an older man in a red-trimmed pilot's uniform, who must have been flying the plane that arrived just before theirs. Before getting in beside the driver, the other pilot saluted Captain Ahearne, saying in an English accent, 'Hello there, Ahearne. See you for a nightcap back at the hotel?'

'Not sure about the nightcap, Bottomley, feeling a bit wrecked to be honest,' the captain answered as he placed Lena's bag in the boot of the second taxi. Then he switched smoothly into French, saying to the driver, 'Lido de Paris, *s'il vous plaît.*'

Lena had heard French spoken before – when August Berger spoke to Decker, he always did so in that language – but she had no idea what the captain just said. She just assumed it was directions to the hotel where he'd said all the crew were going.

Captain Ahearne handed Lena into the back of the taxi and then climbed in beside her, instead of sitting beside the driver like Captain Bottomley had done. Lena started to think it would have sent a better message if she'd insisted on getting into the taxi with the other two women, even if it would have been a bit crowded. Was she imagining it, or was Captain Ahearne sitting closer to her than was strictly necessary? He slid further towards her as the taxi sped round the first corner and didn't move away again.

'Are you tired?' he murmured in her ear. 'I was thinking we could go to a club. The Lido de Paris is very famous. It's on the Champs-Élysées...'

So much for him being too wrecked to have a nightcap with Captain Bottomley, she thought. She had to shake this pest off. 'I won't, thank you, Captain. I need to telephone my husband. He's hoping to join me in Strasbourg, so we need to make arrangements.'

Refusing to be rebuffed, he tried again. 'It's a bit late to be ringing husbands, don't you think? Poor chap will be fast asleep.'

She could almost feel the warmth of his smile, the same one he'd used to great effect on other women, she was in no doubt. Most girls would swoon over a handsome pilot who spoke French – they would find him dreamy – but not her. She had no interest whatsoever, and he needed to hear that loud and clear.

'Oh, he's waiting up to hear from me. We've never been apart before, not even for one night, so he'll be sitting by the telephone.' She smiled sweetly, rummaging in her handbag. 'We have three children – would you like to see a photograph of them?' She pulled out the picture she kept in her purse, pointing out each child in turn. 'That's Emmet, and in the middle is Sarah and the baby is Pádraig. It's wonderful he's out of nappies now. He used to get terrible nappy rash, and as for when his teeth were coming through... isn't he gorgeous?'

It finally seemed to sink into Captain Ahearne's brain that he was barking up the wrong tree, and he sighed and said to the driver, *'Excusez-moi, emmenez-nous plutôt à l'hôtel Cheval Blanc, s'il vous plaît.'*

The driver frowned, slowed, did a screeching U-turn and shot off in the other direction. Lena pressed herself against the door, keeping her bag and coat between herself and the pilot, and gazed out the window. They passed over a bridge called the Pont de Flandre, and the lights of the city of Paris were perfectly reflected in the water below.

When they reached the hotel, the other taxi had already arrived, and Captain Ahearne, with a sulky 'goodnight', turned off into the bar area, where Captain Bottomley was sitting at the counter having a whiskey. A very sleepy porter showed Lena up to her bedroom, a lovely spacious room with a wide bed and a silky bedspread, and another room with a bath and toilet for her own use and what looked oddly like a second toilet next to the first. The room was very warm, and she opened the window. The sounds of the city flooded in, people laughing and shouting even though it was the middle of the night. Under the window was a tiny bookshelf, and once she'd undressed, she selected a slim volume, the only one in English in the collection. She felt wide awake and hoped that she could read herself to sleep. Propped up on the luxurious feather pillows, she opened the book to the first page. It was by someone called Choderlos de Laclos, and the title intrigued her, *Dangerous Liaisons*. It sounded particularly suitable for the task she had ahead.

As she dove in, she found she couldn't put it down. The antics and lengths that Marquise de Merteuil and the Vicomte de Valmont were willing to go to, to seduce and use others for their own cruel pleasures, both shocked and delighted her. Eventually by four in the morning, when the streets outside were finally quiet, she reluctantly put it down. She would ask the porter if she could buy it from him, as she wanted to find out what happened next. She fell into a fitful sleep, imagining herself in powdered wigs and tight corsets, getting up to all sorts of depravity with a variety of pre-French Revolution aristocrats.

* * *

SHE WOKE, groggy and disoriented – where on earth was she? *Oh lord*, she thought, trying to swallow the panic. She was far from home, in a hotel, in a country where she didn't speak the language, about to find and confront a murderer. Well, she'd started and now she was here, and she had to go through with it. Like Anthea said, 'Once you start the fight, you have to make sure to take it all the way.'

She got dressed in some of the light summer clothes she'd bought in Clerys and went downstairs. It was nine thirty, and she hoped she wasn't too late for breakfast.

'*Petit dejuner, madame?*' an impeccably dressed very round man asked her, different to last night's sleepy porter. He had a bald head and an incredibly curly moustache that he clearly needed to oil and wax each morning.

'Em...breakfast?' she answered, hoping it was what he asked.

'*Oui, madame.*' He directed her to a small dining room where the aroma of coffee and fresh pastries made her mouth water. There was one table still set with silver cutlers, linen napkins and bone china – she guessed she must be the last down – and the waiter pulled a seat out for her with a flourish.

'*Café, thé ou chocolat chaud?*' he asked kindly.

'Excuse me, I don't speak...' She was embarrassed not to be able to communicate.

'*Moi aussi, je ne parle pas Anglais malheureusment, un moment, madame, je choisirai pour vous.*' He made a Gallic gesture, an apologetic shrug, and she wondered what was going to happen. He disappeared through a door and re-emerged a few moments later with a steaming cup of coffee, another little cup with what looked like melted chocolate in the base and a jug of boiling-hot milk. She looked at it, unsure, and he took the jug, smiling, and swirled the milk into the thick chocolate, stirring it with a little ceramic spoon that rested in a special place in the handle of the cup. He handed it to her, and she took a sip. It was the most delicious thing she'd ever tasted. She'd had cocoa of course, but it tasted nothing like this; this was sublime.

The waiter beamed when he noted her reaction, then went back to the kitchen and returned with a large platter on which was a stick of white crusty bread and a wedge of a very creamy-looking cheese. Beside that were some tiny pastries that looked like seashells and parcels containing a filling of some kind. There were little pots of jam and tiny curls of butter too.

He pointed to the bread and spoke slowly. '*Du pain.*'

He seemed to be waiting for her to repeat it, so she touched the bread. '*Du pain,*' she said hesitantly.

'*Oui, oui, et ici, du fromage.*' He pointed to the creamy cheese, and again she repeated his words. Together they went around all the food on the table. *Du café, du chocolat chaud, une croissant, une pain au chocolat, une tarte au pomme.* Lena repeated each one as she heard it and was quite pleased with herself.

In Ireland and in Wales too, breakfast was hot and savoury, with a lot of bacon and sausage and the like, but these melt-in-the-mouth cakes with chocolate or apple inside, the light-as-air bread with the delicious cheese, this was a whole other world.

Lena finished every scrap of food, and once he was satisfied she'd had enough, the friendly waiter helped her up and withdrew the chair once more. He could teach Imelda in the café in Kilteegan Bridge a thing or two about service, she thought.

'*Bonne journée, madame.*' He bowed.

She decided to repeat this too. It might be wrong, but it would show she was willing, and he'd been so kind.

'*Bonne journée, monsieur?*' she tried. This delighted him and he clapped his hands.

'*Oui! Tres bien.*'

She went back upstairs to fetch her case, handbag and coat, and then, following instructions from the man on the reception desk who spoke English and kindly let her keep the book she had been reading for no extra charge, she walked to the enormous railway station.

The building itself was beautiful, as all the buildings in Paris appeared to be, and she wished she were here with Eli. It was so romantic and atmospheric. The huge sleek trains huffed and puffed. They looked like something out of *Murder on the Orient Express*, and she wondered if it was from here people left for Istanbul. Though Strasbourg was enough of an adventure for her today, she decided as she bought her ticket.

By eleven o'clock, she had finally found the train. It was due to depart at 11:04, so she congratulated herself for making it in plenty of time, then got a shock when it actually did leave at four minutes past. She was used to the bus that went from Skibbereen to Cork, passing through Kilteegan Bridge. A rough estimate within an hour was the best anyone could do as regards the timetable, and a complete no-show wasn't unheard of. Timmie Mac, who drove the bus, might have to go to a funeral or a doctor's appointment, and therefore all plans to go to the city would be thwarted without a word to anyone.

In France, things were clearly different.

As the train moved eastwards, leaving the tall grey buildings of the City of Light behind, she gazed out at the enormous flat landscape. Fertile farmland turned to vineyards, and soon there was only an occasional house. It looked so different from the green, rugged and mountainous place she came from. At lunchtime, she discovered the dining car and had the tiniest, tenderest lamb cutlets she'd ever seen, pink inside, which would have had most Irish people having a heart attack. Everyone charred their meat at home. The meat was served with exquisite green beans – she'd never tasted them before – and sliced fried potatoes, and she even had a glass of wine because the waiter seemed to expect it and everyone else was having one. Afterwards she had a dessert she was told was called crème brûlée, which was like a smooth thick custard with a crunchy top of burnt sugar. It was divine. Then for the rest of the afternoon, she buried her head in *Dangerous Liaisons*.

After almost the entire day, the train finally pulled into the Gare de Strasbourg, yet another very impressive building with statues and frescoes and an enormous concourse. Everything about this country seemed to be on such a grander scale than anything in Ireland.

A taxi took her to the hotel that sour-faced Marjorie had booked for her, and she found La Belle Étoile lived up to its name, the beautiful star. It was even grander than the hotel in Paris, all white marble and brass, and she wished her heels didn't make such a loud *click clack* as she crossed the lobby to check in.

Behind the desk was a dark-skinned young woman, with the most perfect features Lena had ever seen on a person before. Her skin was luminous, and her dark eyes were circled with kohl, accentuating the almost-black colour of her irises. Her long hair was braided in tiny plaits across her head and gathered in a bun at the nape of her neck. She was dressed in what looked like a length of canary-yellow and vermillion fabric wrapped around her slight figure. She was by far the most exotic person Lena had ever seen.

She'd seen Black people in Wales – she even knew one to say hello to – but they looked just like darker versions of the white people she knew, nothing like this bird of paradise.

Lena said her name, and the woman smiled and handed her a key while beckoning over a boy in a royal-blue and gold uniform to carry her bag. 'Dinner will be at eight, madame. If you have any questions, don't hesitate to ask. My name is Fatima.' Her full lips enunciated the words, and her French-accented English was mesmerising.

'Thank you, Fatima, you're very kind. And thank you for talking to me in English. I'm afraid I don't speak French.'

Fatima smiled and her face lit up, her pearly white teeth straight and even. 'That is quite all right. Everyone in Strasbourg speaks other languages – this is an international city.'

'And where are you from?' Lena asked, then immediately worried she was being impertinent. She would never have asked if Fatima was white; she would have assumed she was French.

Fatima didn't seem to mind. 'I grew up mostly in Algeria. My father is from Algiers, but my mother is French. And you?'

'I'm from Ireland.' She had an idea Algeria was in North Africa but wasn't completely sure.

'Ah, I believe it is very beautiful, no?' Fatima asked.

'Yes, I suppose so. Wetter and colder than here, though.'

Fatima gave that Gallic shrug that seemed to be a universal mode of communication here. 'Well then, I would not like it. I find Strasbourg too cold in the winters. I am from a very warm climate, and I belong there.' She gave a mock shudder, and Lena smiled.

'Well, maybe visit in the summer. You might just about be able to stand it then.' Lena suppressed a smile at the thought of how the people of Kilteegan Bridge would react to the amazing-looking Fatima.

'Maybe I will,' Fatima said, before turning to another guest needing her help.

Lena followed the bellboy up to her room, which was larger than the one in Paris and had a wonderful view of a huge park. It was seven thirty, only half an hour to dinner, but she doubted she'd be able to eat. French food was amazing, but she was still full from lunch, and anyway now that she was in Strasbourg, so close to her goal, her stomach was twisting into knots of anxiety. She decided to go out. It felt too late to ring Pierre Laroche, but she had to do something to burn off all this adrenaline.

After freshening up and tidying her hair, she went back downstairs to ask Fatima for directions to the post office where Decker received his mail.

Fatima beamed at her again. 'You can walk easily. It is on the other side of the gardens. Just cross the street, go through the garden, pass the fountain and the big house – you cannot miss it – follow the signs for the Quay, and you will emerge from the park there. Cross the bridge and keep on straight – it's easy to find. Ask someone else if you get lost.'

* * *

LENA DID as Fatima instructed and walked through the beautiful gardens, shaded by vast canopies of trees and brilliant with vivid floral displays. There was a lake with fountains and even a little zoo, and she felt a pang of loneliness for her children; they would have loved to see the ducks and monkeys. Then to her amazement, huge white birds with black-tipped wings and long beaks, bigger than she'd ever seen, started flying from tree to tree, and the noise they made was like a hammer on a wood surface, or a much louder version of a toy Pádraig had at home, a wooden frog with spines on its back that he could run a stick over.

She stood and stared and then realised that their huge nests were everywhere, in the trees and on roofs of the surrounding houses. One swooped so close to her, she screamed and leapt back, much to the hilarity of a group of boys who were cycling past.

Leaving the park, she asked again at a corner shop for Rue des Glaciers, and despite the man not speaking English, he gave her remarkably clear instructions using hand gestures and counting on his fingers.

The street of the post office was lined with four-storey buildings, many of which housed shops on the ground floor. The second and third floors had windows and ornate metal balconies, and the top floors were simply dormer windows jutting out of the roof slates. She noted that the even numbers were on one side of the street and the odd ones on the other. The post office was at number 23. So this was where he came, she thought. She studied the open times – from nine until five thirty, if she was reading the sign right.

There was a café almost opposite, and because the evening was so warm, she decided to sit outside. She had no real plan, except maybe to learn about him by soaking up the atmosphere of the place he inhabited. A man handed her a menu, and she had no idea what to do. Should she order tea? A drink? Food? She looked around; people seemed to be drinking beer or wine.

She knew the French for wine but not for beer. When the waiter reappeared, she said, '*Vin, s'il vous plaît.*'

He looked confused. '*Quelques vin, madame?*'

She looked at him blankly, and he touched his finger to the menu. In her panic she pointed to where he'd touched, and he seemed fine with it. He nodded and said, '*Bon,*' then disappeared into the café while she sat wondering what on earth she'd ordered.

The man returned with a little bowl of dark-brown breadsticks rolled into a twist and a drink in a little glass, and he stood waiting as if for her approval. She sipped and found the drink to be effervescent, like a lemonade but wine.

'*C'est bon? Le Crémant?*' he asked as she wrinkled her nose in surprise.

'Yes, yes, *oui. Le Crémant. Bon. Oui,*' she managed, feeling herself blush, and he bowed and mercifully left without asking her opinion of the breadsticks. She tried one after he'd gone. It was salty, with a light fluffy centre, and whatever it was called, it was delicious.

* * *

SHE SAW him a split second before he saw her.

He was wearing his hat low over his face, but he walked right past her table, within inches of her, and he was unmistakeable.

He glanced sideways when she gasped, then stopped dead, looking straight at her. He was dressed in dark trousers, an open-necked shirt and a jacket that had seen better days. He was as short as she remembered, no more than five seven or eight, clean-shaven and his hair still dark, but he was thinner, his skin more weather-beaten and his eyes more creased.

What is he going to do now? she wondered as she sat there, speechless with astonishment. *Run? Ignore me?* His eyes were fixed on hers. Would he attack her? Her mouth was dry and she swallowed.

Then he did something she didn't expect. He put his hand on the vacant chair on the opposite side of the small round table and pulled it out. '*Bienvenue en France*, Madame Kogan,' he said, a little drunkenly, as he sat down. And then, with a crooked smile, 'Welcome to France, Mrs Kogan.'

Lena stayed silent, unsure what, if any, sound would come out if she tried to speak.

The waiter appeared, and Decker said something to him in French, then addressed her again. 'I assume you've come to find me?' He looked…not smug exactly, but certainly not discomfited.

'I have,' she managed to say.

'And how may I be of assistance?'

Lena felt a rush of sheer hatred. Here he was, the man who killed her father in cold blood. But she had to keep calm. She'd rehearsed this speech over and over in her head so many times, and now was her chance to make it before he decided to disappear again, maybe for good.

'I want you to give up the claim to our home and never again in your life set foot on Irish soil.' To her relief her voice sounded firm and steady. 'I know what you did, I know how you murdered my father, and I have a witness to corroborate what August Berger said on his deathbed. And if you don't leave me and my family in peace, I will see you arrested and stand trial for his killing.'

The waiter appeared with another glass of Crémant and a glass of water, placing them both assiduously in front of Decker. Her speech hung between them as the waiter ensured everything was just so.

'Two things,' Decker said slowly once the man had retreated. 'Firstly, I was given that house and the estate in return for the care I gave August throughout his life, but in particular since he was injured and confined to the chair. It wasn't a gift – it was payment. Secondly, as I'm sure you know, I did not kill your father.'

'Don't lie to me.' She spoke flatly, trying to stay calm. 'Berger admitted it on his deathbed.'

He shrugged as if he didn't believe her.

She leaned forwards, raising her voice slightly. 'That gun never backfired. It wasn't an accident. August told you to kill my father, and you did.'

'Except I didn't.' Decker took a sip of the Crémant.

She wanted to dash the glass from his hand. 'Why would Malachy's father lie? He had nothing to lose at that stage – he was dying.'

Decker laughed, a small sound, one breath. 'Maybe he was confused. Maybe you misheard. Most likely, you are lying to me. You want to accuse me of this so you can keep the house.'

She was dizzy with hatred for him, his evasions and lies. Did he think he could get away with this, just denying he knew anything, over and over again? 'If you didn't do it, why did you run away?'

'I didn't run away. August gave me money to leave. He had things he wanted done in Strasbourg, wine sold, accounts set up and money transferred to Kieran Devlin for Malachy. And he said he wanted to talk to you and Malachy alone before he died. He promised me the house would be sold at once and the money sent on to me. He said he was going to leave instructions with his son, and I am sure he did.'

'He didn't.'

'I wouldn't expect you to say anything else.' He took another sip of his drink and placed it back on the cardboard coaster.

It was infuriating, the way he just kept denying things. Yet despite everything she'd ever believed, a tiny splinter of doubt forced its way into her mind. Was it possible it had been an accident, and Berger had simply lied to push her and Malachy even further apart, to kill any chance he imagined there might be of them getting back together? 'Mr Decker, are you trying to claim my father wasn't murdered?'

'Oh, I'm not saying that, Mrs Kogan. I'm just saying nothing that happened was my fault.'

It was like being on a roller coaster, or on that awful plane journey as the Starflight plunged up and down in mid-air. She felt sick to her stomach, but she did her best to keep the shake out of her voice. 'Then what did happen, Mr Decker? Maybe you could tell me who you think was at fault.'

He signalled to the waiter for another glass and nodded at her empty one with his eyebrows raised. She pushed it towards the waiter. She hadn't imagined there was a world where she would accept a drink off Phillippe Decker, but the world as she knew it was spinning around her and she needed something.

Decker folded his arms on the table and smiled at her, clearly emboldened by her accepting his offer. 'First and foremost? It was your father's fault.'

She instantly felt sick again, like her heart was going to explode with rage. 'How dare you!'

Again, that shrug. 'He should never have had an affair with Hannah Berger.'

She wanted to slap his face, and she gripped her hands together in her lap. 'When it happened, everyone thought August Berger was dead and my mam had been locked away for months, maybe forever...'

'Maybe so, but after it ended, Hannah continued to hanker after your father, following him around, watching him work. Leaving all the care of August to me. It was disgusting, animal-like. August became very, very angry with her. And so...' He shrugged, making a gesture with his hands. 'And so she...'

'Hanged herself,' said Lena, when he seemed unable to complete the sentence.

He inclined his head. 'Hannah died for your father's sins.'

The waiter returned with two more glasses of Crémant and two more glasses of water.

Lena sat, cradling the cold glass in her hands, tense, speechless.

This felt like a very brittle moment, a moment that could go either way. If she could stay cool, focused, maybe Decker would tell her the truth about what happened next. Or at least his version of the truth. If she got too angry with him, there was nothing to stop him leaving, melting away into the city, going underground again. 'And Berger blamed my father for her death?'

He nodded. 'Yes, he did. August felt he had been robbed of his wife by Paudie O'Sullivan. August was a man of honour, a decorated war hero. He wasn't going to accept it.'

She noted he said nothing about what type of soldier. Perhaps he imagined she didn't know. She said carefully, 'And then what happened?'

He looked at her. 'Hannah was buried.'

Lena sat very still and decided to stay quiet. It was like she was in the hide her father had built for her in the corner of the woodland on their farm so she could secretly watch for wildlife. Birds and squirrels, rabbits and pine martins would appear and play around without noticing she was hidden there. Sometimes just by being very quiet, one could coax wild animals out of their lairs.

Decker sighed heavily and drained his glass, beckoning for another one. 'So it was just us two again. I tried to shake August out of the black mood he was in, but instead of making him better, I seemed to be making it worse. He was obsessed with your father. He took out his old sniper rifle, the Karabiner 98k with a telescopic sight, and practised for months shooting birds out of the trees, until he was as good as he ever was. He could drop a robin at a thousand yards. One day, he told me to take your father's old shotgun from his shed and tamper with it to make it backfire if anyone used it. It's easy if you know how.'

Lena breathed slowly, twisting her hands under the table.

'I asked him if he wanted me to return the shotgun when that was done, but he said no. We knew a fox had been stealing all the local farmers' chickens, and August had me tell your father that its lair was in your top field, in the nearest corner to our land. August could see that spot from Malachy's bedroom window.'

She knew that was true; Malachy had shown her one day when

they used to play together as children. 'I could nearly even see your house from here,' he'd said. 'If that stupid hill wasn't in the way, I could signal to you.'

'So I told him and he thanked me.' Decker's voice was slightly louder. He had drained his third glass since sitting down, and he'd been drinking already. 'And August waited and waited, all the following day. Until Paudie came up the field, with a trap for the fox.'

She wanted to scream out loud, as if after all these years she could still warn her father to keep away. But she remained silent.

'I heard the shot, and then August called me up to the bedroom. I didn't see the body at first. Your father had died instantly, so there was no movement. August told me to take Paudie O'Sullivan's shotgun, fire it and leave it by the body. So that's what I did. We watched as your brother came looking for him a couple of hours later, and then the priest and the doctor.'

She stared at him, incredulously, as he signalled the barman for another glass. How could he think he had no responsibility for what happened? He'd known about the plan, he'd acted to cover it up – any court would surely find him guilty of being an accessory to the crime.

'We were both in the army, you see,' Phillippe Decker said with a drunken smile. 'It wasn't my fault, it wasn't my idea, I didn't squeeze any trigger. I never even lied, because nobody ever asked me about it. I just followed my orders. I'm an honest man, Mrs Kogan. You've asked, so I've told you. You have to understand and forgive me, because I did not do it, and now I'm being honest.'

'An honest man?' she repeated blankly. Her mind was racing, wondering how to keep Decker from leaving. She thought of asking the barman to call the police. But she didn't speak French and anyway, if she left the table, Decker might be gone when she got back and she'd never see him again.

He was nodding. 'Yes, the way Rebecca will forgive me if I ever find her.' He was slurring his words a bit more now.

'Rebecca?'

'Rebecca Loeb...'

Something about the way he said that girl's name, Rebecca, made

Lena pay attention. He seemed to become softer, more human or something. Maybe there was a weak spot. 'Tell me about Rebecca?'

He smiled and it softened his hardened features. 'Ah, my darling Rebecca, she was beautiful, so beautiful. I begged her to leave without her parents, but she couldn't abandon them... We lay there, holding each other, kissing.' He gave her a small smile. 'Wishing so much that things would be different. It was her parents' fault that she got taken to Auschwitz.'

'She died in Auschwitz?'

'No! Why does everyone think all the Jews were murdered?' he hissed. Drunk as he was, he knew such words would attract attention. 'They were worked a bit too hard maybe – the war was hard on everyone – that's all. No, August found her and made sure she lived in comfort until the end of the war, when she went abroad. And once I have money...' His voice trailed off, and he seemed to be half dreaming.

'Once you have money?' she prompted. He seemed to have forgotten who she was. She saw then the knuckles of his right hand were bruised and scabbed over, like he'd been fighting.

'Yes, once I have money, I'll hire a private eye in America to find her, and then it will be like the past. Time has gone by. She will forgive – it's the Christian thing...' He started laughing then. 'Except she's not a Christian! But I don't care. Others cared, but I didn't and Rebecca didn't.' He rested his cheek on his hand. 'I'm sorry, I'm a little drunk. *Eau de vie*, it's stronger than your poitín, you know...'

It came to her what to do to keep him in her sights, not lose him again, to get him to trust her while she figured out what to do. 'Phillippe,' she said softly, 'where do you live?'

Without lifting his head from his hand, he looked at her with a sneer. 'And why would I tell you that?'

'Just so I can get in touch. I know someone, you see, a man here in Strasbourg, who finds out what happened to people's Jewish relatives. I know you're not Jewish yourself, but he's a friend of a dear friend of mine, so I know if I asked him, he would do us this favour. He's even expecting me to call him.'

153

His eyes flickered in surprise and hope but then became dull and cynical again. 'Why would you help someone like me?'

'Why not?' Even though it turned her stomach to do it, she patted his hand. 'Like you say, it wasn't your fault my father died. You've told me the whole truth, and that helps me a lot. So now I want to help you in return. And if you don't tell me where you are, how can I get in touch with you?'

He looked at her for a long time, then said, 'I'll be there after five,' and scribbled an address on a paper napkin. Before Lena even had a chance to read it, he pushed back his chair and left, leaving no payment for the drinks he'd had, within seconds blending into the shadows of the city.

CHAPTER 15

The night porter, a smirking lad of no more than twenty who stank of cigarettes, let her in. She thanked him in a whisper, then crept up the stairs. She had no idea what he was grinning about and cared less. As she was getting her key out of her purse, she noticed light seeping under the door. Her heart nearly stopped. She definitely hadn't left the light on; she was far too careful with electricity. Then who...? And then she knew. It was Captain Andrew Ahearne. He'd said the crew stayed here every time they were in Strasbourg, and he would have been able to find out her room number from the dreadful Marjorie.

She thought about going back downstairs again and getting the porter to help her get rid of him, but from the way the young man had smirked at her, he was probably on the captain's side. No doubt they knew each other from when Ahearne had stayed here before, most likely playing the same tricks on other poor women.

So instead, she channelled Anthea. *I am a strong, independent young woman*, she told herself sternly. *I coped with Phillippe Decker without a man by my side, and I can cope with this.* She reminded herself that the vial of Librium Anthea had given her was in her bedside table, and if the worst came to the worst...

She slipped the key into the lock, turned it as softly as she could, braced herself and threw open the door. 'If you think I wanted you to follow me here,' she said loudly, 'then you couldn't be more wrong...'

Eli stood sheepishly in the middle of the room, looking very uncertain of himself.

'I mean, right! Oh, Eli!' Laughing with joy and relief, she ran to him and threw her arms around him.

'I'm sorry if you didn't want me to follow you –'

'No, you were *right* to follow me! You couldn't *be* more right! I thought you were someone else.'

'Who? Was it Decker? Oh, Lena...' His long arms enveloped her, holding her tightly.

'No, not Decker, just some very unimportant little man who didn't frighten me at all. He only annoyed me. I'll tell you about him later, I promise.'

'I'm not checking up on you – I trust you. I know I've been a jealous fool.' He covered her face with kisses. 'Oh, Lena, I've missed you so much.'

'I've missed you too,' Lena murmured as his kisses along her collarbone became more insistent.

'I love you, Lena.'

She took him by the hand and led him to the bed, all their squabbles forgotten. She needed to be with him now, and whatever their problems, they would face them together.

* * *

AFTERWARDS, she lay in his arms, his fingers gently drumming on her back in a way she loved for some reason, and she rested her hand in the tangle of hair on his chest. The familiar beat of his heart, now returned to normal after their passionate lovemaking, filled her with pleasure. This was her Eli.

Then she remembered about London, and her fears. She turned her head on the pillow to look at him. His eyes were half-closed; he was sunk in pleasure.

'Eli, how did you get here? I thought you were in Cardiff, and then I rang your mother and she said you'd gone to London. I was scared you'd gone to see a lawyer.'

His mouth twitched with amusement. 'A London lawyer? Devlin wouldn't be pleased. Why would I do that?'

'I don't know, but, Eli, I really don't want a divorce...'

He burst out laughing. 'Well, that's good, because I don't want a divorce either, you mad woman. Of course I wasn't seeing a lawyer. I was just getting the ferry to Calais – it's the quickest way to France.'

'But how did you know I was here? I only told Katie I was going to Dublin.'

'And I guessed you were heading to Strasbourg, so I didn't want to waste time. I went straight to London and then got in touch with Anthea from there. I have to say, she gave me a fine talking to, by the way, saying I had no right to impose my will on you. She made me feel like some kind of Victorian *Father Knows Best*, but she relented in the end and told me where you were staying.' He pulled her towards him and kissed her again. 'I've missed you, Lena, and I'm so sorry for being such a donkey about everything. I did feel jealous about Malachy, and I never really wanted to live in that house, not because it's not lovely, but it felt like you wanted to keep some connection to him or something. But I know it's not true.'

'It isn't. You're the one I love – I'm blue in the face telling you.' Lena rested her head on his shoulder.

'I know, I'm thick, and I'm sorry.' He kissed her hair. 'And what you said about me dealing with my past my way, Lena, you're right. I have no right to impose my way on you. I don't talk about what happened because I just can't. That's the truth. I honestly can't. It's too hard. It's not that I've forgotten, or put it behind me. And I know enough about psychology to know it's not good to have something like that bottled up inside. That's one of the things I went home to Cardiff for, to talk to Charlie.'

'Wait...' She reached to switch off the light; she knew it was easier sometimes to talk about difficult things in the dark. They lay together under the sheets, and she hoped he would talk now, for the first time in his adult life, about the awful things he'd endured. 'Tell me,' she said into the dark.

'I...I don't know where to start...' His normal jokey confidence was gone.

'Maybe just start with what Charlie said.' She reached over and took his hand.

'Oh, Charlie... Well, he thinks I need to talk about it. He reminded me how when I was thirteen or fourteen, I kept getting into fights. Poor Mum was called into the school several times. She said she didn't know what was wrong with me, and I didn't know either, but Charlie decided it was because I was so angry about my childhood and had nowhere to put it. I never talked about Germany. I'd got rid of my German accent as soon as I could, and I tried to forget every word of that language as soon as I could – I refused to allow it to enter my consciousness in any way. In the end, Charlie took me playing rugby. It was the obsession of Wales, and it was good for me. I could channel all that energy into something less problematic than fighting. He really saved my life.'

'Charlie always was one of my favourite people in the world, and never so much as now. Go on.'

'Yes, and so we got to discussing life now. And then he wanted to know why I was so angry, and what was going on in my life. I said I wasn't angry, but he said he knew me well enough, that he'd been my stepfather since I was a little lad and to tell him. So I told him about the house, and how I wanted to pay Decker off, just move on and leave everything behind me, how I felt dirty even living in that house if a Nazi owned it. And I told him how I kept getting so angry with you when you wanted to confront him and drag it all out – that's what it felt like – and how I messed up badly when we discussed it and how I mixed it all up with Malachy in my head and accused you of awful things.' He caught his breath. 'Oh, Lena, I can't believe I was so stupid to risk losing you like that. I don't know what I was thinking.'

She held his hand tighter. 'You didn't risk losing me. If you want to get rid of me, Eli Kogan, you'll have to try a lot harder than that.'

He laughed. 'Oh, I have missed you.'

'Well, you've found me. And what did he say then?'

'He said he thought my mother, and especially my Uncle Saul and me, had collectively decided to deal with what happened by putting it behind us and getting on with our lives. Being as happy and as productive as we could be and not giving what happened to us all any room in our minds. And he said it wasn't such a bad plan. There were some survivors he knew over the years who could never forget, and even now, years later, they lived it like it all happened yesterday. Then he made a joke about a certain amount of suppressing being no bad thing. He said, "Have Bessie Evans as a mother, and I assure you, you learn to suppress a lot."'

Lena chuckled at the mention of Charlie's tyrannical mother who never thought a Jewish widow with a child was good enough for her boy. 'So he thought it was OK to just forget and move on?' She felt a touch of disappointment in Charlie, but he was a wise man, and if that's what he thought, she would go along with it.

Eli shook his head. 'No, he didn't think it was OK. Well, a bit maybe, but he thought there was also a problem with trying to forget too much. He said we are emotional beings, whether we like it or not, and when we bury things, it works, for sure it does, but not very well and not forever. He said he remembered one day coming home from work when Rhys was a baby, and my mum was sitting on the floor, sobbing her heart out because one of his little socks was missing. Charlie said he thought she was going a bit doolally from sleep deprivation – that little tyke didn't sleep for a year. Charlie and my mum were like zombies by the time he was two, I remember it myself. But it wasn't that. She told him that the day we all left the apartment in Berlin, thinking we'd go to Leipzig to reunite with the rest of the family, she had no time to pack properly, just grabbed the nearest things to hand, and she never closed one of the bags properly. A little sock of mine fell out on the stairs, and my father told her to leave it and just run for the train. The missing sock years later, of a different child, at a different time and place, opened the floodgates.'

'Oh, poor Sarah.'

'I know, and I knew exactly what she must have felt like. Sometimes the slightest thing can set it off for me. A smell like the Tarr aftershave that my father wore, the taste of a fresh pretzel, the words of a Yiddish folk song that my father would sing badly when he was washing the dishes after our evening meal – it takes me to such a dark place, and I have to immediately shut it down.'

Lena turned towards him and took him in her arms again, pressing her face against the rough skin of his jaw. 'I'm so sorry. I didn't know.'

'Why would you? As Charlie kept reminding me, I've never talked about it to you.'

'And I wanted you to come and confront Decker with me. I didn't understand why you couldn't bear to see him. I'm such a fool.'

'In a way, I want to confront him too, though. But what would I say? "Are you sorry? Do you know what you did? Do you care?" No matter the answer, it wouldn't change anything. It can't bring back the millions of Jews, gypsies, homosexuals, Jehovah's Witnesses, trade unionists, resisters... Nothing can do that.'

She kissed his neck, not knowing what to say.

His voice strengthened. 'Sometimes I wish I was more like my Uncle Saul. I mean, he's the same as me and my mother – he doesn't like to talk about the war – but at least he's a committed Jew. He observes all of the rules of his faith. He attends synagogue, prays and keeps a kosher house. I mean, he has an identity, in the way I feel robbed of mine. His wife is Jewish as well – her father was a rabbi in Southampton.'

Her heart turned over. 'Do you wish I was Jewish?'

He laughed. 'Don't be silly, that's not what I was trying to say. You'd be the love of my life if you were a Martian.'

'What, green?'

'Yes, Lena, even if you were green. No, you mad woman, what I'm trying to say is Uncle Saul has rebuilt his Jewish identity. He's involved with Zionism as well – he's consistently made the case for it through various organisations – and he was involved with Britain's support for the state of Israel. He was so disappointed when support for Israeli nationalism faded after the war, with senior members of the parliament opposing the creation of a Jewish homeland. I suppose they just weren't willing to rock the boat in the Middle East, and supporting a Jewish state would have done just that. But he wasn't going to give up – being a Jew means so much to him. Against all the odds, however, the state of Israel does exist, and that's down to the likes of Saul. And there are others who have dedicated their lives to hunting down the perpetrators. But I don't do anything. I don't live like a Jew, and I don't get involved.'

'Do you wish you didn't live in Ireland? We're so far away from all that, it must be hard to feel part of it.' It was true. To a great extent, Ireland was removed from those dark years by virtue of geography and politics. It was something she had been grateful for, that her father hadn't had to go off and fight. The Irish had been so busy fighting the English for eight centuries, they'd had no energy for other wars.

'No, I love Ireland, Lena, and I'm grateful nobody seems to mind where I'm from, even though they all have me down as British.'

Lena smiled in the dark and hugged him again. Those divides and seams of resentment and bitterness still existed in the country, and the Irish still had issues with the British establishment but not with individual British people any longer. In the 50s there was huge emigration out of Ireland, largely to the building sites of the UK, reconstructing that country after the decimation of the war. 'There's very few families in Kilteegan Bridge that don't have some relatives over there,' she said.

'I know, and that's good, because we have to close these divides between us. You know, Lena, as a doctor, I see life at its best and worst. I know that people are all the same. Lungs, kidneys, hearts, livers, a mother's love for her newborn, the loss when a spouse of decades dies, the worry about a sick child. It's the same for everyone, German, Jew, Irish, English. But mankind seems hell-bent on destruction of others and can't see the shared humanity. It baffles me.'

'I know, but things will get better. Nobody will ever go back to those days again – we can't,' she said hopefully.

He stroked her hair. 'We all have darkness in our pasts, Lena, but you and I are optimistic and cheerful people, and that's how we'll stay.'

'Together,' she murmured, snuggling into him.

'Always,' he replied. As she began to drift off, he spoke again. 'You never told me about that man who annoyed you?'

'It's not important. I'll tell you tomorrow.' Sleep was wrapping itself around her like a blanket. She was back in her husband's arms; nothing could go wrong now.

* * *

WHEN SHE WOKE, he wasn't beside her, and for a horrible moment, she thought she'd just had a lovely dream. But then she saw him, standing and gazing at a map of the Alsace region on the wall. Maybe he was noting the German-sounding place names: Neudorf, Ostwald, Kehl, Eckbolsheim, Mittelhausbergen…

'Breakfast?' she asked, sitting up.

He spun to face her, smiling. 'Morning, sleepyhead. Breakfast sounds just the ticket. Where do you suggest?'

'We could eat in the hotel, or we could go out and walk around and find somewhere?'

'You're the better-travelled one of the two of us, so I'm in your hands.'

'Then we'll go out. I can't wait to show you the gardens next door, and then when we've found somewhere to eat, I'll tell you all of my adventures and plans.'

She jumped up to shower and clean her teeth, tied up her hair in her Audrey Hepburn ponytail, then got dressed in one of her white blouses from Clerys and the black skirt with white flowers. Coming out of the bathroom, she realised Eli might be suspicious about her buying such a nice outfit when she was going abroad without him, but he was only delighted by it, and she had a job to stop him taking her back to bed.

'Eli, stop, come on. I want to show you these huge birds – maybe you know what they are. And I need to make a call from reception to Pierre Laroche. I want to see him today.'

He smiled at her. 'Lead on, Mrs Kogan. I'm at your service.'

In reception, Eli lounged in one of the luxurious armchairs and flipped through the English-language newspapers while Lena waited at the desk. Fatima was dealing with a red-faced German guest who seemed very cross about something, and she was soothing him in what sounded to Lena's ears like perfect German. Eventually he left, after which she turned to Lena and switched into perfect English. 'How can I help you, Mrs Kogan?'

'Hello, Fatima. I have a phone number for a Pierre Laroche, and I was wondering if it was possible for you to put me through to him on the hotel phone if I don't take too long?'

'Of course, Mrs Kogan, we have a line especially for the guests. What is the number?'

Lena handed her the torn-off title page from the book, and Fatima took a phone out from under the counter, set it on the top and dialled. After a few rings, she said, '*Bonjour, Monsieur Laroche? Bon, c'est l'Hotel Belle Étoile. Une Madame Kogan veut vous parler... Oui? Bon, elle est la.*' She handed the phone to Lena, who had just that moment realised there was no reason to think the amateur historian spoke English. If only she hadn't had to leave school at fifteen, she might have done the language for her Leaving Cert, but she'd never had to speak a word of it.

She said nervously, 'Hello? I'm sorry, I can't speak French.'

'Do not worry, Madame Kogan,' said a warm, deep voice with a wonderful French accent. 'I am very happy to speak with you in English. There are many languages spoken in Strasbourg – we are a city of diplomats. You are Klaus's friend, are you not?'

'Yes, I'm Lena.'

'And you want to know about Phillippe Decker and August Berger. I have been researching, but there is little more to say, I'm afraid. Phillippe is what you call...um..."small fry"? Although I would be interested to know more about this Berger man.'

'Actually...' – she glanced at Fatima, who was busy sorting

brochures – 'I was wondering if you could find out anything about Decker's girlfriend, Rebecca Loeb. She was a Jewish girl from his village, and I think she was in Auschwitz, but Decker is convinced she survived the war.'

There was a long silence at the other end of the phone, but she knew Pierre hadn't gone away because she could hear him breathing and shuffling papers. Eventually he said, 'I have four Rebecca Loebs who were in Auschwitz, one of whom survived, two of whom died and a fourth I am still investigating. Have you any further details? Date of birth? Place of origin?'

She was as astonished as when Klaus announced Decker was alive and living in Strasbourg. 'No, but I know someone who would know all that about her.' She glanced behind her; another guest was hovering to use the phone after her. 'Phillippe Decker.'

'You've found Phillippe Decker?' The professor sounded impressed. 'Perhaps we should use you as a researcher for our organisation, Mrs Kogan. I would very much like to talk to Decker about his friend August Berger.'

'Berger is dead.'

'I am aware. However, I always like to have more information about what happened, to fill in the gaps. Could you persuade him to meet with me, do you think?'

Lena glanced towards Eli, but he was absorbed in the London *Times*. 'I think I could persuade him, yes, if he thought you could give him information about his old girlfriend. Perhaps later today, around five thirty or six?'

'That's perfect, Mrs Kogan. Have you my address?'

'Yes, Klaus gave it to me.'

'Then I'll see you at five thirty, Lena. *Au revoir.*'

'*Au revoir,*' she said, feeling fairly confident it meant goodbye, and the phone clicked off.

* * *

LENA LED Eli through the Jardin d'Orangeries where she'd been only
yesterday, and he told her that the huge birds were the white storks of
Alsace. 'I know about them from my childhood in...' He stopped
before saying the word 'Germany', then carried on. 'They come up
here in the summer from Africa, and there are a lot of legends about
them.'

'Tell me some?'

He grinned at her. 'Well, if a woman has a baby, it means the stork
that nests on her roof has flown off to the lake where the souls of the
dead are reincarnated, fished out a brand-new baby and flown back to
her house with it hanging from its beak, swaddled in a sheet.'

'Oh, if only women had it that easy,' Lena said, laughing.

Walking hand in hand, they admired the flowers and the fountains
in the summer sunshine, and Lena smiled as a mother duck led her
tiny flock of ducklings across the path and landed in the lake with a
gentle plop. The air was scented with the delicate fragrance of lilac
planted beside yellow roses swaying in the gentle warm breeze.

As they came out of the gate, the flags of all the members of the
Council of Europe were blowing in the wind in front of the council
building, symbolising a united peaceful Europe once more. There was
a small *gelateria* on the corner of the street, with a few tables and
chairs outside.

'What about ice cream for breakfast?' she asked daringly. 'It's not
full Irish breakfast, I know, but it's so hot already...'

'Lena, if you want ice cream, then it's ice cream we shall have.'

'*Madame? Monsieur? Avez vous choisi?*' a smiling young girl asked,
standing behind the glass counter with a waffle cone in her hand.

'*Bonjour.*' Lena smiled back, then hesitantly looked at the ice cream
on offer. In Ireland the flavours of ice cream were vanilla and possibly
raspberry ripple if it was a Sunday, so the staggering array of colours
in the trays in front of her seemed amazing. She pointed at a tray
marked '*chocolat*' and another deep-purple one labelled '*cassis*'. 'Chocolate and blackcurrant, please?'

'*Bien sure, et pour vous, monsieur?*' She turned to Eli once she'd
handed Lena her cone.

'*Chocolat et vanille, s'il vous plaît,*' he said.

She handed over his ice cream and took the coins to pay for them.

'Listen to you with the French!' Lena teased as they sat down at a table with two chairs. It was so wonderful to be back on good terms again with him. It was as if part of her were missing when they were fighting.

He shrugged. 'When Saul made us learn English in the Isle of Man, I used to play with a little Jewish boy from France, and we managed to communicate using three languages. Marcel was his name.'

She smiled at him in surprise. 'You were on the Isle of Man?'

'Yes...' He looked away, his voice trailing off. Then he turned back to smile at her and changed the subject. 'Now, Mrs Kogan. I want to know everything about what you've been up to. Who was the annoying man you thought had followed you to the hotel?'

'The man was a pilot who thinks he's God's gift to women. He was useful at first, but then he got a bit too helpful.' She told him the story, and Eli laughed out loud about sourpuss Marjorie, and then, when he heard about the taxi journey and the pilot's reaction to her wittering on about nappy rash, he laughed even harder.

'Eli?' She looked at him over her ice cream cone. 'Eli, can you bear to talk about Phillippe Decker?'

He winced. 'I can. I assume you've already been to Pierre Laroche and he's found out more about him? Is that what you were talking to him about on the phone?'

'No, although I do want to visit Pierre later today. And...Eli, this is going to be hard for you, but I've already met Phillippe Decker. And I want to meet him again and bring him to see Pierre with me.'

His face tightened and paled. 'I think I'll order a coffee. Would you like one?'

'Please.'

He went to order two coffees in French and, to her surprise, returned with a small glass of brandy as well. He grinned when he saw her looking first at the glass, then up and down the street. 'Don't worry, it won't shock anyone. This isn't Kilteegan Bridge. The French drink brandy for breakfast all the time.'

'How on earth do they get any work done?'

'Maybe they have harder heads than we do.' He poured the brandy into his cup, then picked up his coffee. 'Now tell me what I need to know.'

As she talked, Eli never interrupted or asked any questions; he just listened until she'd finished the entire story, to the point where Decker disappeared into the night. When she stopped, he asked simply, 'Is he lying, do you think?'

She sighed. 'I honestly don't know.'

'So what do you want to do now?'

She thought about it. 'I'm not sure yet. Of course I want him arrested and convicted, but maybe for that I need to bring him back to Ireland? So for now I'm acting like I agree with him that none of it is his fault. And I'm trying to get his trust. I promised him Pierre could find out what happened to an old girlfriend of his, a Jewish girl who he thinks survived the war.'

'Find a Jewish woman on behalf of a Nazi?' For the first time, Eli looked shocked.

'But it's just to coax him out into the open, Eli, and get him to trust me, that's all. If he thinks I'm his friend, he won't run away, and then I can work out what to do, who best to report him to. I know it sounds stupid, but if I don't do something, if I lose sight of him again, it will kill me.'

He nodded and forced a smile. 'Lena, if it's what you want to do to make yourself feel better, then do it.'

'The weird thing is, Pierre might actually know what happened to this Jewish girl, Rebecca Loeb. She might even have survived the war. Isn't that extraordinary?'

'Rebecca.' Eli looked down, twisting his coffee cup in its saucer. 'I knew a girl called Rebecca when I was a kid. She lived down the street. Rebecca Linderman. She and her whole family tried to get to relatives in America – she had an uncle who was a rabbi in St Louis, I remember – but they couldn't get them out.' His eyes gleamed with unshed tears. 'The Lindermans went the same way as everyone else, I suppose.'

Lena shivered. It was the first time Eli had ever spoken to her about a small, special memory of something like a childhood friend, and she almost couldn't bear to hear the depth of sadness in his voice. How could she ever have thought his experiences hadn't affected him? Reaching across the table, she put her hand on his.

CHAPTER 16

*M*alachy Berger parked the Alpine A110 outside Kieran Devlin's office and went in to see him. It was a short meeting, Devlin being a man of few words, but they agreed on the next step in the process, which was for Devlin to go through the second will with a fine-toothed comb to see if it was flawed or faked in any way.

Days earlier, Malachy had driven up to Dublin to the engineering conference and gone to see Ignatius Hayes. Hayes had been obsequious but stubborn when it came to handing out any information about Decker's whereabouts. 'I don't give out information about my clients to anyone,' he'd said in an oily voice, although Malachy suspected that if he had gone to Blackrock College rather than Larksbridge, or been a doctor or lawyer rather than an engineer – however rich – it might have got him further. At least Hayes gave Malachy a copy of the will to bring up to Devlin. 'I'll think you'll find everything is in order, Mr Berger.'

Now Malachy stood gazing down the main street towards Kilteegan House. After the row he'd had with Eli Kogan, it wouldn't be easy to go back there; it would have to be cap in hand, and he didn't feel ready for that. Yet he would have loved to have seen more of the house, the library and sitting room, maybe the bedroom Emmet slept in. Would it be his own old room, from where he could just make out a corner of the O'Sullivans' top field? A memory came back to him of telling Lena when they were children that if only that hill wasn't in the way, he'd be able to see her house. Maybe he'd known he loved her even then, when they were children.

'Ah, I don't believe it!' He heard a voice behind him coming from the direction of the town library. 'Malachy Berger, isn't it?'

He turned with a smile and saw Lena's mother. She was carrying a canvas shoulder bag embroidered with a beautiful peacock. She looked well. She'd always reminded him of a mermaid when he was a child, as she was willowy and tall, with long fair hair that she often wore loose, something never really seen on married women, and today she was dressed in a longish green dress, completing his childhood vision.

He knew from Lena that Maria O'Sullivan suffered from nerves and that she was up and down all the time, but today she looked bright and friendly, not troubled at all.

'Yes, Mrs O'Sullivan, it's nice to see you again.' He shook her hand and smiled, noticing that she seemed to have a small smudge of paint on her cheek.

'Well, haven't you grown up to be a fine, handsome man? And what a smart suit, quite the fashion. What brings you back around here? I thought Lena said you went to America. Is that right?'

He didn't remember her being so animated before; she was usually much quieter. He also remembered Lena saying her mother didn't approve of him, but none of that was on show today. 'I did. Boston first, then California. I've been there a good few years now. I just was in Ireland on business and thought I'd pop down to see the old place. It hasn't changed much, I see.' He doubted Maria O'Sullivan knew anything about the Decker challenge to the house. He was pretty sure it wasn't the sort of thing Lena would reveal to her fragile mother.

'My goodness, America. Imagine that? I was never there – I was never anywhere really. My brother, Ted, went to Germany before the war. I don't know where he is now, though…'

Her eyes filled with tears, and Malachy felt a stab of panic. Was she going to start crying to him in the street? He glanced up towards the hardware store, hoping to see Emily or Blackie – maybe they could take care of this. They were clearly a capable couple, judging by the new look of the shop.

'But he'll be back I'm sure, some day.' She grinned then and gave a tinkly laugh. 'It's such a pity you're missing Lena. She and Eli are up in Dublin. They are visiting an old friend of Doc Dolan's – do you remember him from when you were little? He and my late husband were very close, but poor old Doc died a few years ago now. He's a huge loss to everyone, and of course Lena adored him – we all did really. Anyway, this lady friend of his turned up and Lena met her and they became friendly, so she and Eli are visiting her. Or maybe Eli went to Wales... I don't remember. Eli's a doctor, you know.'

'Oh really?' Malachy tried to sound neutral. 'And do you know when she'll be back?'

'Yes, this woman is a doctor up in Dublin – a lady doctor, would you believe – and she's quite high up too, I think. Lena was telling me about her a few weeks ago. She actually runs her own hospital. A huge hospital, bigger than the one in Cork. The one in Cork is very big. Do you miss living in your house?' Her words came fast, almost garbled, and he wondered if she was quite well.

'Well, I –'

She slapped her head theatrically, a gesture that made him start. 'I forgot, Lena and Eli bought your old house, didn't they? I expect you'd like to see what they've done with it. It looks much different now from when your father lived there. Much brighter. Why don't we go and look at it? I have the key, and I'm sure she wouldn't mind me showing you around, since you came all this way.'

So Lena hadn't mentioned his recent visit. It was as if he wasn't important to her, didn't matter in her life any more. And Maria thought her daughter and Eli had bought the house; she had no idea he'd given it to Emmet. He wasn't surprised the Kogans would let the town believe that, but her own mother... Did Lena want everyone to forget Malachy Berger ever existed?

'Well, if you're sure, I would love to see the place again,' he said with a bright smile. 'I have a car, so I could drive us there?' He knew Lena wouldn't like Maria showing him around – her mother shouldn't have offered, and he should refuse – but this was an opportunity he didn't want to miss, even though he wasn't sure what he wanted from it.

'Lovely.' Maria linked his arm as they walked back up the street towards where he'd left his car. He could feel the eyes of the town on them. He knew Lena would find out about this – her mother would tell her – and she'd probably be furious when she heard. But still, something compelled him on. Just to be in her house again, maybe stand in Emmet's bedroom, see his books and toys, get a better sense of him... The memory of Emmet appearing in the kitchen doorway while he and Eli were shouting at each other had haunted him the last few days. All the way to Dublin, he'd racked his brain as he drove, trying to remember what was said, what the boy might have heard.

'So did you get married yourself, Malachy? I'm sure a lad like you, with a fine education and a big job, must have had the ladies queuing around the block. You must have a fine wife and children of your own now.'

'No, Mrs O'Sullivan, I didn't find a wife and I have no children. I set up an engineering company, and to be honest, no woman could have put up with the long hours and all the time away on jobs. At the start anyway. It's settled a bit now. I have a good few engineers working for me, so the pressure isn't quite so much, but I'm a bit of a workaholic, the truth be told.'

'All work and no play, Malachy, it's not good for you. I'm always saying the same to my son, Jack – you remember Jack? He took over our farm when my husband passed away, a terrible accident. But Jack's like you, working morning, noon and night. I know a farm is different, when you have animals and that, but honestly the boy never takes a day off.'

'He sounds very committed. I remember Lena saying he was into all-natural farming methods, the old ways without chemicals.'

She nodded vigorously. 'That's exactly it. He loves it. Always reading books and getting things sent from England and America. His friend Skipper is from Montana, imagine that? But he came back here with Jack a few years ago and never left again. I honestly don't know how we'd survive without them, and while Jack is a quiet one, you'd be wondering what's going on in his head at all. Skipper is all chat, and he wears a cowboy hat all the time.'

She was trilling away quite loudly now, and Malachy thought her slightly overexcited, but he didn't know her before and figured maybe that was the way she was.

'Skipper sounds a character.'

'Oh, I enjoy him. He has a belt buckle that would take your eye out, and when he talks, he sounds like John Wayne in that picture...what was it now? Jack took us to see it. *The Man Who Shot Liberty Valance.* Oh, it was marvellous. We went to Cork, to the mart – he was selling calves – and afterwards Skipper and himself and me went to the Pavilion to see the film. I'd seen a few pictures years ago, when Paudie was alive, but nothing like this. It was marvellous altogether. But anyway, Skipper told me he sounds nothing like John Wayne, but I think he does.'

Malachy smiled. 'Well, I suppose it's a bit like here. We can tell someone from Dublin or Belfast or Galway in a second, but to an American, we all sound the same. So I think it's the same with them, and the longer I'm there, the more I notice the differences. I had a fellow from Louisiana working for me one time, and honestly I'd no idea what he was saying – not just the accent, but different words and everything. And where I used to live in Boston, it sounds very different to, say, the Bay Area, where I am now.'

They reached the two-seater sports car, and he held the door open for her to climb into the passenger seat.

'My goodness, this is a lovely car,' she said, stroking the leather interior. 'Emmet would love to have a spin in this. He knows all about cars. He's such a clever little boy, he could probably even tell you what this one was called. He's got such a wise head on him.'

'Tell me about him?' Malachy prompted, and he listened in pleasure as she recounted every clever phrase Emmet had ever said and every smart thing he'd ever done, from his first bit of writing to what a great horse rider he was.

Driving out of town and up the hill to the gates of Kilteegan House, Malachy noticed this time that the long winding avenue up to the house, once thickly lined with trees, had been thinned out to make it brighter and more open, revealing the rolling parkland beyond and even a view of the fields that were divided between grazing sheep and swaying golden grain.

Maria was still chatting away. 'Jack has the Kilteegan House land for grazing and planting – it backs on to ours. And the orchard there on the right was my Paudie's pride and joy when he worked here. Nobody could grow apples like he could.'

'I remember,' Malachy said, recalling so many days playing there as a child, Paudie O'Sullivan lifting him up to reach the sweetest apples to crunch. And then he remembered that photograph his mother had taken of Paudie helping him down from the tree. The last time he'd seen it, his own father had been showing it to Lena. He wondered where the photo was now.

'You do of course,' Maria was saying. 'He worked here when you were a child, and even after your father came back from the war.'

'He did. He was a great help to my grandfather, and later my mother.'

An awkward silence hung between them then, the air heavy with things unsaid. He wondered how much she knew about her husband's affair with Hannah Berger. When Lena had said that her mother didn't approve of him, she'd blamed it on Maria thinking posh boarding-school boys like him only picked up local girls like her for a laugh, then dumped them as soon as they went to college. A stereotype Malachy had played right into, thanks to his lying father. But maybe it was because Maria had sensed something going on between Hannah and Paudie?

'He was a great husband, loyal and true.' Maria O'Sullivan gazed over her shoulder towards the orchard as Malachy pulled up on the gravel outside the big house.

'I know he was,' he said quietly. There was no point in telling her the truth now.

'People sometimes thought... Well...I don't know what they thought, but they didn't know him, not like I did. Nobody knew him like me.'

Malachy didn't respond. There was nothing to say.

Then, with that disconcerting way she had, she was bright and bubbly again, pulling a large, long key from her handbag, the same key he remembered hanging on a string inside the kitchen door. He and his mother used to use the back door rather than the huge ornate door at the top of the front steps, but now Maria trotted up those limestone steps like a girl, still carrying her peacock shoulder bag, and turned the huge key in the lock.

The door opened easily, not sticking like it used to, and he followed her in. This time, not distracted by Lena's presence, he took in the changes properly, admiring how open and spacious the hall had become without being cluttered by heavy furniture and dark colours.

'She's done a smashing job, hasn't she?' The pride in Maria's voice cut through his thoughts. 'The upstairs is lovely too.' She hesitated, then added, 'I'd better not take you up. Lena might not like that.'

'Of course, that would be too private,' he said, disappointed. He wanted to see where his son slept, but it looked like that wasn't going to happen. 'Just show me the downstairs. They've made an incredible job of the place. It's so much nicer than I remember.'

'They have put a lot into it, Lena especially. Eli works so hard. He took over Doc's practice, and he's exactly like him, devoted to his patients.'

'So they're happy here?' he asked, trying to make his voice light.

'Really happy. Lena was in Wales for a while, years ago, and she met Eli there. They are as suited to each other as two people can be. They love each other and their three children deeply, and this home is such a reflection of who they are.'

'They're lucky,' he managed. 'I'm glad the old place is in such good hands, and I'm glad Lena's happy.'

'She really is. Come on, let me bring you around. You won't recognise it.'

In room after room downstairs, the darkness was gone. Floral patterns, bold stripes, functional, comfortable furniture had replaced the hard, dull, forbidding décor of his childhood. Lena had filled the wide fireplace in the library with tory tops and dried flowers, and the sofa in front of it begged to be sat on. The cushions were squashy, and on each end, pastel-coloured blankets were folded neatly.

The little sitting room had a silk Persian rug, and there was a lovely old rosewood writing desk in the corner, which he instantly imagined Lena sitting at to write her letters. The heavy fireside chairs were gone, and a small sofa and a selection of mismatched easy chairs were dotted around the room.

The kitchen was tidier than when he'd last seen it, the crayons and colouring books now in a neat pile on the sideboard. The door to the garden was bolted, but Maria pulled back the bolts and showed him outside, pointing out all the flower beds Lena had planted. 'She's got such green fingers! Now you must come and see what I did in the playroom...' She ran off, leaving Malachy to come back in and close the door.

The playroom on the other side of the hall was full of toys and books and paints and musical instruments, and Maria showed him the animals she had painted on the walls, lions, elephants, giraffes, all skilfully done. 'And Emily gave her the piano. Wasn't that kind of her?'

'Very kind.'

Everything in this house conveyed family unity and warmth and love and belonging and happiness. In his day it had been so dark and forbidding. His mother had crept around, afraid to modernise anything, and after she'd died, it had only got worse, the drapes always pulled and chairs covered and rooms locked up like everywhere was full of ghosts.

His own home in Palo Alto, California, was open-plan and light, but he hadn't been entirely able to shake off his father's influence, because it was also hard and minimalist, all steel and glass. It had won awards and was featured in several architectural magazines, and every girl he had gone out with loved it, but it didn't feel like a home, not like this.

As they crossed the hall again, he allowed himself to imagine Lena in California, decorating his hard metallic house with rugs and throws and pretty things. She could grow her flowers in his 'yard' – a word he always smiled at because a 'yard' in Ireland was a place full of machinery or tools or coal bunkers. Gardens in America, he'd discovered, were simply where people grew vegetables. It was true what the Irish playwright George Bernard Shaw had said – they were two countries divided by a common language.

Would Lena have grown to like America given the chance, despite all the differences? He knew his friends and colleagues would have loved her; she was so bright and funny, and well able to stand up for herself. He could imagine them having cookouts in the summer, inviting all the other guys in the firm, with their wives and kids, eating hot dogs and splashing around in the pool...

'Aren't the photos lovely?' Maria broke into his thoughts.

With a start, he looked where she was pointing and recognised a walnut side table with turned legs that his mother had loved, now polished and gleaming and placed against the wall beside the library doorway. On it were several silver photograph frames. There were Lena and Eli, then one of Lena and Eli and three children together, then four children in separate oval frames. He spotted Emily and Blackie, Jack, and Jack again standing with a man in a cowboy hat he assumed was Skipper. He thought a group of other adults and small children must be Eli's family from Wales.

He longed to pick up the photo of Emmet, but with a bright eager smile, Maria insisted on showing him the photo of a girl he didn't know, a miniature version of Maria herself, with long fair hair.

'That's Nellie. She's Emily's, and she adores her cousin Emmet. They're the same age about. She's the absolute ticket – she'd buy and sell you, that child. She still sleeps in Emily and Blackie's bed, you know. Em was trying to convince her to go back to her own bed and asked her how long more she intended to sneak into her parents' bed, and do you know what Nellie said to her?' She giggled wildly.

'No?' Malachy found himself amused and interested. He remembered sweet, kind Emily O'Sullivan from junior school, and it was hard to picture her as a mother now.

'She said, "Mammy, we both know the answer to that, so let's not go upsetting ourselves now, will we?"' Maria pealed with laughter. 'She would have you in stitches, that child, she really would.'

She took the picture of Nellie back and gave him another photo. 'This is her cousin Emmet.'

His heart missing a beat, Malachy studied the boy closely, in the way he'd not had the chance to do before. Emmet was pale-skinned, with huge green eyes and a mop of dark-red curls. He was slight, and a gentle smile played around his rosebud lips. He looked exactly like Malachy in that photo of Paudie and himself in the orchard.

Malachy felt a physical pain of loss. This was his son. And he would never know him. It was his own doing for abandoning Lena without question, he knew that, but the pain was hard to bear.

'Now look at Sarah. She's called after Eli's mother.'

Reluctantly he handed the photo of Emmet back as Maria gave him the one of Sarah. Then once more, he was mesmerised. The girl had Lena's beautiful face, dark hair and eyes.

'That's Pádraig – he's a dote! He's named after my husband.' Maria replaced Sarah's photo with one of a square, solid toddler, then took that away as well and gave him an oblong frame. 'And that's Eli and Lena of course. That was taken at a wedding recently, I think – I forget who. Lena looks lovely in it, I think, but she wasn't sure about the dress. I had to alter it for her – she's so petite and the skirt was too long – but once we took it up, it was gorgeous.'

'Yes, it's perfect. It really suits her.' He tried not to see the way Lena looked up at her husband, a beam of joy on her beautiful face. She had looked at him once like that. He glanced at himself in the oval mirror that hung over the mantelpiece. She hadn't recognised him when he'd come to her front door, or not right away, and that had hurt. Had he changed that much in the intervening years? His red hair had gone even darker, and his face was thinner. He still played a bit of rugby over in San Francisco with a team of Irish and English fellas he knew, so he still had the physique of a winger, his position on the pitch, not tall but fast and agile.

When he looked back at Maria, she was gazing at him oddly, and perhaps he imagined it, but something seemed to change. He couldn't put his finger on it, as she was still smiling, but it was as if she was trying to remember something. Had she known that he and Lena were out when they were young? Or was he reminding her of Hannah?

'This house didn't always bring happiness, Malachy, but Lena and Eli have chased away all the old ghosts and now it's a happy home. They both deserve it.' Her blue eyes fixed on his, refusing to break the disconcerting stare.

Was she trying to say something to him? But what?

'I'm sure they do. Now I'd better get on. Thanks for showing me the place. Please tell Lena...' he paused. 'Tell her I was asking for her.'

'I will.' She was bright and chirpy again as she showed him out the front door.

'Right, well, thanks for showing me around. It was lovely to meet you again.'

'You too. Good luck in your life, Malachy, and find yourself a wife. A good marriage is a rare blessing. Lena has one – you should too.'

Smiling fixedly, he took out his car key. 'Can I give you a lift home?'

'Not at all. I'll walk today. My husband died in our top field near here, so sometimes I spend a little time in the place to feel close to him. Although I wish you'd drop by tomorrow if you are staying in town, because Emmet would only love to see your car.'

'Emmet is with you?' He stared at her, stunned. Could it be? He'd assumed the boy and the other children would have gone to Wales with their parents, or Dublin, whichever it was.

'They're with me for the whole week – isn't that lovely? I've been doing so much painting with them, and I only ran to the library to get a proper art book for them to copy the pictures. It's got Renoir and Matisse and everything.' She patted her peacock bag, slung over her shoulder.

Was this his chance to finally meet his son properly? It seemed too good to be true. 'The book must be heavy. Please let me run you home, Mrs O'Sullivan.'

'No, no, the place is a mess. Come tomorrow – come to lunch! Everyone will be there, the children, Jack, Skipper… Yes, come to lunch! Will you come?'

His heart was beating very hard now, and he couldn't stop smiling at her. 'Yes, I will, of course I will.'

'Twelve o'clock? Make sure to be there!' And she skipped in her long green dress down the gravelled drive, then turned up the road towards the upper field where her husband had died.

Malachy stood by his car until she'd disappeared from view, then pocketed the car key, went around to the back of the house and let himself in the kitchen door. It was wrong, he knew, but he wanted to see his son's bedroom, so he'd deliberately left the door unbolted. But now he was going to see Emmet the next day, so he would just lock up and then let himself out the front door.

As he passed the sweeping staircase, he stopped, then walked on, then turned back and took the stairs two at a time. He only wanted to see his son's bedroom, just for a couple of minutes, and he'd be gone. He wasn't going to invade Lena's privacy. It was fine – no one would ever know.

All the doors on the landing were closed. The first one he tried was locked, but he remembered it was only a small room, barely bigger than a cupboard. Probably Eli used it as an office and a place to store medicines, which is why he would lock it. Next was a man's dressing room, with a rack of suits and a sofa by the window, covered in cushions. Malachy moved on. The following room was painted a delicate rose pink and had a small white bed and a blue cot in the corner. So Sarah and Pádraig slept here.

After that was the room his mother had slept in, and then his father when he came back from the war and Phillippe Decker would carry him up the stairs to bed. Malachy placed his hand on the door-knob…and froze, his heart racing. Memories of Hannah in this room came flooding back, taking his breath away.

Finding out his mother had committed suicide had shaken Malachy so fundamentally, it had left a lasting impact, causing him to shut off his entire childhood. But standing here now, and seeing that photograph of Emmet, he was dragged back to those early years.

His hand trembled on the doorknob. His colleagues back in the States wouldn't recognise him. There, he was a decisive businessman, a tough negotiator, dreaded among builders because of his exacting standards. Woe betide the chancer who tried to cut corners on any of his projects. But here in this house, he felt just like a stupid, scared kid again.

He'd been only Emmet's age when August Berger came into his life. Before that, Malachy and his mother had had their own relationship and Hannah was her own person. She'd loved life and was full of fun and light and laughter.

Until *he* turned up to ruin everything.

Why couldn't his father have been one of the millions killed in the war, as they'd thought he had been? It would have saved so much heartache. He was dark and dour. He used to drink brandy in the evening and either get maudlin or rant and rave, frightening him and his mother half to death. Malachy now remembered walking into this bedroom and finding his mother curled up on the four-poster bed, crying, and not knowing what to do because he was just a boy.

Like a film, the memories he'd suppressed came flooding back, one after the other.

The time he fell out of a tree and broke his wrist, and his father coldly informed Hannah that she was a terrible mother, that he'd have her committed and take her precious son away from her, raise him with the knowledge that she was unfit. The time she made boiled potatoes and bacon and cabbage for dinner and August threw it at the wall and roared at her to learn to cook properly, like the French, like Phillippe.

The time Malachy heard a crash and a scream and went running to see what happened and she had knocked over a vase while wheeling his father into the library – his father had been gripping her arm, holding a piece of the broken china to her wrist while she sobbed in terror. Malachy had shouted at his father to stop, and August had blinked and seemed to come around from a terrible dream, a faraway place, and then his mother made excuses for his behaviour, saying it was shell shock from the war and they had to forgive him.

Malachy knew now that it wasn't shell shock. August Berger was just a cruel, heartless man, and not a member of the French resistance as he claimed back then, but a Nazi who had spent his time in the camps.

At least this deluge of memories brought back others in their wake, ones that he could treasure, earlier memories of his mother that were picture-perfect. Reading books by the fire with her, baking in the kitchen, throwing wet sponges in the yard in the summertime, her carrying him on her shoulders. His mother laughing with his grandfather, who had died when Malachy was Pádraig's age but who lived on in his heart as a warm and kindly presence. A glossy red setter dog called Rí, the Irish word for king. Paudie O'Sullivan helping Malachy to saddle up his pony. His mother had a horse too, a big chestnut stallion called Gypsy, and she would ride through the fields, her red hair loose and flowing.

She had been so happy then. Why hadn't she just left his father if he made her so miserable? Why didn't she come and take Malachy out of school? They could have gone far away. He supposed she stayed to be near Paudie O'Sullivan, and then when she realised Paudie would never leave his wife…

She killed herself. Abandoned her son.

In a fit of hurt rage, he flung open the door.

The room was unrecognisable. Gone was the huge mahogany four-poster bed with its horsehair mattress and heavy crimson curtains. In its place was a gleaming brass bedstead and a well-stuffed feather mattress and pillows, neatly tucked-in Foxford blankets and a patchwork counterpane. The walls had been stripped of their heavy '30s wallpaper and were painted cream, and the cotton curtains at the window were sprigged with lilacs. It was gorgeous and light and airy, and suddenly he felt so tired and racked with guilt at snooping around the house. It was Lena's bedroom now, not his mother's.

Lena.

How exhausted he was from his love of her. Love, regret, guilt, self-admonishment, longing. It was an endless cycle of pointless, draining emotion. He had told himself over and over it was just a teenage romance, but no – she was the love of his life. If he'd only known about Emmet, he was sure he would have defied his father to find her, forbidden the adoption, got married to her. But ifs and should haves were such a waste of time. *Stop it*, he admonished himself. *It's pathetic. She's married very happily to Eli Kogan, and they have their own family.* He needed to get on with his own life and forget about her.

He closed her bedroom door and went to the stairs. The sooner he got out of here the better. But he had only taken a few steps down before he turned and went back up again. It was no good. He had to see Emmet's room. It was why he'd come here in the first place.

He checked the second-to-last door and found a spacious modern bathroom, then opened the final door, the door to his old bedroom.

It had changed less than the other rooms, perhaps because his mother had always made sure it was bright and cheerful. There in the corner was his old rocking horse, polished and repainted but still his. A shelf of books still contained some titles he remembered: *The Coral Island, Kidnapped, Moonfleet*. The rotating globe of the world was new, and the Meccano set, and the collection of Airfix planes dangling from the ceiling, but he recognised the old school desk and chair, and the model steam train, an absolute beauty that would puff happily around on its big circular track. His father, delighted to have an heir – at least that was one thing his mother had done right – had been a lot more generous to Malachy than he had been to Hannah.

Malachy went to the window and then stepped sharply out of sight. Maria O'Sullivan was standing in the O'Sullivans' top field. She hadn't seen him; she was too far away. She was only recognisable by the sun gleaming on her long loose hair. When he looked again from behind the curtain, she was walking away.

He had to leave the house – now.

No, he thought, *just a while longer.* He wanted to breathe the air his son breathed.

He lay down on the old familiar bed and closed his eyes. The mattress was a lot more comfortable than the one he remembered. He was so tired. *Mustn't sleep...* He forced his eyes open. Directly above him was the hatch to the attic, where the water tank was kept. He wondered what Lena had stored there. Maybe more memories from his youth, even some mementoes of his mother? Surely not everything had been thrown out? He remembered it as a huge attic, spread across the whole area of the house. Perhaps there was something he could take back to California, something soft, a memory of a life that had been simple and full of love.

On impulse, he got up, took the old school desk and lifted it onto the bed, then placed the school chair on top of it. It was precarious, but he managed to climb up without overbalancing. He pushed back the hatch, gripped the sides of the opening and hauled himself up. The attic was dusty and gloomy, but it was floored with rough boards and there was a dangling string that lit up a single bare bulb. Sure enough, there were a few items of the old furniture and some ugly oil paintings that used to hang in the library. There were also some baby items that Lena must have been keeping for her grandchildren, or even for another child of her own: a Silver Cross pram, a wooden cradle, a baby bath. He opened a cardboard box to find folded baby clothes, topped by a hand-stitched christening robe. Had Emmet worn this?

He gazed around him. There were several more boxes lined up against the eaves. The first one he looked in contained the clothes of a small boy, which must have been Emmet's and were waiting to be passed down to Pádraig. He touched them lovingly. How many years of Emmet's childhood he had missed.

The second box was full of the old curtains, which Lena had obviously been reluctant to throw out, maybe because the material might come in handy.

In the next were some very expensive-looking but ugly marble ornaments; he thought he remembered them being in the library. Beyond it, the table from the hall was resting on its side, and he noticed the corner of another box behind. He went down on his knees to pull it towards him. To his surprise, when he had it out in the open, he discovered it had 'MALACHY' written on it in a neat hand. It was his mother's writing. He felt his heart thump in his chest.

He untied the green string that bound the box and opened it. Lying on top of a heap of papers was a small photo album containing black and white photos of himself as a child. He leafed through it, remembering his mother having fun with her camera. The picture she had taken of Paudie, the one in which he was helping Malachy down from a high branch, had been returned to its place. He'd put it back into the album himself, he remembered, after his father had insisted on showing it to Lena. Looking at the picture now, he realised he'd forgotten that a five-year-old Lena had been in the background. It was astonishing to see them both again at that age. The boy could have been Emmet, and the girl could have been Lena's daughter, Sarah. It was an uncanny resemblance.

When he'd stopped studying the photo, he moved on to the papers underneath. Old schoolbooks of his, some childish diaries, the sorts of things a mother would keep to remember her son's childhood. His mother had loved him then, at least a little. He looked through his primary school books with a smile.

Near the bottom of the box, an envelope was tucked into a maths copy, addressed to him in Hannah's handwriting.

His stomach turned over. The envelope was sealed, unopened. Hannah must have placed it there herself for him to find, not realising that after her death this box would be hidden away, no doubt by Decker on his father's instructions. Lena must have stumbled on it, thought it unwanted by him, but had kept it anyway and even added the little album of photos in case he ever asked for it.

He stared for a long time at the envelope, then with a shiver tucked it with the photo album into his jacket pocket. He wasn't ready to read his mother's suicide note – if that's what it was. He'd had enough sadness for one day.

Sitting with his feet dangling through the trapdoor, he gripped the sides and lowered himself to the chair, then reached up to replace the hatch. He'd only just managed it when the chair tottered, and he had to leap sideways to the floor as both chair and desk crashed off the bed. Sweating, he replaced the furniture where he'd found it – luckily nothing was broken – straightened his son's bedclothes, ran downstairs and went to let himself out the front door...which of course Maria had locked from the outside when they left. Stupid of him.

Reluctant to use the back door because he'd have to leave it unbolted, he poked around for a sash window that was already unlocked so he could close it behind him without anyone noticing. Eventually he found a small one in the pantry. Squeezing through it, relieved he wasn't anywhere near as big as Eli, he fell with his arms stretched out to the soft ground, rolled, jumped up and dusted himself off. He closed the window, tried to fix up the flowers he'd crushed, picked up the letter and album that had fallen out of his pocket and headed for his car.

There was a new hotel in Bandon where he would stay while he waited for tomorrow, when he would see his son.

CHAPTER 17

*L*ena squeezed Eli's hand as they walked towards Rue des Glaciers. She was so touched by his insistence on coming with her to see Decker, a man who would bring back everything he was trying his best to forget.

The house Decker lived in had the paint peeling from the front door, which was on the latch. Eli went to knock, but she tugged him back. 'I think I'd better fetch him down by myself, Eli, while you wait here. He's very nervous at being found and might panic if he sees a strange man.'

Eli shook his head. 'Supposing he gets violent? Klaus thought –'

'I don't think he will – he's desperate to find this Rebecca woman. And if he does anything, I'll scream and you'll be there in a flash.'

'You bet I will,' he said grimly.

'So you'll wait here?' He was a remarkable man, her husband, and she was filled with gratitude and love for him allowing her to make her own decisions. 'And you'll try to act friendly when you see him? I know it will hurt, but we need him to trust us.'

'I don't like it, but if you think it's the best way. Just make sure you scream good and loud if he does *anything* at all.'

'I will.' She kissed him, then knocked on the door. Nobody came.

With a glance at Eli, she gingerly pushed the door and was immediately assailed by the strong smell of meat cooking. The smell was mixed with a kind of must and something else, dirt possibly. It was unpleasant.

The faded green linoleum on the floor was torn where the door had rubbed it away, and the walls appeared to be covered in what looked like painted embossed wallpaper, which was peeling off in sections.

She stepped inside, trying not to breathe in the smells, as a wiry woman in a housecoat and with iron-grey hair in a bun appeared from the back.

'Excuse me,' Lena said slowly. 'Monsieur Decker?'

The woman looked her up and down several times before answering, as if she were a streetwalker or something. '*A la troisieme étage,*' she said eventually, her bony finger pointing upwards and a sly grin on her face.

Lena had no idea what the woman had said, but she guessed by the action that Decker was on the floor above. The landlady stood watching shamelessly as she climbed the stairs. Several spindles were missing, and some of the bare treads had been eaten by woodworm.

The second landing had two doors, one that stood open into a room draped with grey laundry and a pot boiling on a single gas ring but which was otherwise empty. From the other door came the sound of a baby crying.

She carried on up another flight.

On the third floor there was a single door straight ahead, and Lena took a few deep breaths to steady herself before knocking.

She gave three sharp knocks.

Nothing.

Maybe he'd gone out, or it wasn't the right door after all. Just as she was about to turn and try her luck on the second floor, the door opened and Decker stood there, looking at her, dressed in just a vest and trousers, with a smudge of shaving foam on his face. Without his coat and hat or shirt or shoes, he looked much more vulnerable than he had yesterday.

'Madame Kogan.' He nodded but stayed standing in the doorway, stock-still, his expression impassive.

'May I come in for a moment?' she asked.

He sighed and looked like he wanted to say no, but then he stood aside, permitting her access to his room.

I'm not surprised he didn't want to show it to me, she thought as she entered. She had never seen a more miserable space; it was like a prison cell. A single bed with a thin mattress was pushed into one corner. A string hung between two nails, on which he had two coat hangers, one bearing his coat, the other holding what looked like his only shirt, presumably he'd washed it. A tiny cracked sink stood in the corner, on which was balanced a broken shard of mirror. He had a single kitchen chair, and a table under the dormer window held a small Primus stove, a battered saucepan, a tin plate, a cup and a knife. That seemed to be the entirety of his belongings. Nothing personal, no photo or picture, nothing to soften his existence even a little.

'Please, have a seat.' He pointed her to the chair and went back to the sink, where he picked up a cut-throat razor and continued shaving.

She sat at the table and watched him as he drew the vicious-looking razor across his chin. It was unnerving to see him holding such a weapon, but she refused to feel intimidated. Besides, she hadn't told Eli, but the Librium that Anthea had given her was in her handbag, already made up in the syringe, and that helped her feel safer.

Once Decker had finished shaving, wiped his face, turned off the tap and folded the razor away, she said, 'My friend in Strasbourg says he has information about four Rebecca Loebs who were in Auschwitz.'

He gave such a violent start, he might have cut his own throat if the razor was still in his hand. He spun to face her, his mouth open. 'Does he know where they are?'

She met his eyes, unflinching. 'Two died, one he is still investigating, one definitely survived.'

'Then that's her! I saw her photo from late 1944, and she was well and happy! Where is she now?'

'I don't –'

'Tell me!' He was shaking, white under his tanned skin.

Lena did her best to stay calm. 'I'm trying to say, I don't know yet, but I've made an appointment for us with my friend, and if you give him more of your Rebecca's details, he'll be able to tell if she's the right one. And if she is, then we can find her.'

'Ah!' His eyes flashed with excitement but then went dark. 'Oh, I understand,' he sneered. 'You want me to come and meet a strange man who will turn out to be some deluded Nazi hunter clutching a fake warrant for my arrest.'

She kept on smiling. 'Why would I do that? If I wanted you arrested, why would I come here by myself?'

'To smoke me out onto the street.'

'Phillippe.' She hated using his first name, but she had to convince him to trust her. 'All these years I thought you'd murdered my father, but now it turns out it wasn't your fault.'

'It wasn't.' He said it angrily, but he still looked pleased.

'I know. I agree, nothing was your fault. You're entitled to the money that was coming to you, and maybe we can come to some arrangement, leave the lawyers out of it.' Judging by the state of his home, he hadn't a penny for Ignatius Hayes.

He softened a bit more. 'Well, I want to live in my house, not sell it.'

'Really? Come back to Kilteegan Bridge?'

'Is there something wrong with that?' He looked angry again.

She smiled at him soothingly. It was a horrible thought, having him in her home town, but she was beginning to realise that getting him back on Irish soil was probably her best chance of having him arrested and convicted for his crimes. He was so open about what he'd done, and so confident none of it was his fault, he would surely confess it to anyone, and then she'd have proper witnesses. 'There's nothing wrong with that at all. It's your house.'

'Anyway, first things first – Rebecca.'

'I have an appointment with my friend in half an hour. It's only twenty minutes' walk.'

His eyes narrowed. 'But have you said I was in the Waffen-SS? Will he tell Rebecca? It wasn't my fault – it was August's idea...'

'I know it wasn't your fault.' She did her best to sound sympathetic. 'As you said, joining up helped August find her, didn't it? So even if she knows, she will surely forgive you. You saved her life.'

He looked at her suspiciously but said nothing. He pulled on his damp shirt; it was so warm in the room, it was nearly dry already. 'Are you sure it's only this man we're going to see?' he asked as he buttoned it up.

Lena kept her voice light. 'There will be one other person.'

His eyes flashed and he stiffened. 'You said it would just be us three.'

'I know I did, but it's just my husband, who arrived last night. You met him before you...left Ireland.'

He frowned but seemed to relax.

'He's only here because I'm here, and I've explained everything to him about none of this being your fault, so you're safe with him, I promise.'

Decker didn't look totally convinced, but he sat on the bed and pulled on his broken-down shoes, brushing off dry mud. 'I don't hate Jews, you know. My girlfriend was Jewish, and when I find her, I'll explain that. August made sure she was well treated, for my sake.'

'I know, you said.'

'Did I?' He looked at her in surprise and then remembered. 'Oh, I told you last night when I was... Did I say he brought me a photo of her when she was in the camp? She looked so happy and well. They hate the Nazis now, but it wasn't true that we starved and gassed the Jews. War was hard on everyone.'

'Of course.' It was an almost impossible task to keep smiling when he came out with things like that, but she managed it. She stood up. 'Will we go?'

He nodded, took his jacket and followed her out onto the landing, pausing to lock the door behind him. But then he unlocked it and went back in, pushing the door almost shut. For a bad few seconds, she thought he'd changed his mind, but he reappeared in no time and went ahead of her down the stairs.

Outside in the street, Eli was waiting for them.

Phillippe Decker hung back, glowering suspiciously, but Eli took a deep breath, stuck out his hand and said in a warm, pleasant voice, 'Good afternoon, Mr Decker.'

CHAPTER 18

Sitting on the edge of the bed in the Bandon hotel, Malachy read his mother's last letter for the third time. The first two times, he'd barely been able to take it in, let alone process it, but this time he began to understand.

Dearest Malachy,

This is a very hard letter to write, but you have to know the truth and I want you to be ready for me when I come and get you from school.

Your father is trying to kill me.

Yesterday, he pointed a gun at me. I was so scared, but he just laughed and said no, he didn't want to be charged with murder, so he'd strangle me to death instead and tell the doctor they'd found me hanging from a tree and that it was suicide. I could hardly believe him, but today I couldn't find Gypsy's leather halter, and now I'm terrified Phillippe has taken it and between them they're going to do as August says.

So I'm leaving him and I'm coming to get you, and we're going to go somewhere far away. Don't tell your teachers. Just make sure to pack your things.

It's hard. The pair of them watch me all the time. I don't even know how I'm going to post this. I'm going to try to hide it in one of your old books until the postman comes to the door, and then I'll run and give it to him and beg him to send it for me even though I don't have a stamp or any money to pay for one. I think he'll do it for me – he's a nice man and his sister worked for my parents in the kitchen here years ago.

And then I'll saddle up Gypsy – I think I can catch him without the halter – and ride away from the house. Your father is used to me riding, so he won't be suspicious, so I'll just keep on riding up to the O'Sullivan farm. Paudie will help me as soon as I explain.

August keeps ranting on that I'm in love with Paudie O'Sullivan, but it's not true. Paudie is a lovely man, and there was a time when we gave each other comfort, back when I thought August was dead and Paudie thought his wife would never come home from the psychiatric hospital. I hope you can understand. I promise that since your father turned up alive, I've been a faithful wife to him, and Paudie loves his own wife with all his heart.

I even thought at first your father and I could be happy together, like we were in Dublin when he was an art student, but the war changed him dreadfully. I don't mean about the wheelchair – I mean in his soul. It was as if he had done and witnessed things too dreadful to bear and had pulled out his own heart. If I ever said to him he should be proud of his war, of being in the French resistance, he would sneer at me and tell me I didn't understand.

I think he has shell shock, so I'm trying to forgive him. But I can't stay any longer. You need your mother, Malachy, and I don't want to leave you at the mercy of such a cold, dark man.

I'll finish now, as I need to hide this, but remember I love you with all my heart and I will protect us from him. Things will be as they were before he came back, I promise.

With all my love, Mam.

PS. In case they kill me before I can get away and then lie to you, I would never leave you, my love. I would never kill myself.

In his luxurious hotel bedroom, Malachy lay face down on his bed and wept.

CHAPTER 19

*P*ierre Laroche's house was very similar architecturally to the house Decker lived in, but the front door was freshly painted and there were flowerboxes on the windowsills. The man who opened the door was in his seventies. He was tall, with sparse grey hair that stuck out at all angles. He wore horn-rimmed spectacles and a crumpled linen suit. Lena introduced herself and her husband, and Pierre kissed her on both cheeks and shook Eli's hand.

'Thank you so much for having us, Mr Laroche,' said Eli.

'You're so welcome, Mr Kogan. And call me Pierre.'

'And I'm Eli.'

'And this is Phillippe Decker,' said Lena, standing aside. He had been almost hiding behind her, his eyes lowered and his hands in his pockets.

'*Bonsoir*, Monsieur Decker.' Pierre favoured the silent Decker with a nod before standing aside to usher them all into his front hallway. 'Can I get anyone a coffee? Fresh orange juice?'

Lena suddenly realised how thirsty she was and asked for juice, and Eli accepted a coffee, but Decker briefly shook his head, his eyes lowered.

'Please wait in here while I fetch your drinks,' said Pierre, opening another door. 'This is my office where I keep my files. There's just about room for us all to sit – I've brought in some chairs from the kitchen.'

Pierre's inner sanctum was cramped but clean and smelled pleasantly of beeswax polish. Files were stacked on the shelves, and boxes full of more files were everywhere. On the leather-topped desk, a fountain pen rested on an ink-stained blotter next to another pile of papers. There was a portrait of a girl, aged around twelve, done in pencil in a frame on the wall, and there were orange tulips in a vase on the windowsill. The room had a woman's touch, Lena thought.

Eli, Lena and Decker sat on the three wooden chairs facing the desk, not saying anything to each other. A minute later, the historian returned with the coffee and juice, and he asked once more whether Decker wanted a drink. Again, Phillippe just shook his head, saying nothing.

Calmly, Pierre sat down behind the desk, fanned out the pile of papers in front of him and cleared his throat. 'Now, Lena, you asked me about a Rebecca Loeb in Auschwitz, and I have four possibilities here. Two died, one survived, and there's another I would like to know more about. So if you could help me with a date of birth, Mr Decker?'

Decker raised his head sharply but still said nothing. He was sitting in the chair nearest the door, perched on the edge of his seat like he was ready to run at a moment's notice, his shabby jacket pulled tight around him, his dark eyes fixed on Pierre.

Pierre peered at him over his horn-rimmed glasses. 'Mr Decker?'

Decker said in a low voice, 'I only know about the one who survived and went to America.'

'Interesting. The survivor I know of is in Shanghai.'

Decker glared at him. 'Then she must be the other one.'

'But maybe she went from America to China? Allow me to check. The Rebecca Loeb you knew…do you know her place and date of birth?'

'Of course I know.' Decker's eyes softened. 'How could I forget?

We were going to be married...' His eyes glazed over as he gazed into his past.

'Mr Decker? *Pardonnez moi*? I need to know your Rebecca Loeb's date of birth and place of origin, please?'

The Waffen-SS soldier shuddered and came back to the present. 'Twentieth of April, 1920. Eguisheim, Alsace.'

Pierre Laroche checked his files and shook his head. 'The Rebecca who went to Shanghai wasn't born on that date. She is quite a few years older, I'm afraid. But nor is she one of the two Rebeccas who I am certain died.'

Decker nodded, pleased. 'She is in America, like I told you.'

'Yes, she may be the fourth, our mystery Rebecca Loeb. Can you tell me more about her, Mr Decker? Any information you might have could help us find her. How, for instance, do you know she went to America?'

'August Berger told me.'

'Ah yes, August Berger of the Waffen-SS. Mrs Kogan mentioned he was involved.' Pierre leaned forwards slightly in his seat. Despite the historian's calm expression, Lena thought she detected a harder edge to his voice.

Phillippe Decker clearly also noticed it and looked annoyed. 'Don't tar everyone in the Waffen-SS with the same brush, Mr Laroche. There were some bad apples – I work for the wife of one – but like most of them, August was a good man. He was my best friend. He found Rebecca and her parents in Auschwitz, and he agreed to arrange American visas. It was very expensive, but her parents paid him with their wine collection – August showed me the receipt. And he arranged for Rebecca to travel back to Alsace because she was feeling a little poorly.'

'Alsace?' The historian pushed his glasses up his nose.

Decker shrugged and spread his hands. 'Not to Eguisheim, you understand, but to comfortable accommodation in the local camp, with three square meals a day and doctors and nurses to see to any medical problems before she would be released and allowed to travel to America.'

'You mean she was moved from Auschwitz to Natzweiler-Struthof transit camp?'

Lena thought there was a slight tremor in Pierre's otherwise steady voice. She wondered what he was feeling. Excitement? Anxiety? It was hard to tell.

'Yes, yes.' Decker gave a careless flip of his hand. 'That's the name of the place, up in the Vosges Mountains. Anyway, August had Rebecca relocated there, along with maybe a hundred other Jews, for rest and recuperation in the summer of 1944.'

'Other Jews? Specifically Jews?'

'Yes,' Decker replied derisively, as if this man understood nothing. 'You should not believe all you hear, monsieur. We treated the Jews very well here in Alsace. It was a holiday camp really. August brought me a photo of Rebecca in the autumn, and she was so well and happy, smiling, her hair glossy, skin like a peach, a little plumper than before the war but it suited her. Afterwards, August told me that her parents used the visas he managed to get them to take her to America. Now all I need from you is to find out where exactly my Rebecca is in America.'

Pierre Laroche sat back in his chair and laid his hand on his desk. 'Mr Decker, if your information is correct, I know exactly what happened to "your" Rebecca.'

'Ah...' The stocky Waffen-SS man took a sharp intake of breath, his brown eyes widening. 'I am grateful.'

'We are still trying to locate some of the other Jews involved,' said Pierre evenly, 'but I can tell you with near certainty that she was one of eighty-seven – fifty-eight Jewish men and twenty-nine Jewish women – who were sent to Natzweiler-Struthof from Auschwitz in 1944, where they were brought back to full health and fed plenty of good food.'

'Yes, yes, I know all that. August told me,' said Decker dismissively. 'Just tell me, where did she go next?'

Lena glanced at Eli. He was sitting on the other side of her, his arms tightly folded and mouth tight, and she remembered his revulsion at the idea of a Nazi being given the address of a Jewish woman.

'The intention behind the good treatment,' continued Pierre, 'was to get them into a fit state to make plaster casts of them, which would then be displayed in a museum. They had been chosen for their looks.'

Decker smiled, gratified. 'Yes, Rebecca was very beautiful of course. So she had a statue made of her?'

'No, no, Mr Decker. The idea was to make plaster casts of their actual bodies.'

Decker stared at the historian blankly, while Eli stared resolutely ahead, clearly determined not to react.

'Their *dead* bodies, Mr Decker,' said Pierre Laroche flatly.

To Lena's astonishment, Decker burst out laughing. 'Don't be ridiculous. What are you talking about? These weren't turkeys getting fattened up for Christmas!'

'Nonetheless, Mr Decker, once "fattened up", as you put it, all the Jews brought from Auschwitz to Natzweiler-Struthof were gassed over the course of three days, then their bodies beheaded and preserved in formalin. The idea was that once the plaster casts were made and on display, people would have visual proof of the subhuman nature of the Jewish race.'

The fleeting joy at being reunited with Rebecca fled from Decker, leaving him stony-faced. His eyes turned dark and his voice trembled. 'You're a liar, Mr Laroche. I've never seen any casts in a museum, and I passed through here in 1945.'

'That is because by September 1944, the Allies were advancing and so the plan changed. Such evidence of their barbarity could not be found, so now the corpses were to be stripped of their flesh in order to make them unrecognisable. In the end, there was no time even for that, so when the Allies arrived, they found the bodies and some heads still floating in formalin –'

'Lies,' said Decker contemptuously.

'Since which time, we have been trying to piece together the identities of the victims, and you have helped us with at least one, Mr Decker, and for that I thank you.'

'Don't you dare thank me. These are stories made up to frighten children.' Decker's voice was full of cold disgust. 'Nobody was murdered, nobody was gassed, nobody was beheaded. What do you think the Nazis were – madmen? Look at this Jew here.' He jabbed his finger at Eli. 'This man is a German Jew. And is he dead? *Non*. He is alive and well and living in Ireland, in the house that belongs to me. As for me, I have been denied my money, all because of made-up stories like these. Even the wealth from selling the Bergers' wine went straight to Malachy Berger – I never got a penny. The Bergers were in with the top brass. They made sure they got the spoils too. August's parents were slippery snakes, made a fortune with wine, but they were up to their necks in all sorts – stolen art, furniture. They had no qualms about it. The Jews had everything, you see, more than their fair share. But August was different. He wouldn't do what you said he did. He didn't approve of how his parents did business, especially with the Jews. I don't know who got the Loeb money – Rebecca told me her father had hidden it, along with his best wines, somewhere safe – but it wasn't August. But I don't care. All I want is to find Rebecca, and if you can't help me, then I'll find someone who will.'

Pierre sat quietly, leaning slightly forwards again but saying nothing, tapping his fingers on the desk.

Lena didn't know what to do or say. Her heart was breaking for Eli, who was stock-still, but she saw a muscle twitching in his jaw. He was clenching his teeth, which he did when he was very stressed. She should never have allowed her beloved husband to come with her to listen to this dreadful story. She'd only wanted to get Phillippe Decker's trust, encourage him to come to Ireland where he could be arrested. But now Decker was getting angrier and angrier. He was going to storm off and disappear, and all Eli's pain would be for nothing.

'Phillippe Decker is telling the truth,' Eli said, his voice steady.

'What do you mean?' asked Pierre sharply, glancing at Lena with his eyebrows raised. She gave a slight shake of her head; she didn't know what was going on, but maybe Eli was trying to keep Decker's trust like she'd asked him to.

'You see, Mr Laroche?' Decker was grinning; he was delighted. 'The Jewish man agrees. It's all bedtime stories.'

Eli's voice grew stronger. 'Don't think I'm not aware every moment of every day that I am alive and well, Mr Decker.'

'That's right, Mr Kogan, and living in my house in Ireland.'

'And please don't think I don't know exactly where I should be instead.'

'In Israel or America or someplace –'

Eli turned his head to face Decker, his eyes burning. 'I should be with my school friends, Heinrich Belau, Chaim Hoffman, Abraham Goldman, Noah Horowitz, all gassed in Auschwitz. I should be with my mother's best friend, Greta, my pregnant Aunt Sarah, my father's only sibling, her husband Benjamin Hershel, their little girl, Rosa who would only sleep when she visited us if she slept in my bed. She was my only first cousin on my father's side, and I loved her and she loved me. But that didn't matter to the Nazis. They were packed in trains to be sent to the slaughter. Uncle Esau, who we know was worked to death. My grandfather too, my mother's father. He was gassed at Dachau with my grandmother. Such a brilliant mind, but they cared nothing for that. All they saw was that he was a Jew. Mr and Mrs Hoffman from down the street, their three small children. Mr Jacobs from the bagel shop and all his family. The Rabbi Joseph, his wife, Rachel, his twin boys, Moses and Mannie. My father, Elijah, dragged away and shot while we were trying to escape. I should have tried to save him. I shouldn't have let my mother pull me away.'

'Oh, Eli...' Lena reached for his hand, but he was on his feet now, looking past her at Decker, who leaned back in his chair, his hands in his pockets.

'Elizabeth and Naftali, Leah, Adam, all the little children from the kindergarten, gone, gone, gone, walked into the gas chambers.'

'Lying Jew,' said Decker angrily. 'Stop with your filthy lies.'

'Nathan was the youngest at two years old –'

'Shut up with your stupid lies!' Decker stood, facing them square on. 'This did not happen! My Rebecca is not dead! She's in America!'

Decker jerked his right hand out of his pocket, and Lena screamed because he was holding a gun, pointing it past her at Eli. It was what he must have returned to his room to fetch.

'Stop, Phillippe!' She scrambled to her feet, throwing herself in her husband's way, feeling in her bag for the syringe of Librium. 'Don't do it! Listen to me – what about your dream of returning to Kilteegan Bridge? If you shoot anyone, you'll be arrested, and you'll never find peace at home in Ireland.'

'I don't believe you ever meant for me to come to Ireland!' he roared, waving the old-fashioned Luger at her. 'You hate me! You blame me for everything, but you're wrong. None of it is my fault, none of it, nothing, nothing, not your father, not even Hannah. It was August who strangled Hannah. It wasn't my fault! I only held her down because he ordered me to.'

Lena felt sick and faint. August strangled Hannah? She gasped out, 'No, I know it's not your fault, Phillippe. Put down the gun, give it to me.' She had her hand on the syringe; if she stepped forwards quickly...

At that moment, Eli grabbed her and in one swift movement swung her out of the way of the gun and pushed her behind him, shielding her with his big body. 'Samuel and David Rosenthal,' he continued steadily to Decker, as he held Lena back. 'Eli Horowitz and Rueben – they were the boys from the choir – all put on the train still wearing their black and white choir uniforms. They were so young, they still sung soprano, pure as birds.'

'It's not true!' screamed Phillippe, brandishing the Luger at him.

Pierre Laroche was on his feet as well. 'Rebecca Loeb, twenty-four years old, from Eguisheim, Alsace...'

Decker swung the gun towards Pierre. 'Not true,' he snarled.

'But it is true, Mr Decker,' said the historian, cool as ice, not even blinking. 'August Berger was lying to you about everything, and you believed his lies. He inherited his parents' ill-gotten fortune, but he was greedy, wanted more, so he took the Loebs' too. I've no doubt he told them he would use their money for visas and so on, that was a standard practice, but once Loeb told him where the money was, he'd have taken it for himself and left that family to their fate.'

'It's you who is lying. August was my friend. He saved Rebecca.'

The gun was shaking furiously in Decker's hand, his finger half squeezing the trigger.

Eli said quickly, 'Think, Phillippe, think for yourself, for once in your life. Receipts for wine? Visas for America? Seriously? Obviously August Berger wanted the Loebs dead so he could steal their wealth, and to secure your lifelong loyalty into the bargain.'

The gun switched back to Eli. 'Not true!' said Phillippe Decker between his teeth.

'Please, Phillippe, it's not your fault,' begged Lena, trying to get in front of her husband again, the syringe hidden in her hand. She had to do this. Maybe she could stab him in the neck before he fired. 'Phillippe, put the gun down. Whatever happened, it's not your fault.'

Again, Eli pushed her back, but she ducked and slipped from his grasp – sometimes it was useful to be small – and sprang forwards. And with a mighty effort before anyone could stop her, she thrust the syringe into Decker's throat and pressed the plunger.

Reeling, gasping, Decker staggered back, nearly dropping the gun. With his left hand, he felt for and ripped out the syringe that had dangled by its needle from his neck, and as he did it, he met her eyes. Lena would remember that look forever. It was the look of a man stripped down to nothing, his mind disoriented, his world in chaos, his layers of denial falling away as the sedative broke apart his carefully constructed world, exposing his small, cowardly, hopeless soul, the truth rising from his suppressed subconscious into the light.

'Oh, oh, Rebecca,' he gasped in a lost little voice. Already he was slurring his words and staggering. 'Rebecca, I'm sorry...' And he turned and walked away unsteadily, staggering and bumping off the door frame as he went.

The three of them left in the room stared at each other, shaking, and Eli took Lena in his arms. 'Lena, my love, are you all right? What on earth did you give him?'

Before she could explain, from the hallway of Pierre Laroche's house came the sound of a shot and the heavy collapse of a body falling.

CHAPTER 20

'The teacher came in. There were only five of us in the class by then – most of my classmates had left the city or their parents were keeping them at home. It was the winter of 1939. November. We had not been allowed in German schools since '33, so I was sent to a boys' Jewish school. Me, Heinrich Belau, Chaim Hoffman, Abraham Goldman and Noah Horowitz were told by our teacher, Herr Levi, to leave, and that we would not be coming back to school. He told us to take all of our things and go home. My mother used to collect me, and so I'd never walked home alone before. It was about three kilometres away and lots of turns, but the teacher said we were to go that very minute. The other boys lived closer and in opposite directions, so I walked alone. I was scared but excited too. My mother would never have allowed it, but the teacher had ordered us, so I remember feeling quite grown up. I had no real idea then, you see. I was so young, and my parents didn't talk about it in front of me.'

Lena reached across the café table for Eli's hand and squeezed it ever so slightly. The moon was up over the river, and the silvery reflected light glimmered around her husband from behind. On the shadowy table between them stood two glasses of brandy. They both needed it; they'd spent a difficult three hours being interviewed by the police, with Pierre Laroche doing the translating. Lena had explained about the Librium and everything, and at last the police had allowed her and Eli to go on their way.

Pierre shook their hands as they were leaving. Nothing seemed to faze him, not even the dead body in his front hallway, which an ambulance had just arrived to remove. He said he was just glad to have identified another lost Jew. 'It's vital to piece the history together,' he told them. 'We must never forget a single human being who died in those camps.'

Lena was afraid Eli would be left traumatised by all the horror, the story of Rebecca's murder and Decker's suicide, but the confrontation had opened him up in a way she wouldn't have thought possible. As soon as he'd finally stopped praising her bravery, he began talking about his past, and now they were in a café on the edge of the old town, which was lapped by the moonlit river Ill.

'*Mutti* was at home,' Eli continued after taking a mouthful of brandy. 'The bookshop she'd worked in was long closed down.'

Lena nodded. Eli's mother, Sarah, had mentioned the bookshop when she explained to Lena about the scar on her face. She'd said a Brownshirt had come into the shop and hit her with the butt of his gun, although other than that, like Eli, she'd told Lena next to nothing about her time in Germany.

'Papa was at home too,' said Eli. 'My parents had moved from Leipzig in 1930. I wasn't even born. Papa had got a consultant's position at Charité hospital. But in 1933 he was fired under the law that forbade Jews to hold positions of authority, so he'd been seeing Jewish patients privately at home. Hardly anyone could pay the doctor's fee and he treated most of them for free, so we had hardly any money and very little food. Patients might bring us something if they could spare it, but it was not much. I remember being hungry a lot.

'Anyway, I walked into the kitchen in the middle of the day, and they nearly had a heart attack. I told them I'd come home alone because the teacher told me to take my things and that me and the others wouldn't be going back there. My father was furious, absolutely livid, and *Mutti* was trying to calm him down. He'd had enough.

He said he was going to demand the fees back, he was going to have it out with the headmaster, he was going to do this and that... *Mutti* stopped him. What was the point?' Eli shook his head, remembering.

'So what happened then?' Lena asked softly.

He sighed. 'There was a woman who lived downstairs, Frau Klipper, and her husband was in the Wehrmacht. She had a daughter, Elise, and she and I used to play. One time, Elise got very sick. They took her to the hospital, but they sent her home, said it was nothing. But that night she got worse, so in desperation they called my father. He was able to save her by diagnosing what the hospital missed. I forget what it was, but he was able to save the child. Three days after that, we had a visit from the Gestapo saying they had information that he was practising medicine illegally on German people. He was arrested, roughed up a bit, but released. They told him it was our neighbour who had reported him.'

'Oh, Eli...' Lena had no words.

'So *Mutti* convinced Papa we should leave the city, go back to Leipzig where at least we had family, Aunt Sarah and Uncle Esau, my grandparents, cousins. The only family we had in Berlin was Uncle Saul – he was a doctor too and had also lost his job. It was impossible to get a visa to anywhere outside Germany. Britain officially closed its borders to refugees in 1939, no other country would take us, and we had no papers to get anywhere abroad. But we had to go somewhere.'

He paused for a long moment, and she wondered if he was going to say any more.

Then he continued. 'So the next day, we packed up our few things. It was before they introduced the decree that all Jews had to wear the star, and my father was tall and fair-haired, like me, so we didn't attract too much attention. Uncle Saul came too. I don't remember much about the apartment we lived in except I used to roll my toy cars on the landing. But I remember the train station.'

He stopped again. She held his hand, not speaking. He took a gulp of brandy.

'A soldier stopped us. Demanded to see our papers. He had a gun, and there was another one with him with a big dog. I tried to pat the dog, but he growled and my *mutti* pulled me close to her. It had been raining, and her coat was wet and smelled of damp wool.' He inhaled like he could remember that smell and sighed deeply.

'Papa gave the soldier the papers, and when he saw my father's name, the soldier said he had to come with them because he was a known troublemaker. *Mutti* was crying, begging no, and the other soldier dragged her away roughly. My father tried to fight back to protect her, but they beat him. Two more came to join the first two with the gun and the dog, and they kicked and used the butts of their guns until he was all bloody, curled up on the ground. Saul went to help, but my father shouted at him, "No, get Sarah and Eli on the train!" Blood was gushing out of his mouth. He was spitting out teeth. The soldiers dragged him to his feet, and the man put his gun in my father's back, and they shoved him out the train station. They seemed to have no interest in the rest of us, just decided it was him who needed to be punished as a troublemaker.'

Eli turned his face to stare at the sparkling river, his eyes disappearing into shadow. 'We heard he was shot at the local police station that day. They said he was trying to escape or some such rubbish, but they just shot him.'

Lena sat there, silent, fighting back the tears.

'So we got on the train to Leipzig. *Mutti* was crying, Uncle Saul was trying to get us seats, and as the train pulled out of the station, a man we didn't know approached us. He quietly told us that the Germans further up ahead were taking people off the trains with Jewish papers, so it wasn't safe. He told us to get off at the next station and follow him. We had to trust him, he said, because he knew my father, but he wouldn't tell us his name.

'We got off after him as he told us to, and he was walking a few yards ahead of us. It was terrifying, not knowing who this man was, whether we could believe in him, but there was nothing else to do, so we just followed him. He hid us in his house. I remember being under a bed with my mother, and then in the middle of the night, the man came back and told us to come quickly. We drove in a car and then walked a long way – Uncle Saul carried me – then another car, then someone else. Somehow this escape route got us out, passing the three of us like batons in a relay from one to the other. It was all a blur, but I knew we had to stay quiet and only move at night, avoiding check-points. During the day we hid in people's houses or barns. We never knew these people's names or who they were really. They hardly spoke to us, but I do remember one lady giving me an apple dipped in powdered sugar. It was delicious. Eventually we got to the coast and got a boat to Sweden that smelled of diesel and fish – I must have vomited the whole way there. That's why I hate fish to this day.'

Lena smiled slightly, despite her sadness. So that explained it. She had tried all kinds of fish on her husband, and he detested it all but had never explained; he always just said he didn't like the texture.

'I remember getting to Sweden. It was a neutral country. And from there my uncle wrote to some colleagues of his father in England. My grandfather was a fairly famous physician in the field of cardiac medi-cine, and he collaborated with several colleagues in Harley Street before the war, met them at conferences and so on back in the 1920s. And after a while, they must have pulled some strings and we were allowed to go to the United Kingdom as refugees.'

'That must have been such a relief,' Lena said gently.

'Yes, though we were put in an internment camp first, on the Isle of Man.'

'Oh my goodness, Eli, as if you all had not been through enough.' Her heart broke for little Eli, a little child not knowing what was going to become of him.

'*Mutti* and I were separated from Saul, and I cried and cried. The last time some strange people took someone away, it was my papa, and I was scared they'd kill Saul. I remember clinging to my mother. I was so tired then, so thin and frightened of everyone and everything. I started wetting the bed. I wouldn't let my mother out of my sight. I had nightmares.'

She pressed his hand. 'Did the people running the camp treat you badly?'

'No, they realised we were no danger even though we were Germans, so it was all right. It was run by civilians, and they took care of us. We could go shopping, or borrow books. There were other children to play with, English classes, that sort of thing. Saul insisted we learn to speak English without accents – he said it was important not to sound remotely German in case people suspected us of being spies after we were released. My mother could never shake hers completely, but I did.'

'And then when you were let out?'

'Saul got a job at the hospital in Cardiff, some more connections of my grandfather, and we all cramped into a tiny flat. That's when we shared with Doc, but I don't remember much from that time. Saul told me Doc had rented the flat, but he had got to know Saul in the hospital and offered that he and we share it. We had nothing, so we lived on his charity until we got on our feet. *Mutti* got a job in a clothes shop, and I went to school and worked hard on listening to my friends so I'd have a real Welsh accent. Nothing about Germany remained in me.

'Then things got better. We had a bit more money, I suppose. *Mutti* met Charlie, and they got married, and life became a version of normal. Except everyone else was gone.'

'And when I told you Klaus had found someone... Oh, Eli, I'm so stupid. I can't believe I got your hopes up for nothing.'

He took her hand across the table and looked at her, his eyes shining in the moonlight. 'Lena, I have you, I have the children, I have so much to live for. I have my mother still, my uncle, Charlie and my little brothers and sisters. And maybe one day – who knows? Maybe Klaus or someone will find someone else who belongs to my family, or they'll just turn up out of the blue. But even if that doesn't happen, I am content with the family I have. I will never forget, I will never forgive, but with you I am happy, because you are my light.'

* * *

LENA TELEPHONED the farm from the hotel reception the following morning to ensure all was well, and Maria answered. She told them Jack and Skipper had taken Emmet and Sarah to feed the chickens, that she was in the kitchen with the twins and Pádraig and that Katie had gone home to her family for a day or two. 'Her granny got sick, and she had to go and mind her until her other sister could come.'

Maria sounded bright and chatty. Lena hoped she was just happy in an ordinary way and not beginning another bout of mania. It was worrying about Katie being called away. She wondered if she should ring Klaus and ask him to take a trip up to the farm, although that seemed excessive if there was nothing too wrong. 'That's great, Mam... Are you feeling well?'

'Very, very well. I cleaned out the attic yesterday, and I'm going to get back painting again. I've been painting with the children. I got an art book from the library, and I thought we might make a little studio up there. I've asked Skipper to take all the old stuff that was there to the dump.'

Lena's heart sank. This was how it started. Her mother would be hugely enthusiastic for a task, go into it like a dervish, but after the manic energy burst was the inevitable crash. It would take a week or two, perhaps longer, but it would come. The farmhouse was a shrine to her mother's notions. Maria was very creative, but her creativity was linked so closely to her mood, and once it was ignited, it started on a course from which there was no returning until another stay in St Catherine's ended it...for a while.

When he was alive, poor Doc – and Eli after him – had tried everything, every drug, every therapy, every approach, but nothing really worked. Lena's mother couldn't help her illness, but it was so tiring.

'I hope they're behaving themselves, Maria,' Eli called. Lena held the receiver out so he could hear what her mother said.

'They are such lovely children. I love them. Sarah is so like Paudie too. He would have adored them, wouldn't he, Lena?'

'He would have, Mam, no doubt about it.' Lena felt a pang. She was glad her mother had never stopped talking about Daddy. It was the good side of her obsessiveness, better than her constant searching for her brother, Ted. Although Klaus had been wonderful with that by letting Maria talk to him endlessly and helping her write letters to the authorities.

'Emmet found Paudie's hat yesterday – it was in a bag upstairs – and he was playing with it, dressing up, you know.'

Lena got goose bumps. There was an occasion years ago when Jack wore Dad's watch and Maria went so mad and said some horrible things to Jack about him never being as good as his father was. It hurt Lena to even think about it. Maria had to go into St Catherine's then, and she had stayed for months.

'I'm sure he didn't know who it belonged to, Mam –' she began.

'Ah sure, of course not. Paudie would love Emmet to be playing with his things, and sure what harm was he doing?'

'All right, but draw the line if you want to.' Lena smiled and relaxed. Clearly this time it wasn't a problem. It sounded like her mother was doing just fine; Lena didn't need to phone Klaus. And anyway, she and Eli would be home tomorrow.

'And are you two all right?' her mother asked. 'Are you in Dublin?'

Lena caught Eli's gaze. He gave her a nod.

'I got the train up and Eli followed me. We'll be back tomorrow, though, around midday.' She didn't lie exactly, but her mother would be so agitated and distressed if she knew where they were and what they had been doing.

'No rush coming home, love. They're good as gold. We'll see you both soon then. I have to go – we've got company for Sunday dinner...' The line began to crackle.

'Who's that, Mam?'

The crackling was getting worse, and all Lena could hear was her mother saying faintly, 'Bye, love, bye, lo –' And the phone cut off.

'I feel terrible, but she wouldn't understand,' Lena said as they left the hotel to find somewhere nice for breakfast. 'She's heading for another crash. The clearing out of the attic is a frequent indicator. I can't tell you how many times she's done that before. I'm just hoping she stays stable till we get back.'

It was such a relief to speak openly about her mother's mental health. Eli was a doctor, but he also was a loving son-in-law and knew that Maria never meant to hurt anyone. In fact, the person most frequently hurt by her disordered mood was herself.

'Yes, well, this is what it is unfortunately. I wish there was something I could prescribe, but you know yourself how many things Doc and then I have tried. God love her, the poor woman. But now, whatever about Maria, the children are safe because the twins and Jack and Skipper are around, so don't worry.' Eli took her hand as they strolled along beside the park.

After breakfast, maybe a buttery croissant and a coffee, they would pack, then catch the train back to Paris and a flight that night to Dublin, then the morning train to Cork. It was a rushed schedule, but they were so looking forwards to being reunited with their children, and Lena was now especially anxious to be home.

CHAPTER 21

$\mathcal{M}$alachy parked his two-seater sports car at the gates of the Kilteegan Bridge graveyard, then reached into the narrow space behind for the two climbing rose bushes and the trowel he had bought from Blackie and Emily's new store in Bandon.

Emily had been in the shop when he came in. It had only just opened, and she was unpacking a case of kitchenware. She'd greeted him with a startled look that she tried to turn into a smile. She only really relaxed when he told her he was on his way back to America the following day. Then Blackie appeared and chatted happily about the business; he clearly knew nothing about all the drama with Phillippe Decker.

At Hannah's graveside, Malachy knelt on the marble surround, and with the trowel, he dug the roses into the grassy earth that covered her. They would climb and intertwine as they grew. They'd hide August Berger's name behind their thorny stems and flower around his mother's name.

'I hope you can hear me, Mam. I hope you can forgive me for thinking you didn't love me enough to stay and for believing my father's lies...' His voice cracked. 'Oh, Mam, he made me think badly of you just like he made me think badly of Lena. I'm so sorry.'

As he knelt by her grave, a southerly wind whispered through the chestnut tree in the corner of the graveyard, where Paudie and Doc lay side by side. And after a while, a butterfly settled on the pink rose and swayed with it in the warm breeze, then glided to the white rose, then back again to the pink, where it perched with its wings spread out in the sun. It was a peacock butterfly. He remembered his mother pointing them out to him whenever she saw one. She loved butterflies.

* * *

As he drove past the turn to Kilteegan House, and then the field where Paudie O'Sullivan had been murdered, he felt he was passing through a cloud of darkness, but then the road went over the hill and the view opened up to the sea. The O'Sullivans' small white farmstead shone below him in the sun, and the dark mist lifted.

Soon he was going to see his son, play with him, touch his hair, listen to him chatter. The rest of his day would be about life, not death.

When they were teenagers in love, he'd always parked at the far end of the lane and waited for Lena to come to him, because she said she was afraid of what her mother would say if she saw them together. But Maria didn't seem to mind him these days; he thought she must be much better. So he drove up the lane and in through the open gate into the farmyard, where an old horse cart sat with its shafts resting on the ground.

Two young girls were out in the yard, but neither of them paid him the slightest heed. One was suckling a lamb from a bottle; the other was holding a stocky toddler by the hand, helping him feed a carrot to an old horse through the wooden bars of the fence. 'Like this, Pádraig,' she was saying in a bossy voice. 'Keep your hand flat so Susie doesn't bite your fingers.'

Malachy supposed they were Molly and May, Lena's twin sisters, and he recognised the toddler from the photos as Lena's youngest boy.

In the doorway of the farmhouse stood a much younger girl, who looked astonishingly like Lena. She stared at him with her dark head to one side, and as he got nearer, she said, 'Are you my mammy's friend? Nana said to watch for you. The twins are always busy doing stuff, but I'm good at standing still and watching.'

'Yes, I'm Malachy.' He smiled. 'Are you Sarah?'

'Yes, I am.' She called over her shoulder, 'Nana, Mammy's friend is here!'

Maria O'Sullivan came flying to the door in excitement, her long pale hair messy, her face flushed from the heat of the range and with gravy splashed on her apron. 'I'm so happy you could come! It's so exciting. I told Jack and Skipper there was an American guest, but I didn't say who, and Skipper can't wait to meet you. He's like an adopted son to me.'

'Jack doesn't know it's me?' He felt a twinge of alarm. *This might be awkward.*

'No, it's a surprise for him. Come in, come in.' She chattered away. 'They'll be here in a minute – ah, there they are, my lovely boys.'

A small red tractor was plodding through the gate, and when it stopped in the yard, Jack and the cowboy-looking fellow from the photographs jumped down and strode towards the house. Jack had his hand up, shielding his eyes from the sun, but Skipper didn't need to shield his eyes; he was wearing a cowboy hat, the brim pulled low.

'We're starving, Mama,' the cowboy announced in a strong Montana accent before shoving out his hand to Malachy. 'You must be our surprise visitor from the States. I thought I was the only one. I'm Skipper.'

Malachy tried not to wince as Skipper nearly crushed his fingers. 'Well, I'm over from America – I live there now – but I'm not really American, I'm afraid. I'm from Kilteegan Bridge.'

'That explains it. Thought I knew your face, or someone who looks very like you. You got family in the village?'

'No, he doesn't have family. Jack, look at him, you know who this is.' Maria beamed. 'It's Malachy! He was a friend of Lena's long ago – I think he was anyway. You two boys must know each other from childhood.'

'Malachy Berger.' Jack stared at him in shock; Jack had one of those transparent faces that showed what he was thinking. 'Oh, I –'

'We went to primary school together, Mrs O'Sullivan,' said Malachy smoothly, keeping his own face expressionless. He was used to hiding his feelings because he had to do business with some less-than-scrupulous people in the States. 'Though Jack was two years below me, so we didn't get to know each other that well.' Inside, he felt shaken. It was obvious Jack knew something about him, and that it wasn't good. Lena must have told her brother that he'd betrayed her. Had she also told him about Emmet? And Emmet's murdering grandfather? His palms sweated.

Jack stopped staring at him and walked past his mother into the house, followed by Skipper and Lena's little daughter, Sarah. Maria shouted for the twins, who came slowly, complaining they had things left to do, and for Pádraig, who came at a hungry run, shouting, 'Nana, we feeded Susie!'

Maria swept the chunky little boy up into her arms. 'Well done, Pádraig. Now come and sit in your high chair that Skipper made for you. Emmet and Nellie are already inside. Come along, Malachy, you've to tell us all about America. Skipper is only dying to hear whether Bobby Kennedy is going to be the next president.'

Malachy took a deep breath and stepped into the stone kitchen. For a moment, he had to wait for his eyes to adjust after the bright sunlight of the yard. And then he saw him, the red-haired, green-eyed boy, sitting next to the girl he knew from her photograph to be Emily's daughter, Nellie. The young cousins had their heads together, turning the pages of the art book from the library, Nellie admiring the pictures and Emmet reading the difficult prose aloud to her.

'Rem-brand-T was arg-hab-lee the finest painter of the Ba...roke period – that means poor, Nellie – and his vast hist...hist...pictures and stuff – it *does* say that, Nellie – open up the world of the... Oh, it's you again. Have you got your car?' The boy was looking boldly at Malachy across the table. 'Can I drive it?'

Malachy laughed, and his heart gave a throb of joy. 'Well, not drive it, but I could take you for a drive maybe.'

'I want to come too,' declared Nellie, but Emmet glanced at her scornfully.

'Don't be silly, Nellie. An Alpine A110 has only two seats, and if this man... Excuse me, what's your name, mister?'

'Malachy.' He smiled.

'If Malachy has to drive, then I will have to be the only passenger.'

'Oh.' Nellie looked crestfallen.

'It doesn't matter either way,' said Jack firmly as he sat down next to his nephew. 'You won't be troubling Mr Berger to bring you anywhere. He's here for his dinner, not to amuse little boys.'

'Really, I'd love to do it.' Malachy grinned.

'Uncle Jack, Malachy wants to –'

'Not going to happen, kiddo.' Jack's words were addressed to Emmet, but it was Malachy he was looking at, and his open face said very clearly, *You're not taking him anywhere, so forget it.*

So he does know I'm Emmet's father, thought Malachy, still keeping his own face blank. He turned to Maria. 'Can I help you in any way, Mrs O'Sullivan?'

'Not a bit of it. Sit down here at the head of the table – that's where Paudie used to sit, he's dead now – and tell Skipper about Bobby Kennedy while I finish the gravy for the lamb. Molly, get the roast potatoes out of the range – be careful not to burn yourself. Strain the peas and carrots, May. The colander is in the sink.'

While Maria served up the dinner, helped by her daughters, Malachy obediently turned to Skipper and started a long conversation about the Kennedys, that famous Irish American political dynasty that had already been twice touched by the hand of doom. They talked about how, when Joseph Kennedy was killed in action, it had been tough on John Kennedy to take on his dead brother's mantle, but he had risen to the challenge and won the presidency. And now JFK was dead and the torch had passed to Bobby. If anything happened to Bobby, which God forbid, then Teddy was the next in line, and he seemed like a smart lad...

Jack carved the leg of lamb, and Maria heaped everyone's plates with rich meat, carrots and peas with knobs of bright-yellow butter, crisp roast potatoes done in goose fat and steaming gravy made from the juices of the meat. Soon the adults and children were tucking in. Malachy ate sparingly even though the food was delicious. His stomach was in a knot because Emmet kept staring straight at him with his bright-green eyes.

'Emmet, stop ogling our visitor and eat,' said Maria cheerfully. 'He's not got two heads, you know. Molly and May, why don't you sing our visitor a song?'

'Because we're eating, Mammy,' chorused the twins in patient voices, clearly used to dealing with their mother's odd flights of fancy.

'Oh yes, I forgot.' Maria burst into shrill giggles, gravy spurting from her lips. 'Oh dear, look at me, I'm a fountain, a gravy fountain...'

'Nana fountain!' roared Pádraig in delight, clapping his chubby pink hands.

'Mam.' Jack leaned over, wiping her mouth tenderly with a napkin. 'We have a visitor.'

She pushed his hand away, still giggling. 'Oh, Malachy doesn't mind. Malachy is fun. Do you know I showed him around the house yesterday? He thought it was lovely, and he thought my pictures of tigers and things on the playroom walls were wonderful. And he was very complimentary about Lena's garden, weren't you, Malachy?'

Everyone went quiet, apart from Pádraig, who was spitting gravy and saying he was a fountain. Malachy kept his head down over his food.

A few seconds later, Jack said, 'Really, Mam? You showed Malachy around Lena's house when she wasn't there?'

Maria snorted impatiently. 'Oh, don't fuss, Jack. It was Malachy's house not so long ago, and I knew he'd be interested to see around.'

'It's my house, actually,' interrupted Emmet, with another look at Malachy.

Malachy's heart turned over.

'Emmet, it's your family's house.' Maria was laughing again, busy spooning peas into Pádraig's open mouth. 'Say "peas please", Pádraig.'

'Peas,' spluttered Pádraig. 'Please peas please.'

'But it's true, Nana,' said Emmet more loudly, raising his voice over his baby brother's. 'I heard Malachy saying to Daddy about it. It's my house – he gave it to me. Didn't you, Malachy?'

'Mam is right Emmet. It's your whole family's house now. What's for dessert, I wonder?' said Jack lightly, but his eyes were fixed on Malachy's across the table. *Do the right thing by Lena*, said his open face.

'I...I... Well...' Malachy knew he should be telling Emmet he'd got it wrong about the house, but he just couldn't seem to get the words out. The trouble was, he didn't want to deny the truth; he felt this urge to show his son how much he cared about him.

Skipper was staring from Emmet to Malachy now, his eyes widening as if something had just become very obvious.

Jack shot him a warning glance.

Skipper pulled himself together with a huge smile. 'What's for dessert, Mama?'

'Apple pie and cream.' Maria beamed, jumping up and starting to clear the plates.

'You look like Malachy, Emmet. You both have the same hair and the same eyes,' piped up Nellie. 'It's the same as I look like Mammy. And Nanny too. And Sarah looks just like Aunty Lena, because Aunty Lena is her mammy.'

'And me and May look like you, Nellie,' agreed Molly, 'because we all look like *my* mammy. But why does Emmet look like Malachy? Is he his uncle or something?'

Emmet looked closely at Malachy, his green eyes roaming over his face. 'Are you my uncle?'

'I...' He longed to tell him. But he couldn't, not without Lena's permission.

The boy frowned and shook his head. 'But you can't be my uncle because you're not Mammy's brother, or Daddy's brother. I don't understand.'

'You've got a great-uncle called Ted,' said Maria sadly as she took

Emmet's plate from in front of him. 'He went away a long time ago. We might not recognise him when he comes back.'

'Uncle Ted doesn't look anything like me, Nana – I've seen his photo. Nobody looks like me in this family. Sarah looks like Mammy, and Pádraig looks like Daddy, but I don't look like anyone. Mrs Shanahan told Mr Shanahan I'm so different to Sarah and Pádraig, but when she saw me listening, she said she was joking.' The boy's eyes widened.

'Stop this. Stop this now,' said Jack firmly. 'Emmet, Nellie, go out and play.'

'I look like Malachy, and he gave me a house, I know he did. I heard him and Daddy arguing about it and –'

'Now look…' said Jack warningly.

'I don't want to go either,' said Nellie stubbornly. 'I want apple pie and cream.'

'The apple pie!' Maria looked startled. She'd been staring off into space, but now she turned to the counter where the crusty pie sat cooling on a blue-striped plate, with a jug of cream beside it, and started cutting the tart into big thick slices.

'Malachy, I do own our house, don't I?' Emmet began again.

'Emmet, go outside,' growled Jack. 'Molly, May, take your cousins to feed the lambs.'

'We've fed the lambs,' said the twins unhelpfully, reluctant to leave the excitement.

With a furious snort, Jack leapt to his feet and marched all of the children outside, the twins protesting, Sarah and Nellie fascinated, Pádraig running – he loved the lambs – and Emmet looking mutinous.

'No wait, there's apple pie and cream! I made it specially.' Maria was standing with the plate in her hands, looking confused and upset.

'It's all right, Mam,' said Jack, coming back to her. 'We'll eat it later.'

'No, they must have it now. I said we were having it now.' Maria's eyes brimmed with tears, and her voice rose querulously.

'Mam, calm down,' said Jack quietly.

'Calm down?' she started at Jack as if she had never seen him before.

'Please, Mam, you don't want to get upset. Lena and Eli are home tomorrow. Emily will be here then as well. Just hang on till tomorrow.'

'I want the children to sit down and eat their pie.'

Skipper stood up, and Malachy could see he was torn. He clearly wondered if he should go out to the children or stay here and help Jack with his mother.

'I hate you!' In a sudden fit of blinding fury, Maria raised the plate and smashed it to the floor, blue and white striped china and pieces of pie flying everywhere. 'You're mean and rude, and you lie to me all the time. Paudie would never lie to me, Ted would never lie to me...'

Malachy pushed back his chair, feeling sick. 'I'm very sorry if I've upset things, Jack. I didn't mean to. Mrs O'Sullivan, that was a delicious meal, but I have to go now.'

'You haven't had any pie!' screamed Maria, reaching to grab his arm.

'I couldn't eat another thing, and I have a boat to catch,' he said, trying to free his sleeve from her grip.

'Mam, let him go,' begged Jack, pulling her back. 'The pie's broken now anyway.'

'But me and Jack will clear it up, Mama,' promised Skipper, peeling her fingers from Malachy's shirt. 'Don't you worry about a thing.'

As Malachy hurried to the door, Maria howled after him at the top of her lungs. 'Get out so, you're no better than your mother! She hated me. I could see her watching me at Mass. She was a witch with her red hair, and she wanted my Paudie...' She was hysterical now.

He escaped into the yard, pulling the door closed on her outburst. He could hear Jack and Skipper trying to soothe her. He was literally shaking. He knew Lena's mother suffered from her nerves a bit, but he'd had no idea how bad it was. Behind in the house came the sound of more screaming. What on earth was Lena thinking, leaving her children in the care of a madwoman? He could see their small figures heading across the fields in the distance; one of the twins had Sarah by the hand, and the other was carrying Pádraig on her hip. Nellie was there too, but he couldn't see Emmet – he must have gone on ahead. For a split second he thought he should find him, try to explain. He was full of remorse that the meeting went as it did; the poor boy was so confused.

No. He'd caused enough trouble for one day just by being in the same room as his son. The best thing was to go back to America and only return when the court case about the house was ready to go before a judge. He'd already left Hannah's last letter with Devlin, and the county solicitor said it was circumstantial evidence of murder. While he was horrified, he was also pleased Malachy had found the letter, because it made the case against Phillippe Decker so much stronger. As for Emmet's questions about why he had the house, Malachy would have to talk to Lena on the phone and decide with her when and how to answer them.

Feeling stronger and better in himself, he crossed the yard to the Alpine A110 and jumped into the front seat. Jack's red tractor was almost blocking the gate, but the sports car was small and he managed to squeeze past, just missing knocking off a wing mirror. The car bumped down the rutted lane and out onto the road. When he reached the turn to Kilteegan House, on impulse he swung the wheel and drove in through the open gates, past the little yellow stone gate lodge, right up to the front door. This place was undoubtedly beautiful, but it had caused, and continued to cause, so much pain. Maybe he was wrong to give it to Emmet; maybe he should have left Lena and her family alone. Today had been so hard, so confusing. He needed to go, get back to San Francisco, where life made sense and ghosts and secrets didn't lurk in every corner. He got out and stood, gazing around him. In the orchard, bees buzzed around the swelling apples, and nearby a thrush battered a snail on a stone. Sheep grazed in the surrounding fields.

Such a beautiful spot. Such a dark history.

He remembered every word of his mother's letter. Poor terrified Hannah. What a dreadful way to die. And how dare Phillippe Decker imagine he had a right to profit from her murder? Malachy would make sure he didn't, whatever happened. This wasn't just about Emmet now, or Lena. It was about justice for his mother. Whatever it took, he'd fight that man to the bitter end.

He strode back to the car and threw open the driver's door. Emmet looked up at him from the passenger seat with an uncertain smile.

'Emmet?' Malachy grabbed the doorframe; he felt like he was seeing things. 'How...?'

'I squeezed into that space behind the seats,' said the boy, pointing backwards with his thumb.

'But why?'

'I wanted to be with you.'

'Oh, Emmet...' This was out of control, not what he'd wanted.

'Are you my real daddy?' The boy's green eyes gazed at him with a deep intensity, and Malachy could see he was wise beyond his years. So much of him reminded Malachy of himself as a boy.

He pulled himself together, climbed back into the Alpine and sat facing the anxious child, his arm resting on the steering wheel. He sighed. 'I don't know what to say. I'm sorry. This isn't how I wanted things to happen. Your mother should be here with you to have this conversation.'

'Are you?'

He couldn't lie, not any more. 'I am.'

'Why did you leave me when I was a baby? Didn't you like me?' The small voice was full of hurt, and Malachy longed to take him in his arms. He contented himself with touching his son's shoulder.

'Believe me, I've liked you ever since I first laid eyes on you.'

'So why did you leave?'

'Emmet, I didn't know about you.'

'But how could you not know about me?' The boy looked upset. 'When Mammy had Pádraig, her tummy got bigger and bigger. Sarah thinks babies are left under cabbages, but Daddy told me Pádraig grew inside Mammy's tummy, and Daddy's a doctor so I think I believe him. I don't think he was joking like he does sometimes, like about eating gazelles.'

Malachy took a deep breath to steady himself. He hated this, but he didn't want Emmet to think he'd abandoned him. He'd abandoned Emmet's mother, but not his son. 'This is very hard for me to tell you, Emmet, but someone told me a lie about your mammy and I left her before I knew you existed.'

The boy's eyes widened. 'You believed a lie about Mammy? What was it?'

'I can't tell you.'

'Why not? Was it very bad? Why did someone say a bad thing about my mammy?'

Malachy thought of a way to put it, suitable for a child. 'They told me your mother didn't love me, and I believed them.'

'Why?' Emmet's right eye leaked a single tear. 'I wouldn't believe anyone if they told me my mammy didn't love me.'

'Then you're a lot more clever than I ever was,' said Malachy miserably. 'But I was stupid and weak. And so I didn't find out about you for a long time, and when I did, Eli was already your daddy.'

'But you like me now?' It was heart-breaking, the way his son kept needing this reassurance from him.

'Of course I do. I care for you a great deal.'

Emmet thought about his answer, then nodded. 'Actually, I think you do, because you gave me your house.'

'Yes, I did, and not only because I care about you but because it was my mother's house before, and her mother's house before that, and she would have wanted you to have it.'

'Because I'm your son.'

Malachy took another deep breath. 'Yes.'

Emmet sat in silence for a while, then said kindly, 'I can't call you "Daddy" because I call my daddy that. Will I call you Malachy? Or I could call you "Father" if you wanted.'

'Malachy is fine,' said Malachy faintly.

He settled back in his seat, his hands on the leather steering wheel, but he didn't start the engine. What on earth was he going to do with this child? He couldn't bring him to the farm with all that chaos going on. Jack and Skipper were busy trying to deal with Maria, and the place was dangerous, just like Kilteegan House had become after his insane, raving father came home from the war.

'We can go inside – I can get in the back way – and we can wait for Mammy and Daddy to come home. They'll know what to do?' asked Emmet hopefully.

Malachy started the car; he'd made his decision. 'They won't be back until tomorrow. How about I take you to Emily and Blackie's house?'

'They're in Bandon and won't be back until tomorrow – that's why Nellie is with us. Where are you staying tonight?'

'In a hotel in Cork, but I can't bring you there.'

'Why not?'

'Because everyone will be frightened you've run away or had an accident or something.'

'No they won't. Uncle Jack thinks I'm gone to the Maddens with the others.'

'But Jack will ring Mrs. Madden surely. We have to tell her and Bill what's happening at least.' The loose arrangements of childcare in this family were less than ideal.

'No, don't. She'll make a fuss and not let me go with you. Anyway, Uncle Jack won't call. He'll be too busy with Nana, and the Maddens don't have a phone.'

'But tomorrow…' He felt himself wavering.

'Jack won't expect us back until the afternoon – that's the way it always happens – and Mammy and Daddy will be home by then. All you have to do is write them a note and put it in the postbox by the door.'

Malachy knew he shouldn't be weak enough to let a little boy boss him around. But the trouble was he *wanted* to believe that no one in Kilteegan Bridge would miss Emmet. He couldn't imagine anything more satisfying than bringing his son to Cork with him, buying him fancy food, maybe some fashionable clothes, something useful for his pony, an armful of books.

Not only that, but the idea of Emmet having to go back to the O'Sullivan farm the next day, even if Maria was calmed down with

225

medication or whatever, was unthinkable. The boy had to be cared for properly until his mother came home.

'Do you want me to write the letter?' asked Emmet with a touch of impatience.

Malachy's mouth twitched with amusement. 'No, I think I'll do that myself.'

'I never stayed in a hotel before. Is it nice?'

'Yes, very nice.' Malachy smiled.

And while Malachy penned a long note on a page from his diary, explaining things as best he could and giving the name and address of the hotel, Emmet leaned back in his seat with his little foot resting on his thigh and his slim elbow on the open window, looking very pleased with himself.

CHAPTER 22

'*I* was thinking,' Eli said as the train chugged through the French countryside, 'of converting that little gate lodge to a surgery, so I'm not so far away from you all when I'm working.'

'Oh, Eli, that would be marvellous. I always hoped you would, but a part of me knew you were only in the house under sufferance, so I never suggested it.'

They were sitting in the dining car, having just eaten some gorgeous lobster thermidor. Eli's fish hatred didn't stretch to lobster, and he was thrilled by how the French prepared it, in a rich sauce of egg yolks and brandy and mustard, stuffed back into the shell and served with an oven-browned crust of Gruyère. A half-bottle of delicious cold white wine sat between them.

Eli said apologetically, 'You knew that because I behaved like that, and for it, I'm so sorry, Lena.'

'Don't be sorry. I should have realised you were insecure about Malachy. You do know for sure now that this was never about him or anything like that?'

'I do. Finally I've got it through my thick skull.'

'We have to talk to him about Phillippe Decker, though, and about poor Hannah's murder, and we should warn him that part of his inheritance is the Loeb wine. The money he got from his father was Berger money, but based on what we know now about them, how closely they were connected to the upper ranks of the Nazi party, it's likely that the fortune is dirty money. And then there's the stolen Loeb fortune too.'

'Do you think it's best he knows? They're very heavy secrets to carry.'

'I don't know. Our experience with secrets and lies has been the cause of such division. Actually, lies are what divide us, never truth. Even people who are diametrically opposed can be in harmony if they tell each other the truth. But then the Bergers and Decker and all of it is behind us now – maybe it's best just to let it lie. It's not like we'll ever see Malachy again. He lives in America. And now that the claim on the house is no more...'

'Yes, and aren't some secrets better not told, like you mentioned Anthea said to you when she gave you the Librium?'

'I've been thinking about that, and I think mostly they're better out. Like I think now it was wrong of me and Emily not to tell Jack about our father's murder. Maybe I should even tell Mam. I think maybe part of Mam's madness is half knowing things that everyone around her keeps on telling her aren't true. It's like that film *Gaslight* with Ingrid Bergman. It's enough to confuse anybody.'

'And now that Emmet's definitely going to inherit the house, I suppose we'll have to tell him at some stage about Malachy.' Eli sighed.

Lena pressed her husband's hand. 'I agree. We should tell him the truth, though not yet. He's a very clever little lad – I think he'd grasp it if we told him gently in a way he understood. But I don't want to tell him he's got to keep a secret – we know how bad that is for people – and I'm not sure either of us is ready for the outrage of Kilteegan Bridge.'

'Anyway, I'm sure the solicitor will let Malachy know the claim on the house is gone.'

Lena sighed with relief. 'I should probably speak to him myself, but I'm just as happy not to. Let's let the dust settle and get back to our lovely life, and then we'll open that can of worms if we have to.' She toasted him with her wine glass, and he raised his in return.

'To us, the undefeatable team.' He smiled.

'To us,' she replied. 'I love you, Eli. I always have and I always will.'

'I love you too.'

The journey back through the French countryside, now that she could enjoy the scenery with her husband beside her, was delightful. As the vast vineyards of the Champagne region slid by the window, they chatted on over rich black coffee, making plans for the new surgery.

'We can ask Blackie's advice on who to ask to do it,' suggested Lena. 'He knows every builder for miles.'

'Good idea. And don't forget, we have to go to Cardiff for Charlie's birthday next month. My parents and Uncle Saul and Aunt Ann would love to see us, and it would make a great holiday for them. I'll get a locum, and we'll stay for a couple of weeks?'

'Though the idea of us taking a holiday might have to be explained to Jack.' Lena laughed. 'That boy never takes a single day off the farm.'

'I know. I've never met anyone more hard-working, but he seems to thrive on it.'

'He's ridiculous. What's more amazing is why Skipper puts up with it. I mean, Jack pays him well, I'm sure, and they're friends, I know, but I could never see what was in it for Skipper to stop him going back to Montana.'

Eli gazed at her, an eyebrow raised.

'What?' she asked in surprise.

'Lena, talking of secrets, do you really think Jack and Skipper are just friends?'

Lena's brow furrowed. 'What else would they be? Do you mean you think Skipper has invested in the business? I don't think Jack would sell away Daddy's farm.'

Eli was clearly deliberating on whether to say something.

'What, Eli?' she asked impatiently.

He rubbed his chin. 'I think Jack and Skipper might be more than just friends, or Jack more than just his boss. I think they're together, you know?'

'What are you going on about, together? Of course they're together. They're never apart. You can't see one without the other tagging along...' Suddenly what her husband meant dawned on Lena. 'No, what? Jack and Skipper? No, I mean...no, surely not...' She was so shocked and horrified, she had no words. Was her darling little brother one of those men? The kind that nobody ever dared speak about? She remembered Doc treating a pair of old bachelor farmers who lived together out towards Dunmanway. He'd said when he went out on a house call that he realised there was only one bed. But apart from them, and famous people like Oscar Wilde or Andy Warhol, she'd never even heard of it. Could Jack and Skipper be up to... Well, she didn't know what exactly. 'You can't mean...?'

'I think so. And, Lena, if they are, does it matter to you?' Eli asked gently.

'Oh my goodness...' She loved her brother, and she loved Skipper too, but this was a bolt from the blue. 'Eli, of course it matters. For a start, it's illegal, so it's dangerous. And, well...it's not right. The Church says and everyone says –'

'Well, best that nobody knows then, isn't it?' he pointed out reasonably. 'And then they can't say.'

She was stunned. 'And it doesn't bother you? As a man?'

Eli chuckled, unperturbed. 'Why would it? They have no interest in me that way, nor me in them, but live and let live, I say. It's love, Lena, just the same as it is for us, and why shouldn't they be happy together if it's what they want?'

Lena wasn't sure. Everything she'd been taught, which wasn't much, was that it was very, very bad to be homosexual. 'And do you think they...' She coloured at the thought of her brother and Skipper being intimate, the way she was with Eli. 'I can't picture it.'

'Then don't. You don't think about Emily and Blackie together like that, do you? Or Mrs Buckley and old Johnny?'

'No, of course I don't,' Lena answered hotly.

'Well then, what Jack and Skipper get up to when they're alone and hurting nobody is not anyone's business, any more than what happens between us is anybody's business.'

'I suppose so,' she said slowly, 'but I'm not going to say I'm not shocked. Are you sure?'

'Fairly sure,' he said, and she knew he was more sure than that.

'And should I say anything to him?' she asked.

Eli shrugged. 'Let him bring it up if he wants to, but I suppose there are subtle ways you could let him know you wouldn't fall down in a heap or go screaming for Father Doyle. It might be nice for them to know we didn't mind.'

'Do other people know, do you think?'

'Some people might have their suspicions, I suppose, but I haven't heard anything.'

She shook her head, bewildered. 'My goodness, this has been some few days, hasn't it?'

'It certainly has, my love.' And he leaned across the table to kiss her, ignoring a matronly woman in the seat across the aisle who clearly disapproved of such public displays of affection.

* * *

THE TRAIN PULLED into the Gare de l'Est, and she thought of the last time she was there, just a few days ago, but it felt like a lifetime. She'd been terrified and overwhelmed and miserable after the big fight with Eli, and here she was now, strutting along the concourse in a very chic outfit she'd bought on a whim that morning. She wore a cream pillbox hat and a cream pegged dress complete with little capped sleeves. She wore her light-blue pea coat over the dress and strappy light-blue sandals. She felt quite glamorous and was glad she'd made the effort. Paris was the most fashionable city on the planet after all.

The flight back was not on a DC-3, much to her relief. It was on a Fokker F27 Friendship aeroplane, which was much more commodious and comfortable. She was relieved not to have to face Captain Andrew Ahearne either, though his flirting had proved useful, she had to admit.

She held Eli's hand as the flight, at its maximum capacity of forty passengers, took off; it was comforting to have him by her side. The events of the previous days had taken their toll, and she was soon asleep, only waking with a jolt as the plane touched down at the Dublin airport.

Eli collected their bags and called a taxi, and much to her relief, they made the early train just in time. It would be a long journey home – they would be back at the house by midday at the earliest – but with every mile travelled, they were nearer to the children, so she felt happy and excited the whole way.

CHAPTER 23

ena, Emmet is with me...

Lena stared in disbelief at Malachy's handwriting.

The taxi had dropped her and Eli to Kilteegan House, as it was easier to drop their bags first and then walk up to the farm afterwards. While she was waiting for Eli to unlock the door, she had checked the postbox and found several letters, two rolled-up medical journals and a folded sheet of paper with her name on it.

Lena, Emmet is with me. He knows he's my son, and he knows about the house. I didn't tell him – he overheard something...

'Lena, is something the matter?' Her husband's voice seemed to come from far away. Speechless, she shook her head and kept on reading.

Anyway, he hid in my car, and when I found him, he begged me to take him away from the farm. You see, your mother seemed a little hysterical, and Jack and his farm labourer have their hands full minding her. Your other children are safe at the Maddens', but Emmet says he doesn't want to go there, and Emily and Blackie are out of town, and he was so upset. So we will be at the Imperial Hotel in Cork until late tomorrow night, when my passage is booked to America. I hope you don't object to me taking responsibility for our son's well-being in your absence.

Yours sincerely, Malachy

'Eli, we have to go.'

He looked up in surprise from unlocking the door. 'Just let me take the bags upstairs first.'

'There's no time. Get the car keys from the hall table.'

He frowned. 'Are you all right? I thought you wanted to walk up to the farm.'

'Eli, just get the keys and come.'

'Has something happened?' Now he was alarmed. 'Are the children all right?'

'Yes, but please hurry.'

Still looking very worried, he got the keys, closed up the house and unlocked the car passenger door for her. 'Is it your mother?' he asked as he hurried around to the driver's side, jumped in and started the engine. 'Will I drive straight to the farm? Wait, will I go and get my medical bag?'

'No, drive to the Maddens'. Sarah and Pádraig are there, and I want to check on them. And then we have to go on to Cork.'

'But we just came from –'

'I know, Eli, I'm sorry, but Emmet's with Malachy at the Imperial Hotel.' She couldn't bring herself to tell him that their son knew about his parentage and the house; she'd save that for the journey to Cork.

'What!' Her husband was pale with panic as he sped down the drive. 'Oh my God, he's kidnapped our son…'

'He hasn't kidnapped him, Eli. I think Jack must have let Malachy take him. Mam's had another breakdown.' Tears of remorse were choking her throat, making it hard for her to speak. 'Oh, Eli, I'm so sorry, this is all my fault. I knew Mam was turning, even though Jack said not.' She was furious with herself for her own stupidity. 'I should have rung Klaus when I thought of it yesterday. I should have asked him to go to the farm as soon as I knew Katie had been called away.'

Eli ground the gears furiously, saying through gritted teeth, 'It's not your fault. Your brother should have sent Emmet to the Maddens' or to Emily and Blackie's.'

'Blackie and Emily are away, and apparently Emmet didn't want to stay at the Maddens' with the others, so I suppose Malachy offered to mind him.'

'What was that man even doing here, hanging around our son?'

'I really don't know, Eli. I don't know how he got involved in the first place, but he's being totally open about where he and Emmet are. I don't think we need to worry.'

And yet she was desperately worried. Malachy had seen Maria have one of her spectacular breakdowns, and supposing he decided Lena couldn't be trusted to keep Emmet safe, and supposing they caught an earlier boat? She felt ill. She'd been so careless, running off on her adventures out of pride and a big show of independence, when she should have been at home keeping her children safe.

Grim-faced, Eli roared up the potholed driveway towards the Maddens'.

The place was in chaos, Jack running in and out of the outhouses, the twins and Lucy shouting shrilly in the fields for Emmet, Pádraig wandering around the yard calling his brother's name and laughing, clearly thinking it was some sort of game, Sarah standing on a fence scanning the landscape and little Nellie just sitting on the whitewashed step, her face tear-stained. Taking in the scene, Lena felt hot with fury. It was obvious Emmet had only just been missed and no one here knew where he was. Malachy must have taken Emmet without letting anyone know, but that was yesterday. How could he be missing so long and they only just realised?

As the car screeched to a halt, Deirdre came racing over. 'Lena, love, I'm so sorry, so sorry. I had them all here last night, but I was sure Emmet had stayed behind at the farm – May said he didn't leave with them. He doesn't really like coming here, so I wasn't surprised, but your poor mam is after taking a turn and Jack was trying to settle her. And the locum in for Eli wasn't available to come out, so he had her all night, and Skipper had to fetch Doctor Burke from Bandon. But then when Skipper came to get them this morning and he said he didn't have Emmet... Bill's checking the barns...'

Lena jumped out and hugged the distraught woman who'd filled in so much of the absent parenting for the twins over the years. 'It's all right, Deirdre. We know where Emmet is and he's safe.'

'Oh, thank God.' Deirdre nearly collapsed with relief.

'Mammy! Daddy!' Sarah and Pádraig came rushing towards them, and Lena bent down to hug Sarah and assure her that her brother was fine, while Pádraig simply climbed into Eli's open arms and covered his cheeks with sloppy kisses.

'Sarah, will you go and tell poor Nellie that her cousin is found,' Lena said, giving her daughter another kiss, then straightening up. 'Deirdre, I know you do more than enough for us, but will you keep the children until evening? We have to get Emmet from where he is. I'll explain later.'

'I will, of course.' The woman looked mightily relieved that Lena was still prepared to trust her with her offspring at all after this. 'I'll put the kettle on. You'll be wanting a cuppa before you go.'

'No, we're not stopping. I just want a word with Jack. Eli, will you tell the twins and Lucy they can call off their search? And find Bill and tell him too.' She ran off towards the cowsheds where she'd last spotted her brother and found him crawling over a stack of hay bales as if he thought Emmet might have slipped down in between them. 'Jack, come down. He's found.'

'Oh, thanks be to God.' He slithered to the floor, his face a mixture of joy and guilt. 'Where was he?'

'You mean, where is he. Malachy took him to Cork.'

Jack's eyes widened in shock. 'What? You're joking.'

'Jack, what was Malachy Berger doing at our house?'

'Lena, I swear to you, I didn't know he was even in Kilteegan Bridge. Mam said she'd asked someone to Sunday dinner but didn't say who it was. It was out of the blue. I didn't know what was going on, and suddenly it was like everyone saw it...' He stopped, looking embarrassed.

'Saw what, Jack? Tell me the truth. There have already been enough problems caused by the lies we tell each other.'

'Well, how Emmet looked so like Malachy. All the children and Skipper saw it. And then Emmet was asking all these questions, and

I sent everyone out of the kitchen, and Mam was getting upset at me for sending the children away. She lost it then, the usual, you know, throwing things, screaming, the whole lot. But Eli's locum was gone for the day, so Skipper had to go get Dr Burke. He came and gave her a sedative, but it was late, and I just assumed the kids were all at the Maddens'. I'm so sorry, Lena – I should have checked. But it's a bad one with Mam this time, so Skipper and I were up most of the night with her. We're bringing her to St Catherine's tomorrow.'

Lena could only imagine what the situation must have looked liked to Malachy. She didn't blame him for acting like he did, although he'd done it in such a stupid, careless way. And of course she should have warned Jack that Malachy was in town, and that it was because of the house and Phillippe Decker, which meant telling him about their father. It was such a tangled web, and she had to untangle it.

'And there's something else. Mam met Malachy in the village and took him into your house. She shouldn't have, of course, but she was a bit manic by then. I just thought you should know.'

Her heart went out to her lovely brother. Jack was a gentle soul who always tried to do the right thing; she had no reason to be cross with him.

'Jack, I'm so sorry.' She hugged him tightly. 'I've been... Well, there are so many things I have to tell you, and I will. I have to go now – I have to get Emmet back before evening – but after that, we'll sit down, the two of us, and I'll tell you everything. No more secrets, I promise.'

He came with her to the car, and before she climbed in beside Eli, who was waiting impatiently for her, she turned to him. 'You and Skipper are wonderful to Mam, and great uncles to our three. We'd be lost without you, and that's the truth. It was a lucky day for us the day he turned up here.'

Jack dropped his eyes. His open face spoke of his love for his friend, but aloud he said, 'I'll tell him you said that.'

Lena smiled at her gentle brother and gave him another hug. Jack wasn't ready to tell his secret yet, but she felt he would get there in the end. 'Well, I hope he never goes, Jack. I really feel Skipper is part of the family, and we all love him.'

She didn't feel she was saying any more than the simple truth, but her words seemed to make her little brother very happy.

* * *

'I'M SORRY, Eli. I don't know how he found out about Malachy and the house. Apparently he overheard something.'

'You mean Malachy told him,' said Eli bitterly as they raced down the Cork road. 'He wants to take Emmet away from me.'

'No he doesn't, and please don't worry. Emmet knows who his real father is.'

'Yeah, the one with all the millions and the sports cars. What boy wouldn't prefer that to a boring old country doctor?'

Lena swallowed. She was scared about that herself. She was sure Malachy was busy buying her son all sorts of things in Cork, and maybe Eli was right – maybe Emmet would prefer expensive presents to what she and Eli could offer him. What if Emmet decided he wanted to go to America and live with his biological father, who was a millionaire and drove lots of different cars and could stay in a hotel every night of his life if he wanted to?

Aloud she said, 'Eli, Emmet loves us, and Kilteegan Bridge is his home.'

'But San Francisco is a lot more glamorous, and Emmet does think he's a cut above the rest of us, Lena.'

She felt a rush of annoyance. 'I know you think he can be a bit superior, but you know, I think it's because he realises deep down there's something we're not telling him, and he pushes and pushes to find out what it is and why he's different. We were wrong about not telling him, that's all. I think that's why he's been so troublesome at times.'

'Maybe you're right,' said Eli, sounding unconvinced.

'I am right. There are lots of things we've been doing that must have confused him, like me being too protective because of nearly

losing him as a baby, and you and Emily worrying he's getting arrogant, but that's because you remember who his grandfather was while
Emmet doesn't understand anything about that.'

'I know, and we will try to explain the past as best we can to him,
but the most important thing is that Emmet understands he's our son,
that he's Sarah and Pádraig's brother, and we need to get all this
Malachy Berger nonsense out of his head. Where would it end
otherwise?'

'I know, you're right.' She knew it was true; it was just hard. And
besides, she also knew for a fact that Malachy was treating Emmet
right now like he was very special indeed.

It was nearly six when they pulled up outside the Imperial Hotel,
and when she asked for Malachy Berger, the nice receptionist directed
them to the dining room. Lena almost cried with relief when she saw
the two of them sitting at the table in the bay window. She hadn't
realised how somewhere in her heart, she'd been convinced they were
already on the boat to America.

As she and Eli crossed the dining room, Emmet got eagerly to his
feet, but then he glanced anxiously at Malachy and sat down again, as
if torn between them all. Lena's heart turned over and she sensed Eli
stiffen beside her, but she squeezed her husband's hand, smiled at
him and whispered, 'We're just going to act natural. We mustn't make
Emmet feel he's done something wrong. It will be all right, I
promise.'

When they reached the table, Malachy greeted them with his polite
unreadable smile. 'Lena, Eli, you're very welcome. Sit down and join
us – my treat. We haven't ordered yet – we're still choosing between
the *salmon en croûte* and the *coq au vin*. What did you decide on,
Emmet? I'll have *coq au vin* please.' He handed his menu to the waiter.

Clearly not understanding the French words, the boy said some-
what wildly, 'Um, I don't really know...'

'How about we both have fish fingers and chips, Emmet? That's
our favourite, though it won't be as nice as when Mammy makes it,'
Eli said, and the child's face registered relief.

Malachy looked bemused. 'I don't think they do that here?'

'Oh, I'm sure they do, if we ask,' said Eli, and the waiter agreed and wrote it down.

'Lena?' Malachy urged.

Lena wasn't remotely hungry, but she could see the trepidation on Emmet's face.

'I'll have fish fingers and chips too, please.'

'That's one *coq au vin* and three fish fingers and chips, no problem.' The waiter smiled and departed.

'So, Emmet, how are you?' Eli turned to his son with a big smile. 'We've missed you so much, but I'm sure you've been having a lovely time.'

The boy beamed, relaxing now that he realised he wasn't in trouble. 'Oh, I have, Daddy. Malachy bought me lots of books and a purple and gold blanket for Ollie and these clothes and shoes...' He jumped up and did a twirl. He was wearing a very white pressed shirt, a silk waistcoat, narrow trousers and polished shoes with smooth soles, all totally unsuitable for Kilteegan Bridge. 'Don't I look very smart?'

'You look very handsome,' said Eli, suppressing a smile.

'Yes, you do,' Lena agreed, also feeling like laughing.

'And when Ned has his blanket, he's going to be so cosy, and one of the books is *Treasure Island* – Malachy loved that when he was a boy. And I asked him to buy Sarah a doll and Pádraig this big squishy green frog – you know how he loves frogs.'

'Malachy's been very generous,' said Eli a little stiffly, and Emmet picked up on it. He was as quick as Maria for noticing when a person was thinking something different from what they were saying.

'Was it all right to ask, Daddy? Malachy has a lot of money, I think, so it's fine.'

'Of course it was all right to ask,' said Malachy warmly. 'You can always ask me for whatever you want.'

Eli and Lena exchanged a glance; this was exactly what they'd feared. Lena would have to have a quiet firm word with Malachy at some time in the future.

The food arrived, and Emmet was delighted to see his favourite dish in the world – crispy fish fingers, home-cut chips and tomato ketchup. Lena felt a rush of warmth as her husband and her son exchanged a big conspiratorial grin. And she found she had a lot more appetite than she'd previously thought and tucked in too.

Malachy said politely, digging his fork into his *coq au vin*, 'So you were in Dublin for a few days?'

She threw a quick glance at Emmet, but he wasn't listening because he was deep in explanation about the Golden Gate Bridge in San Francisco. She shot her husband a look.

Eli took the hint. 'You know what, Emmet, I forgot to wash my hands before eating. How about you and I go to the bathrooms and do that and let this delicious food cool down?'

Emmet knew his father was a stickler for hand hygiene, claiming it was how so many germs spread, so he was used to it. Eli had everyone wash their hands all the time, especially after being on the farm as TB was still an issue.

'All right, Daddy. And they have a big fish tank here, did you see it?' Emmet hopped off his chair and walked out with Eli, chatting nineteen to the dozen.

Lena took her moment. 'In France, actually. I've got to tell you about Phillippe Decker.'

'Ah.' Malachy paused with his fork halfway to his mouth. 'You found him?'

She lowered her voice. 'He…um…he died. On purpose. His choice.'

Malachy flushed, furious, though like her, he managed to keep his voice down. 'I wanted him to stand trial, the coward.'

'Over my father?'

'And my mother. Decker helped my father murder her.'

Lena felt her blood run cold, hearing him say it. She could see the pain there. She knew it on a deep personal level. She'd been going to tell him, of course, but not here and now. 'How did you find out about that? It's true, by the way – he confessed.'

'Good, better again.'

'But how did you…?'

'I discovered a letter from my mother to me in your attic. I'm sorry, Lena. Maria showed me around the house, but not the upstairs.

I crept back in as I so wanted to see Emmet's bedroom, you know, and then I looked in the attic. I'm sorry for invading your privacy, but I'm glad I did, because I found a letter from Mam saying what she thought might happen and how she was going to come and get me and we were going to run away together. They must have killed her before she sent it.'

She felt so sorry for him, she instantly forgave him for sneaking around her house. 'Malachy, that's an awful way to find out.'

He nodded sadly. 'At least I know now she loved me and wanted to stay with me. Devlin has the letter, Lena. Ask him to show it to you. It explains about Mam and your father. She never killed herself because of Paudie. They were still friends. It was all lies.'

'Oh, thank God.' It wasn't until the weight went off her that she realised what a heavy burden she'd been carrying, thinking her father had caused Malachy's mother to commit suicide or be murdered. This would make it so much easier to tell the truth to Jack, and maybe even Maria when she was feeling better.

Malachy was looking at her hopefully. 'Lena…'

'Mm?'

'I was thinking. Now we three are getting on fine, would you and Eli consider letting Emmet come on holiday with me to the States? My ship sails tonight, and there's an extra berth in my cabin. I'm friends with the consul here in Cork, and he could write out travel papers for Emmet if I bring him there after dinner. And there are so many exciting things for him to see in America.'

Lena stared at him in shock. 'No, Malachy, that's crazy. He's much too young.'

Before the conversation could go on, Eli and Emmet arrived back. Eli and Lena shared a silent conversation. *I kept him as long as I could.*

'Did you ask her, Malachy?' Emmet's face lit up with hope.

'I did, Emmet, but –'

'You're not going to America, Emmet. You're too young.'

'I'm not, and I'd be with my…with Malachy.'

'You might feel grown up but it's too far, maybe when you're older…'

Emmet looked mutinous. 'I'm old for my age – Mrs Shanahan says so – and I want to see all the things Malachy's been telling me about, like Alcatraz Island and the Golden Gate Bridge and Fisherman's Wharf, where the huge sea lions bark so loudly, and we're going to go to the funfair in Santa Cruz and –'

'I'll take care of him, Lena,' said Malachy eagerly, looking like a kid again himself. 'I promise he'll be safe with me.'

'Malachy, no.'

'Aw, Mammy! Please, please, please, please, please –'

'Emmet, we've said no,' Eli interjected. 'It's too far to go for a visit now.'

'Well, it need not be just a visit. There are wonderful private schools in the Bay Area, and he'd have so many advantages compared to here. He's clever – anyone can see that. He could go to Stanford, Lena, I have the resources, and a huge house with a pool.'

'Are you mad? Are you seriously suggesting you'd take my son to live with you? Malachy, stop this rubbish this instant!' Lena was furious, and other diners were beginning to look now.

'Why don't you let Emmet decide where he wants to be, who he wants to live with?' said Malachy, and suddenly there was a hard edge to his voice. Lena thought she glimpsed in him a man like his father, his cheekbones prominent in his thin face, his eyes narrowed.

Lena was dumbstruck. She stood up to leave. She'd drag Emmet with her if she had to; she needed to take her child away from this man. But Eli put his hand on her arm and gave her a slight nod.

'Yes, how about it, Emmet?' said Eli calmly.

'Eli, no, he can't decide for himself.' Lena was deeply shocked. Did her husband really not care about their eldest son because he wasn't his own blood?

Emmet was staring at Eli with his mouth open. He looked utterly crestfallen, and she could see his mind turning over. Did his daddy want him to pick Malachy?

But then Eli dropped him a huge wink and said with a grin, 'Stay here with Mammy and me and Sarah and Pádraig and Ollie and all the family eating fish fingers and Nana's apple tarts, or go to live in

America with Malachy, go to school there and everything, Emmet? Go on, you decide.' And her son grinned back, showing his missing tooth.

'I can't go for a long time, so maybe I better not. I'd miss fish fingers and you too much, Daddy. Sarah needs me to read the big words, and Skipper said I can help him fix the old radio at the farm. We're going to take it all apart and get a part from Cork – Blackie has ordered it – and we're going to make it work again because Nana likes listening to the plays on there at night.' He turned to Malachy. 'Can I come when I'm bigger instead?'

Malachy kept his face expressionless, and Lena thought how different he was from Jack, who could never hide his emotions. It was strange how difficult it had become to read what Malachy was feeling. There was a time they were so close, but he was a stranger now.

'Of course, Emmet,' he said. 'You'll be welcome any time.'

'I have to stay with my family, you see,' Emmet explained. 'I'm very important to them.'

'He is,' said Eli, smiling at his son, who beamed right back at him. 'We couldn't manage without him. He's teaching Sarah to read, and Pádraig adores him, and his mother and me think he's the best boy in the world.'

'Better than Pádraig, Daddy?'

'Well, you're the best oldest boy in the world, how's that?'

Emmet thought about it, then grinned. 'All right. Are we going home now? I want to show Ollie his new blanket.'

* * *

MALACHY CARRIED out Emmet's new possessions and Sarah and Pádraig's presents to the car. Emmet helped him pack them in the boot, then rather formally shook his biological father's hand and said, 'Thank you very much for everything, Malachy. And thank you from my little sister and brother too. When I'm old enough, can I drive your car?'

Even Malachy's impassive exterior crumbled a little as he bent to give his son a quick squeeze. 'I'm afraid that one's a rental and I have to give it back, but I have a Chevrolet Corvette in America, and you can drive that when you're old enough.'

'OK. Goodbye then.' Emmet jumped into the back of the Kogans' much more ordinary car.

Malachy shook Eli's hand, then gave Lena a kiss on the cheek. 'Thank you,' he said, holding her a little too close while Eli pretended hard not to notice.

She stepped back, flustered. 'Thank you? What for?'

'Just...thank you for our son.' And Malachy Berger turned and walked away.

EPILOGUE

$\mathcal{E}$mmet, Sarah and Pádraig were all dressed in their Sunday best – for as long as that lasted, Lena thought. She sometimes wished she could have a photograph of her children taken and pinned to themselves every morning to prove they started out each day clean. Emmet wasn't too bad, but Sarah and Pádraig were forever stuck in the stickiest, dirtiest part of the house or grounds they could find.

They were all strictly banned from the building site that was the former gate lodge while Eli's new surgery was being renovated, but like everything banned, it was a magnet. Pádraig especially sprinted about like a mad thing, and trying to stop her from catching him was his favourite occupation. Her blond-haired, blue-eyed baby was an absolute character, but as her mother often said, you'd need your wits about you to mind him.

And poor Maria's wits were not the best.

The high, followed by the inevitable crash, had landed her back in St Catherine's; it was just how life was for poor Maria. Lena wondered if her father had lived if things would have been different; they'd never know, she supposed. Maria had come out and was calm, if a little subdued. There was the promise of a new drug on the

246

horizon for the treatment of Maria's condition – Lena thought it was called lithium – but it was still in the experimental stage and Eli said it might be another couple of years before it became available, although perhaps they could get Maria into a trial.

Lena carried a jug of homemade elderflower cordial to the picnic table laid for lunch outside. Klaus was coming to Sunday dinner; he said he had some news. Mam was looking forwards to the visit. Klaus and Maria really had a connection. He seemed well able to manage her moods.

Eli was down at the building site. He'd had a toilet and sink installed, along with a separate consulting room for a nurse he was going to employ to deal with things like injections and dressings. Doc's place in town already housed a physiotherapist, a dentist and an optician, and now a chiropodist would be taking Eli's old surgery.

In Wales, Charlie's birthday had been a great success, and it had been lovely to see Sarah and the children, who were all growing into fine young women and men now. They'd gone to the seaside at Tenby, and the children rode donkeys on the beach. Ice creams were licked and fish and chips consumed in abundance, and it was a wonderful holiday. They talked openly about what had happened in Germany before the war for the first time, and she could feel her husband's reticence and fear of recalling it dissipate slowly. He'd even sat her family down and told them the whole story. It felt better to have it all out in the open, and of course they were nothing but compassionate and full of love. Lena and Eli even told them a sanitised version of why they were in Strasbourg and how they met Pierre Laroche.

'Emmet, please, watch your brother,' she called. Pádraig was happily throwing all the pebbles from the driveway into a little water feature she'd placed on the terrace.

'I tried to stop him, Mammy. Before that he was eating Brandy's cat food,' Emmet said in exasperation, as if he would never have done something so strange. To be fair, Emmet was a much less messy child than her youngest little scamp. The cat had been a mistake in hindsight, but Jack had given Emmet a kitten from the litter, and how could any of them refuse that tiny tortoiseshell face?

'I know darling, he's a menace.' She picked her little son up, much to his dismay, and took him away from the water to a cacophony of loud objections. 'Where's Sarah?'

Her little girl was cut from the same cloth as her little brother, always up to mischief. Silence was terrifying when it came to the youngest two. Yesterday poor Brandy the cat had been covered in Lena's lipstick, a brand-new one at that. Eli joked that the cat was begging to go back to Jack and Skipper and a life of peace.

'I think she's in the bathroom,' said Emmet, racing away to investigate. He took his role of big brother very seriously these days.

Lena followed him into the house and up the stairs, where she found him with Sarah in the bathroom, looking worried.

As Lena entered, Pádraig in her arms wriggling furiously to be released, Emmet asked, 'Mammy, which colour toothbrush is Daddy's?'

'The blue one, why?' Lena answered.

'Don't say it, Emmet!' Sarah begged, and Emmet hesitated, not wanting to get his sister in trouble but clearly feeling there was something Lena needed to know.

'Can you just ask Sarah, Mammy? I don't want to tell you myself.'

'What is it about Daddy's toothbrush, Sarah?' Lena asked, dreading the answer.

Sarah feigned wide-eyed innocence, her signature look. 'Well, I didn't have one to clean Brandy's teeth, so I thought Daddy wouldn't mind sharing – he always tells us to share,' she burst out in a rush.

Lena didn't know whether to laugh or cry. 'So you used Daddy's toothbrush to clean the cat's teeth, did you?'

'Every day this week, sometimes lots of times. She only just told me,' Emmet said wearily.

'Right.' Lena gave Sarah the blue brush. 'You can use this for Brandy, but only this one, and we'll buy Daddy a new one, all right?' She looked at each of them separately. 'And we won't say a bit to Daddy, all right?'

'See? I told you it was fine, tell-tale tattler.' Sarah stuck her tongue out at Emmet, who stuck out his own back at his sister.

Normally Lena would scold such behaviour, but not today. She didn't need tears, because everyone was coming for dinner.

She changed Pádraig and Sarah, who were both wet from messing with water, delivered them to Katie and Mrs Shanahan in the kitchen and then went back to laying the picnic table outside. Eli had reappeared and started helping her, and she directed him to set out nine places.

Eli gave her the sweetest smile. 'I'm not surprised everyone loves you, Lena.'

She blushed. 'I don't think they do.'

'Oh, they do. We all do. More than you know.' And he came and held her closely, stroking her back and kissing her slowly.

She pushed him away with a giggle. 'Ah, stop. Here comes Emily and Blackie up the drive. They're bringing Mrs Crean too. Dick was back last week causing trouble as usual and Blackie had to put the run on him, so Em thought she'd like a bit of a day out. She was so embarrassed – he stole from the plate at Mass. And Jingo is in jail apparently. So however mad our gang are, at least we're not having to put up with the likes of Dick and Jingo Crean. Best behaviour, all right?'

He groaned and laughed. 'Wait till I catch you later, Mrs Kogan. Unless we get interrupted yet again by all the children you insist on having.' He winked, and she punched him on the shoulder with a laugh.

'Stop that. You were perfectly happy to go along with it.'

'And I might want to go along with it again.'

'Shh.' She quelled him with a look. Emily was getting out of the car, and Lena knew her sister's many lost pregnancies weighed heavily on her heart. She didn't want Em to hear her and Eli joking about having even more children.

'This looks very posh altogether,' Blackie joked. 'How's things?' He kissed Lena's cheek and shook Eli's hand.

'Great, though our youngest two are a pair of criminals,' Lena grumbled good-naturedly.

'I heard about the lipstick. Emmet was telling Nellie last night, and they were hilarious in their disapproval. You'd swear they were a pair of auld ones to hear them.' Emily laughed as Lena handed her and her mother-in-law a drink. Poor Mrs Crean had always looked so downtrodden, but she'd gained confidence of late, with Blackie and Emily making such a go of the shop and buying her a little cottage of her own in the village, a just reward for years of drudgery. However, the re-emergence of her awful husband seemed to have depleted her again.

'Here come Mam and Jack and Skipper.' The little Morris Minor had just turned in through the gates.

A few minutes later, everyone was settled, the men with a beer and the women with a sherry, when Klaus turned up in his silver Ford, dressed neatly as ever in a pressed shirt and a suit that should be too hot for the day, but he still managed to look cool. Mrs Shanahan appeared with bowls of salad and cuts of cold meat and cheese, all from Jack's farm – *Jack and Skipper's farm*, Lena reminded herself; that's the way she should think of it now, the same as she called the hardware store Emily and Blackie's shop – and baskets of bread rolls, which Lena had made that morning.

'Here's to us all,' Eli toasted. 'And here's to family. Klaus, you're included in that, and you too, Skipper. May the roof above us never fall in and those beneath it never fall out.'

Maria looked pale but she smiled. She was clearly glad to be back with her family but looked worn down by all she'd endured. Lena's heart went out to her.

Everyone laughed, and the chatter at the table was warm and loud as everyone talked about their week. It was becoming a tradition to do Sundays together. Emily and Blackie hosted in their place over the shop, and Jack and Skipper had taken to doing fabulous things with ribs and hamburgers, a new concept but delicious. Skipper had even had some spices sent over from America by his sister-in-law, and he made all kinds of things with beans and tomatoes; he was a marvel.

Once everyone had eaten their fill and had second helpings of Lena's famous lemon meringue pie, she turned to Klaus. 'So what is it you want to tell us, Klaus?'

The history professor cleared his throat. 'Well, the fact is…that when Pierre Laroche met you, Eli, you mentioned a name, one of your relatives, and it rang a bell with him, so he did some researching...'

'What do you mean?' Eli was intrigued.

'It seems he's found someone for you, a survivor, alive and well and living in New York.'

The End.

AFTERWORD

I sincerely hope you enjoyed this second book in the Kilteegan Bridge Series. Lena and Eli turned up in my imagination a while ago and refuse to leave, which I'm delighted about. The family are one I've warmed to enormously and I hope you have too.

If you had time and you felt like it, I was so appreciate a review on Amazon or wherever you write reviews. Here's the link.
https://www.amazon.com/review/create-review/error?ie= UTF8&channel=glance-detail&asin=B09YMBVS5S

If you would like to join my readers club and receive a free full length novel to download just pop over to www.jeangrainger.com and tell me where to send it. It is 100% free and always will be and I promise I would never share your details with anyone else. You can unsubscribe at any time.

Finally, if you would like to pre-order the next book in this series, called More Harm Than Good, you can do so by clicking here:

https://geni.us/MoreHarmThanGoodAL

ABOUT THE AUTHOR

Jean Grainger is a USA Today bestselling Irish author. She writes historical and contemporary Irish fiction and her work has very flatteringly been compared to the late great Maeve Binchy.

She lives in a stone cottage in Cork with her husband Diarmuid and the youngest two of her four children. The older two come home for a break when adulting gets too exhausting. There are a variety of animals there too, all led by two cute but clueless micro-dogs called Scrappy and Scoobi.